AVALON FALLS

A *not yet* BOOK

AVALON FALLS

L. B. GRAHAM

And for the Ed…
who give of themselve…

They were silent till the man passed, and then Kumalo said, in all my days I have known no one as you are. And Msimangu said sharply, I am a weak and sinful man, but God put His hands on me, that is all.

—Alan Paton

1

Jimmy walked down the alley through the falling snow. The small, powdery snowflakes landed gently in his hair and on his shoulders. A single, stray flake swirled down past his eyes and landed on his nose like a light, cold kiss. He quickened his pace, shrugging his shoulders and shaking his head as though to ward off any more.

He paused to secure his grip on the crystal vase in his right hand. He was pretty sure he had it tight, but his gloves were bulky and his feel for the vase inexact. With the forefinger of his left hand stuck through the knot he'd tied in the plastic trash bag, he wasn't concerned about dropping it. It was light and the contents unwanted.

The buildings on either side of the alley were largely dark, save for the occasional flicker of a T.V. through semi-frosted windows. It was well after midnight now, and aside from the streetlights at ground level, the world lay in shadow. The alley itself was fairly bright, for all of the darkness above him and on either side—one reason why he and Nina had picked this apartment and stayed so long, relative safety, for Nina of course. Even had the alley been darker, Jimmy wouldn't have been worried. He had a .38 under his jacket and knew how to use it.

Arriving at the large metal dumpster, he stopped in front of it and set his trash bag and the crystal vase down in the snow that now lay a few inches deep. He took the hard plastic lid and gently lifted it up and over the back of the dumpster, lowering it equally gently. He peered inside. It was empty, which wasn't entirely surprising since today was pick-up, but it was still a little surprising. He'd been making more trips than usual out here, and he'd been surprised at how quickly this thing filled up.

He stooped to pick up the trash but stopped midway down. Changing his mind, he picked up the vase instead. With a single fluid motion he lobbed the vase up into the air. It rose in a gentle arc a few feet above the front lip of the large empty dumpster and then began to fall. It struck the floor near the middle of the back wall and shattered. He peered in at the fragmented remains. A large chunk of the bottom lay intact though on its side, the epicenter of the waves of crystal shards that had radiated outward across the bare metal floor.

He bent over now and took the trash bag in his hand. With the same fluid motion he tossed it up and over the front of the dumpster as well. It landed almost silently, but Jimmy didn't bother to look. He was already closing the lid. This time he didn't lower it gently. Instead, he let it drop like a weight, and it closed with a thud.

The snow was already filling in his footprints as he retraced his path to the rusty gate he'd come out of. Sergeant, the old German Shepherd that belonged to the Griers in the ground level apartment, padded slowly out to greet him. Jimmy stooped down and pulled off his right glove.

The fur down close to the dog's body was still warm and soft, and for a long while Jimmy ran his hand peacefully up and down Sergeant's back. Sergeant, unused to this kind of attention during the long watches of the night, sat staring at Jimmy. Sergeant always had a look in his eyes that made him appear lost in thought, but tonight he seemed positively nostalgic, though Jimmy knew he was probably imposing his own frame of mind onto the dog.

"Goodbye, Sergeant," he said quietly as he slid his hand up onto the dog's head. "Give Mr. Whiskers hell in the morning."

Jimmy rose and walked toward the bottom of the stairs that ran all the way up the outside of the back of the building. Sergeant followed him to the first step but stopped, knowing full well he was forbidden to go further. He sat and watched Jimmy go up all four flights.

Inside, Jimmy wiped his feet carefully on the worn welcome mat that had once greeted visitors at the front door before it had become too ragged and had been demoted to the back door. Jimmy locked the door behind him while he kept assiduously wiping his feet. Wherever else in his life he might be negligent, he loathed making unnecessary messes and leaving them for others to clean up after him and took great pains to avoid doing so when possible. When he was sure his feet were dry, he moved forward into the kitchen.

He walked to the sink and flipped the faucet up and on, realizing as he did so that the last of the plastic cups he'd been using was now in the bag in the dumpster. He rinsed the dog hair off of his lone bare hand and then cupped and drank from it, not minding that the water was still lukewarm in his hand. He was just glad that it didn't taste noticeably of dog. He had no paper towels left either, so he reached down when he was finished and wiped his hand on his pants.

The bare bulb light above the sink was on, and as he went to remove his key ring from his coat pocket, he caught a quick glimpse of himself reflected in the kitchen window. His black hair, flecked with grey, was wet and a little bedraggled, and he could use a shave. He looked away, concentrating on the task at hand. With his ungloved hand he worked the worn brown key free from the ring and set it down on the counter beside the envelope for Mrs. Johnson. He traced the cold metal of the key with his forefinger for a moment, then turned and walked away.

At the door leading from the kitchen to the dining room, he looked down the hallway that led to the bathroom and two bedrooms. The door to the bathroom was open, like the door through which he could see the empty master, but the other dark wood door was closed. He'd emptied that room first, and he'd not been able to enter it since.

A few weeks ago he had been planning a nursery, now all he was planning was an escape.

Beside the front door lay the last of his things. He bent over and picked up his CD collection, the most prized of his meager possessions. The box was heavy but sturdy, and balancing it on his knee, he reached out and opened the front door. Turning the latch on the inside, he pulled it to behind him and headed without pause down the inner stair.

He was soon outside again in the swirling snow. As fate would have it, tonight of all nights he'd gotten a great parking spot, right in front of the building. He went around to the passenger side door and opened it, as a small dusting of snow-flakes fell in on the seat. He set down the box and leaned over to pick up his brush. With a few deft strokes he had the front and back windshields clean as well as the front two windows. He was careful also to take care of the snow laying in wait for him above the driver's side door. He intended to put a lot of miles between himself and this place before dawn, and he didn't want to be sitting in snow while he did it.

He slipped into the car and started it up. In the rearview mirror he saw the exhaust billowing up like a cloud. Checking over his shoulder, he pulled out onto the road. A street sweeper was already at work up ahead, its yellow light flashing silently. He went around it and turned left at the corner. In a few minutes he'd be on Lake Shore Drive. After that? Well, he'd cross that bridge when he came to it.

2

"Car Dealers," Jimmy mumbled under his breath.

He stood where Wayne, his helpful sales associate had left him, looking through the big picture window into the manager's office where Wayne was discussing Jimmy's proposition. Wayne had offered him a seat and a drink, but Jimmy had refused both. He was strongly resistant to any attempt to create a feeling of reciprocity, even if sincere. He'd make the deal he wanted to make, when he wanted to make it. He wouldn't buy or sell a car because he felt he owed anybody anything.

He'd driven more than half the way to Great Falls that morning, since the Bob Bateman Chevrolet Dealership was the largest between Helena and Great Falls. The air was brutally cold, and when he'd pulled into the dealer and started walking, not inside the showroom but around the used cars on the lot, it had taken a few minutes for a salesman to show up at his side.

Eventually Wayne had braved the elements, but Jimmy hadn't really been disappointed to have a few minutes of peace as he scanned the options. He'd had a pretty good idea of what he was after long before he'd arrived, and it had only taken a moment for him to find the vehicle that best fit that vision. In fact, he'd already returned to the side of his own car and was leaning against it when Wayne arrived.

"Good morning," Wayne had chirped somewhat cheerfully. His high-pitched voice didn't seem to fit his rotund figure, but Jimmy acknowledged the greeting with a nod and went straight to business.

"How much could I get for my car as a trade in," Jimmy said, matter-of-factly.

Wayne walked around the car once, peering at it intently. "2003?"

"2004."

After getting permission to sit inside it, he disappeared for several moments into the driver's seat and then reemerged to ask Jimmy several questions about the vehicle. When he appeared to have all the information he needed, he'd waved to Jimmy to follow him and headed back inside.

The warm air inside the showroom was quite pleasant, and Jimmy welcomed getting in out of the January cold, even if it meant conceding to Wayne the psychological advantage of the tall leather chair behind his large oak desk while Jimmy either stood or sat in the tiny padded chair reserved for customers. Wayne settled in and pulled over a simply enormous calculator with buttons so large even the thickest of fingers could negotiate it skillfully, and he started clicking away furiously.

When he was finished at last, Wayne looked up with a warm, practiced smile and said, "I could give you fifteen thousand—assuming my mechanic says everything checks out. That's a healthy jump forward toward any vehicle we have on the lot."

Jimmy restrained the urge to laugh. Wayne probably expected a straightforward counter and was no doubt prepared to barter upward a bit, but Jimmy didn't like to do the expected.

"I'll take twelve thousand five, and the blue Bronco over there near the front left corner of the lot."

Wayne stood out of his sleek leather chair and leaned forward across the desk to peer out the large glass wall of the showroom in the direction Jimmy was pointing with his outstretched hand. Jimmy knew that Wayne, like any good car salesman, would already know exactly what car he was talking about, but this little show of seeing for himself what Jimmy meant was giving Wayne a chance to think through his options. After a moment, Wayne sat back down, folded his hands on the desk and fixed his attention once more on Jimmy.

"Mr..., I'm sorry, I didn't catch your name?"

"Wyatt," Jimmy answered. "My name is James Wyatt."

"Mr. Wyatt, that Bronco is a $5,000 dollar vehicle, so I couldn't possibly give you the car and twelve five for your Honda."

"If the Bronco were truly a $5,000 dollar vehicle, I wouldn't ask you for it and twelve five," Jimmy replied. "However, since we both know my car, a single owner, 2004 Honda Accord with less than 35,000 miles and an impeccable maintenance record is worth a good bit more than the fifteen thousand you offered, and that the Bronco is worth a good bit less than the $5,000 you want, my offer is very reasonable."

"The Bronco is in excellent shape," Wayne started, "as you can see."

"I can see that it has been washed and waxed wonderfully," Jimmy answered. "The shine really accentuates that whole bi-tone blue look with the dark and light blue portions glistening in the morning sun."

Jimmy smiled at Wayne. "Why that was ever popular, I can't really guess, can you? Still, I suppose even I liked it at the time, but let's be clear, the important facts of the matter have nothing to do with how nicely the Bronco washes up. Much more important is the fact that it's more than ten years old, it's what, a '94?"

"'95."

"With what, a hundred and fifty thousand miles on it?"

"Something like that."

"Which means more than a hundred and fifty, and on top of it all, it's a Ford, right? I mean if you were showing me a Chevy—a Blazer or a Tahoe or whatever—and I mentioned that I was thinking about an Explorer or an Expedition, you'd tell me all the reasons why I shouldn't get a Ford, right?"

Wayne didn't say anything in reply. He sat, probably not as blank-faced as he wanted to be as Jimmy continued. "As I see it, the Bronco and the twelve five is a good offer. The Bronco can't really be worth more than four. In fact, you probably just use it to show people a mediocre vehicle so that when you show them the newer Jeep Cherokee right next to it or one of those new Blazers over there, they can really see the difference. Am I right?"

Again, Wayne was silent. "Look, Wayne, I'll be candid. I've just taken a place a little west of Avalon Falls, and I've just started at the mill. I've been fortunate with the lack of snowfall since arriving in town, but living in the foothills of the Rocky Mountains, I want to change to a more practical car for the area, hence the Bronco."

"What's more," Jimmy continued, lowering his voice so-as to sound semi-confidential, "I'm a little strapped for cash, so again, hence the Bronco."

"At the same time," Jimmy said, his voice returning to its previous, brook-no-nonsense tone, "I'm not an idiot, and I know what my car is worth and that there are plenty of dealers around who'll be happy to have a not quite three-year-old Honda on their lot. They're like gold, and you know it. So here's the deal. I'll take the Bronco today, with the check for twelve five, and I'll leave my Honda Accord keys in your hands—assuming your mechanic says everything checks out. Once you've washed and waxed it as nicely as the Bronco, you'll set it out front with a sign asking eighteen five or so for it and turn a nice little profit. So what do you say?"

"I'll have to talk to the manager," Wayne said.

"That's fine," Jimmy answered. "Go right ahead. Just let him know that a simple yes or no will do. If he's not inclined to accept, that's fine, I'll just move on to the next dealer on my list. If he wants to barter some more, let him know my next offer will be the Bronco and thirteen five."

With that, Wayne had shuffled through the door to the manager's office, leaving Jimmy standing in the showroom for about five minutes while the two balding men stood close together, talking furtively. The manager had stolen a quick glance at Jimmy, but Wayne hadn't looked back.

A moment later, the brief meeting was over and Wayne came out of the office, "Subject to inspection, we'll give you the twelve five and the Bronco for the Honda Accord."

"Excellent," Jimmy said, smiling for the first time since entering the showroom and extending his hand to Wayne.

Wayne took it without visible enthusiasm and motioned once more to the little padded chair by his desk. "Shall we start on the paperwork while the mechanic has a look at your car?"

"A wonderful idea," Jimmy said, settling into the seat.

About an hour later, Jimmy was sitting in the Bronco, heading back west. He was surprised by the surge of nostalgia that had come over him as he'd climbed up into it. Now, as he drove with the remarkable vista of the always expansive Montana sky spreading out before him, he surveyed its beauty in wonder.

He drove on toward Avalon Falls, a town he'd never seen before a week ago, and he was flooded with memories of home. It wasn't hard to figure out why, since Red Lodge wasn't that much different than Avalon Falls, and this Bronco, though a decade newer, wasn't that much different than the Jimmy he'd driven in high school. *Here comes Jimmy in his Jimmy*, his friends had used to joke.

He resisted the nostalgia, warm memories and even the rugged physical beauty that surrounded him. However much things here looked and felt like the place where he'd grown up, it wasn't home. His life was in disarray, and he was in exile. Self-imposed, perhaps, but exile nonetheless. He hit the gas and accelerated down the narrow road.

A few days later, while online, he surfed by the Bob Bateman Chevrolet website out of curiosity. He wondered if his pal Wayne was somewhere inside, working a live one or perhaps out on the lot killing time in the blustery cold with a tire-kicker. He was almost amused by the thought until he caught sight of his sleek, black Honda Accord, pictured beautifully in the Used Cars' section. He had to scroll down to find the price that no doubt, at that very moment, was painted on the front windshield as the car sat primed and alluring beside the road.

$19,500.

Jimmy snorted. They'd probably get it too, or close to it.

"Car Dealers," he mumbled.

3

Jimmy reached over and turned on his lamp. Sitting up, he swung his legs around over the side of the bed. He rubbed his face and pushed the hair back out of his eyes as they slowly adjusted to the sudden return of light.

The dream again, as vivid as the first time he'd had it. He looked up. Light was shining in brightly through the side of his closed blinds. He looked over at his clock. 8:06 AM—he'd only slept for four hours, but he was finished now and he knew it. He never went back to sleep after the dream.

He rose and walked out to the kitchen. At the sound of his footsteps across the bare wooden floor, Major came softly padding from his favorite spot on the rug in the living room. Jimmy stooped beside the young, large, grey and white husky, scratching him playfully while Major licked his face affectionately.

"All right, all right," Jimmy said after a moment of fending off Major's advances, which reminded him pleasantly of the namesake that Major outranked in name if not age. "Since I'm up, we'll go to the park."

For a relatively small town, the main public park of Avalon Falls was quite a civic accomplishment. In addition to the centrally located playground, picnic tables and basketball court, there was a walking/jogging track that ran for two miles around a manmade pond and through a long, beautiful wooded stretch that took one's breath away, even after it had long since become familiar. And of course, all this was nestled like the rest of the town at the foot of the Rocky Mountains that rose immediately west of town in the direction of the Continental Divide, the Scapegoat Wilderness and the towering peak of Scapegoat Mountain itself. For aesthetic pleasure at least, Grant Park had nothing on Avalon Falls' own small piece of urban parkland.

Jimmy often walked Major in the park before going to work, but that was usually at midday or in the early afternoon. Arriving a little before nine, he was a good bit earlier than that today. The weather was beautiful, wonderfully warm in fact for early June, and since he'd now been in Avalon Falls more than half a year, he'd acclimated to the change in altitude. It seemed to Jimmy, even, that it might be fortunate he was up and out earlier than usual. The day felt like it was going to be a hot one.

There were only a handful of cars in the lot when he arrived, and he went around to the back of the Bronco and let Major out. Major leapt down and danced with excitement around Jimmy as they walked through the park. Jimmy reached into his pocket and pulled out the old, gnawed tennis ball. "All right, boy," he said at last to Major, rearing his arm back and throwing the ball across the expanse of grass beside the playground. "Have at it."

For a long time they walked through and around the park, and no matter how many times Jimmy threw the ball, Major never tired of fetching it. It was almost ten o'clock by the time they had returned to center of the park and Jimmy had taken a seat on one of the picnic tables while Major lay panting in the grass beside him. "You wore me out today, boy."

Major sat, staring at him innocently, and Jimmy knew that if he stood or reached back into his pocket, the dog would be up in an instant. As though in answer to a question that hadn't been asked, Jimmy just shook his head and turned to survey the park.

A basketball game had started up a little while back, while they had been otherwise engaged, and Jimmy had assumed from the sound of it that some boys from the high school on summer break were enjoying a fine morning at the park, but now that he looked at the players more carefully, he didn't think so.

They were an odd mixture. At least one of them looked like a senior citizen, an older, balding, white fellow, who moved at least a step slower than the rest of them. There was another, not as much older than the rest as the first guy, but he was in his early forties probably. He was a tall, slender black man with quite a fluid jumper.

The rest of them seemed a good bit younger, perhaps high school age, though most looked a bit older. They were a motley assortment, to be sure, and while some of them seemed to know what they were doing with a basketball, some obviously had no idea. Even so, the game was being carried on with some intensity as it flowed up and down the court.

Jimmy watched the play go back and forth for a few minutes as he caught his breath, and while he was watching, a bit of an altercation broke out. One of the younger players, a dark haired boy with no shirt covering his broad chest and muscular arms, had been driving a little awkwardly toward the basket when he was fouled pretty hard by one of the guys who seemed to have a better feel for the game. The dark haired boy reacted strongly, turning and shoving the guy who fouled him so he fell back over on the asphalt.

Both of the older men and several of the boys immediately broke things up before retaliation could lead to escalation, and the dark haired kid soon found himself on the side of the basketball court with the tall black man. If the kid was getting an earful, Jimmy couldn't hear it, and he wasn't all that far away. The man was certainly doing plenty of talking, and even though the dark haired boy wasn't looking at him, Jimmy could tell from the kid's posture that he was paying attention. After a few minutes, the black haired boy walked away from the game and took a seat in the grass, lying back with his hands behind his head.

The man started back toward the court, but then he hesitated and looked around. Jimmy and Major attracted his attention pretty quickly, and soon the man was walking in their direction.

"Excuse me," the man said as he drew closer, "do you play any ball?"

"Once upon a time," Jimmy answered, not entirely comfortable with the attention.

"Well, as you probably noticed, we're short a man. Care to join us?"

"I don't think I'd be much help," Jimmy protested.

"Don't worry about that," the man replied with a warm and inviting smile. "Nathan tries, but basketball isn't really his game. He was a state qualifier in wrestling two years ago though."

Jimmy thought momentarily about playing the time card, but he didn't have to be anywhere, anytime soon, and something inside him recoiled from the outright lie. Besides, the level of play wasn't so good that he wouldn't be able to keep up, even if he was a bit out of practice. So in the end, he nodded to the other man and rose from the table. "I'll be there in a minute."

"Great, take your time."

Jimmy turned to Major, and squatting down beside the dog, he scratched his head. "You don't mind do you?"

Major stared impassively back into Jimmy's eyes with what looked like bemusement. Stay longer in the park? Jimmy knew Major wouldn't care. He dropped the tennis ball for Major to gnaw. "All right, stay put, then."

Jimmy walked over to the court and scanned the players who were watching him come. As he joined them, the man who had solicited his participation stepped over to where he was. "I'm Edward Carlson, by the way, but my friends just call me Eddie."

Jimmy took Eddie's outstretched hand. "Jimmy Wyatt."

"Nice to meet you, Jimmy," Eddie said. "Let me run down the names of the guys, but don't worry, you won't be tested over this later. Your team includes Dan and Steve, who aren't to be confused with Daniel and Steven—we'll come to them later—as well as Mark and Coach."

The older gentleman was one referred to as Coach, and Eddie added, "His real name is Sam McAllister, but everyone calls him Coach."

"Hi," Jimmy said to the rest after shaking Coach's outstretched hand, not knowing what else to say as he tried to store the faces of his teammates in his mind. He didn't care if he remembered their names, but he didn't want to pass the ball to the wrong team.

"All right, the other team includes myself, as well as Tim, Jon, Daniel and Steven. We're up two, but the last play was

Steven's foul on Nathan, so it's your ball." Eddie clapped his hands and the guys sprang into motion. "We've only got forty minutes left, so let's play ball."

Jimmy warmed up to the game gradually, but the longer it went, the more he found himself thinking less about how he was playing and the more he just played. Jimmy realized a few things pretty quickly. Eddie was easily the best player on the court, but he didn't showboat or dominate like Jimmy was sure he could have if he'd tried. Coach was well past his prime, but if you were on his team, you'd better be looking for a pass if Coach had the ball. He didn't move well and rarely shot, but he made some seemingly impossible passes.

The rest of the guys were pretty average with varying degrees of ability, but they all played hard and took the game seriously. This struck Jimmy as especially interesting, since despite the brief conflict he'd witnessed, no one got too heated when things weren't going his way. Last, but not least among his varied realizations was the inescapable knowledge that he either wasn't as acclimated to the altitude as he had previously believed, or he wasn't in basketball shape—or maybe both. He tried to keep his wheezing quiet. He still had his pride, no matter what else had been lost along the way.

About a quarter of eleven, a large blue van pulled into the parking lot of the park, and Eddie signaled to the guys to get their stuff and a drink and head to the van. Jimmy was tired, but he was also a bit disappointed. He looked over at the place where Major was lying in the grass, and noticed for the first time that the banished player, Nathan, was sitting beside him, patting his head gently. Jimmy walked over.

"What's his name?" Nathan asked.

"Major."

"Cool," he replied, wiping the dog hair on his hands off in the grass as he rose to follow the others toward the van. "See ya."

Jimmy nodded and watched him go. Eddie drifted over. "Thanks for playing."

"Sure," Jimmy said. "I enjoyed it."

"Well, we play every Thursday morning, about 9:30. Join us any time."

"Thanks," Jimmy said, then added, "but 9:30 is probably a bit early for me."

"Early?" Eddie laughed.

"Yeah," Jimmy answered, "I work the 3 to 11 at the mill."

Eddie nodded with understanding as Jimmy continued. "I've tried to keep semi-normal hours, you know, going right to bed after, but I can't get unwound that fast, so I've stopped trying. I'm generally late to bed and late to rise—guess that's why I'm not healthy, wealthy or wise. Today I was just up earlier than usual."

"Well, if it happens again, come and join us."

Jimmy and Major were now walking with Eddie from the court up toward the parking lot. He could see now that the blue van said Calvary Baptist Church on the side of it. "You guys are a church group?"

"Yes," Eddie answered, hesitating near the van, "and no. I probably should explain. Calvary is small, only about eighty people, tucked away northeast of town where you'd have to look pretty carefully to find it. Still, they have plenty of land and the pastor and the congregation decided several years ago to have a different kind of outreach. That's where I come in, I run an alternative program called New Start for first time offenders in the Montana penal system."

"Really?" Jimmy said, taking a second look at the guys he'd been playing basketball with, now sitting not that far away, inside the van.

"Yep, really. I started New Start twelve years ago. The program was designed to accommodate four guys. We've doubled since, and now we normally have eight—and maybe before long, twelve. Nathan is our most recent addition. He's only been with us about a month."

"What did he do?"

"Well," Eddie said, hesitating. "What he did is something I talk to him about privately, like I do with the others. Outside of those conversations, we don't talk about the boys' offenses. I work hard to stress with them that they aren't what they did, and they don't have to do it again. The whole point of New Start is to avoid recidivism. I don't know what you know about the penal system in this country, but you wouldn't believe how many people in prisons are repeat offenders."

"No, I would, actually," Jimmy said grimly. "I know a bit about what you're talking about."

Eddie was looking at Jimmy curiously, and he didn't really want to become the next topic of conversation, so he said, "So this group of guys, they look too old to be juveniles—at least most of them do."

"That's right, they're all at least eighteen. We've had guys as old as twenty-five, though that's unusual for our program. We target a younger crowd. Still, we're that rare program that deals with guys in the adult system. I felt strongly from the beginning that we could do something effective in that age group."

"And have you?" Jimmy asked. "Been effective, I mean?"

"I'd say so," Eddie answered, glancing back at the van. "The program is entirely voluntary. No one is sentenced here. If they fit the criteria and we have an opening, the presiding judge or the D.A. handling the case might offer New Start as an option. The program is for two years, and in a lot of ways, even though there are no bars and no fences, New Start is a lot stricter with their time then a lot of prisons would be. There's no loitering all day here watching T.V. We're pretty regimented, and not everyone who comes likes it—and if they don't want to stay, they don't have to. They can go serve out a traditional sentence in a traditional facility if they'd rather.

"We've found, though, that if a guy makes it through the first three months, they're almost guaranteed to make it through both years of the program. What's more, we've only had two guys in our twelve year history end up back inside if they stuck with the program all the way through."

"That's pretty impressive."

"Statistically impressive, yes, but not surprising. Prisons just aren't set up well to effectively reach the reachable. Trust me, I know they all aren't reachable, not by any program I know about, at least. But some of them are."

Eddie stared at the van for a moment, then turned back toward Jimmy and repeated his assertion. "Some of them are. A lot of these guys have never had anyone even try to understand them and where they've come from. Nathan, for instance, you wouldn't believe what that kid went through at home. What some people do to their own kids, man, it's staggering."

"Well," Jimmy said, "I've long since stopped being surprised at what people can and will do to one another."

Eddie was looking closely at Jimmy again, so Jimmy said, fumbling for something to talk about. "So are you a pastor too, or this a full time gig for you?"

"I'm not a pastor," Eddie grinned, "Though some of the folks at Calvary and around town call me Brother Eddie. My salary is covered by a grant from the state of Montana."

"Well," Eddie said a moment later, "like I said before, join us any time. I should get in the van now, or Big Johnny will come and throw me in. We have a strict schedule at New Start, and he's the enforcer."

"Big Johnny?"

Eddie's smile widened. "Yeah, check this out."

Eddie turned to the van, "Johnny, come here for a second, would you?"

The driver's door opened, and Big Johnny stepped out. Jimmy had been to Soldier Field and seen NFL offensive linemen who didn't compare to Big Johnny. He was only 6'2 or 6'3, but he was as big as a house. And, from what Jimmy could see. It was all muscle. There didn't appear to be an ounce of fat anywhere.

"Big Johnny," Eddie was saying, "This is Jimmy."

"Hey," Johnny said bashfully, taking Jimmy's much smaller hand carefully in his own and shaking it gently.

"Nice to meet you," Jimmy said, a little bit in awe.

"Well, we should be on our way," Eddie said as Big Johnny started back around to his seat behind the wheel of the van. "Remember what I said about joining us on Thursdays. Or, if you ever want to come out to New Start and find out more about the work we're doing, or even just hang out and chat, give me a call. We're in the book."

"Sure," Jimmy said, taking Eddie's offered hand and shaking it again.

Eddie got in the van, and in a moment it had backed out of the parking lot and was on its way. Jimmy motioned to Major, and they started across the parking lot toward the Bronco.

4

Traffic on Main Street, as per usual on a weekday afternoon, was pretty light. Jimmy drove slowly along until he was opposite Cabot's and then pulled in. He nodded to the Mail Carrier walking past him as he got out of the Bronco and then crossed over to the diner. He'd gotten into the habit of parking opposite the restaurant rather than in front of it. Cabot's was on the east side of the street and nothing was more beautiful to Jimmy before getting out and crossing over than looking up through his windshield and surveying the Rockies looming grand and still beyond.

Cabot's was run by Alice, a pretty, mid-thirty-something single mother with two kids who always wore her long red hair pulled back in a pony tail and a clean, neatly kept yellow and white waitress outfit that looked to Jimmy like something out of the movies. The older of her two kids was twelve or thirteen, and Jimmy had seen her around a few times with her younger brother, more of late since school was out for the summer. Perhaps the kids were better known to the supper crowd, but as Cabot's was closed before he got off of his shift, he was rarely in during the evening hours.

Jimmy had never asked and specifics had not been volunteered, but he was pretty sure that Alice—who appeared to be waitress, cashier and manager all rolled into one—was a Cabot, even though her last name was Miller. He'd gathered from things said here and there that the restaurant had been in Avalon Falls and in her family for at least a couple of generations.

There were black and white photos of it hanging on the wall from the forties, with a man that Jimmy imagined to be Alice's grandfather standing out front with his arm around a pleasant looking young woman, not entirely unlike the current proprietor. Alice was friendly without being nosy, and Jimmy liked her, the food and the place so much he had taken to coming to Cabot's every day for lunch before his shift. Today, even with taking Major back to the house and grabbing a shower after the basketball game, he'd had plenty of time to get to get there by 1:30.

He walked in and enjoyed the cool air laced with the scent of good food. A lot of places like this around the country talked about offering home-cooked meals, but at Cabot's, it really smelled and tasted like it was true.

"Hey, Jimmy," Alice said with a smile as he walked in.

"Hey, Alice," he replied, taking an open spot up at the counter.

"What can I get you?" Alice asked, stopping in front of him.

"The usual," Jimmy said.

"Creature of habit, eh?"

Alice poured him a cup of coffee. "Habit gets me out of bed in the morning. Habit gets me to work, and habit keeps me going, hour by hour, day by day."

Jimmy sipped the coffee. "Habit keeps me alive."

Alice, who usually managed to maintain two or three conversations at once while moving ceaselessly from customer to customer, paused in front of Jimmy and looked at him steadily. "Sounds a little too familiar."

Jimmy shrugged. "Don't pay any attention to me today. I didn't sleep well."

"Yeah?"

"Yeah," Jimmy answered, thinking about the dream, the abbreviated night and his morning at the park. He looked up at Alice who had resumed her activities, mainly cleaning up after recently departed lunch customers. "Do you know a guy named Eddie Carlson?"

"Sure," Alice said as she kept at her work. "Everybody knows Eddie."

"Not everyone. I just met him this morning."

"O.K., not everyone. How'd you run into Eddie? Did you go out to New Start for something?"

"No, I met him at the park," Jimmy said. "He was there with the guys, playing basketball."

"Yeah?" Alice asked, looking over. "Did you meet my brother, too?"

"Your brother?" Jimmy asked, thinking about Eddie, Coach and the boys. He wondered momentarily if Alice had a brother in the program, but then she continued.

"Yeah, Johnny."

"Big Johnny?" Jimmy asked, his eyes growing wide.

"So you did meet him," Alice said.

"Briefly," Jimmy answered, re-evaluating Alice in the light of this revelation. "Wow, Big Johnny is, well, you know, enormous, and you look so normal…"

Alice paused in front of him, eyebrows raised, "Normal? Wow, you really know how to flatter a girl."

Jimmy blushed, realizing he had strayed unintentionally onto risky ground. "You know what I mean. By normal I didn't mean bland or average. You're very pretty, Alice. I meant normal-sized, as in, not larger than my Bronco like your brother."

Alice laughed, and Jimmy relaxed. "Yes, I know what you mean. My dad was a big guy. Johnny always took after him, though he hasn't always been quite this big. I mean, he was always a big boy, but all the weight-lifting and muscles—that's more recent."

"What inspired the change?"

Alice hesitated, then looked around the diner. "I'm sorry, Jimmy, do you mind if we talk about Johnny another time? I'm a bit busy."

"Sure, Alice," Jimmy said, and she went around the end of the counter with the coffee pot to check on the table in the back corner with the old guys who seemed to be as much of a fixture there as Alice. Jimmy looked around at the rest of the place, and aside from the corner table, there was only one other customer from the lunch crowd still there, and his plate was empty. He was just sitting, nursing a cup of coffee and staring out the front window. Jimmy had seen Cabot's and Alice busy, and this wasn't it.

A few moments later, Alice came back with his lunch and refilled his cup, then she disappeared into the back. The guy by the front window left, and the guys in the back corner sat, talking about something that had apparently happened in Avalon Falls back when Eisenhower had been president. Jimmy ate his lunch in silence.

When he was finished, he rose from his seat to get out his wallet. Alice appeared again in front of him with a brown paper bag. "Jimmy?"

She sounded tentative and looked nervous. He smiled as reassuringly as he could and said. "Yes?"

"I'm sorry…"

"Don't be," Jimmy said. "You don't have to tell me anything about Johnny you don't want to."

"Thanks," Alice said. "I don't mind, telling you about Johnny, that is. It just caught me by surprise."

"A story for another day."

"Sure," she smiled. "Here, I want you to take this with you."

He reached out for the offered bag. "What is it?"

"A treat for your dinner break."

"You didn't have to do that."

"I know," Alice said, "but in just five months, you've become one of my best customers. Consider it a thank you."

"Good food, good service—what's not to like?" Jimmy smiled. "You don't need to worry about losing me as a customer any time soon."

"I appreciate that," Alice answered, "even if the best you could do was 'very pretty' after your gaffe about my being 'normal.'"

"All right," Jimmy said, taking a whiff of the warm brown bag, "I guess I didn't get myself out of that hole after all."

"No, you didn't," Alice said. "I chose to be merciful."

Jimmy looked at Alice, standing behind the counter with her hands on her hips, watching him. For the briefest of moments, he saw something in her eyes he'd not noticed before. Then she blushed and took the money he'd dropped beside his plate and walked over to the register.

"Have a good afternoon, beautiful," Jimmy said as he walked past her to the door.

"Too little, too late," she said, not looking up as he went out. He did notice a bit of a smile playing at the corners of her mouth, though.

He stepped outside, put on his sunglasses and walked across Main Street to his Bronco. He'd be a little early for his shift if he went straight to the mill, but he didn't care. He had time. He always had plenty of time, and he might as well kill it there as anywhere.

5

A new habit gradually took root in Jimmy's life of routine, as summer waxed and began to wane in Avalon Falls. Despite his protest, the Thursday after his first encounter with Eddie and the guys in the New Start program, he managed to get to the park by 10:30. Coach was more than willing to take a seat in the dry grass, and Jimmy played in his place for the last half hour. The week after that he was only fifteen minutes late, and every week thereafter he was in the park with Major by 9:30, dressed and ready to play.

Other than that simple change, his days and weeks proceeded much as they had before. His slight connection with Eddie, Coach, sometimes Big Johnny and the New Start program participants each week, and his almost daily contact with Alice at Cabot's, were starkly contrasted with his isolated existence in his remote house and his work at the mill where he knew everyone's name and almost nothing else about them, which was precisely as he wished it.

For this reason, among others, it came as a surprise to Jimmy as much as to anyone else, that he found himself asking Alice on the Friday after Labor Day if she wanted to meet him Saturday after Cabot's closed for a drink at The Rusty Nail — an establishment not nearly as wretched as its name implied. For a moment Alice looked somewhat taken aback, even stunned, before her "greet the customer face" as Jimmy called it—a look of welcome, friendliness and complete confidence in herself, returned as she said, "Sure, Jimmy. That would be nice."

"Great," Jimmy replied. "I don't work tomorrow, so just tell me when you'd like to meet there."

"I'm not closing, so nine, maybe?"

"Nine it is," Jimmy said, rising from his seat at the counter. Alice handed him his brown bag supper, another habit that had become routine during the summer. "Looking forward to it."

"Me too," Alice said as she took Jimmy's money and walked to the register.

"Well," Jimmy said a little awkwardly as he took his change, "See you tomorrow then."

"O.K., Jimmy. Have a good evening."

"You too." Jimmy slipped out of the door and walked with his head down and a jumble of confused thoughts running through it. Without much forethought or planning, he had suddenly come to a threshold and crossed over it. He reached the Bronco, and the driver's side door creaked as it swung open. This or something like it had been bound to happen sooner or later. He was just surprised that it was sooner, though he supposed he shouldn't have been.

People rarely did what you expected them to, himself included.

The next day Jimmy took Major to the park about noon for a good long play. When he pulled out around a quarter to two, he felt strongly the urge to head to Cabot's for lunch, but he was already a little nervous about seeing Alice later on. He decided to give it a miss and headed home for lunch, though he wasn't entirely confident that there was much in the house worth eating. He could have run by the store, but he preferred shopping at night, just before close, when few others wandered the lonely aisles.

He stopped at the bottom of his drive for the mail, though he didn't look carefully at it until he was inside the house. When he'd discarded the dross, he examined what was left—a plain white envelope. He saw the familiar return address as he opened it. Inside was another, smaller envelope, with familiar writing and no return address. He pulled out this second, smaller envelope, and went to his tiny kitchen table and sat down. The first envelope fell on the floor with a swoosh. Inside the second there was a folded, blank white piece of paper, and inside of that was a photo. Jimmy held the photo in his trembling hand for several minutes, then set it down on the table, left the house and got back in his Bronco.

When exactly Jimmy arrived at The Rusty Nail was something no one was later clear about. It was early evening sometime, that much he knew, because he'd wandered for a long time in a bit of a daze around the Avalon Falls' park before heading over. What was clearer, to Jimmy and the bartender at least, was that he hadn't wasted any time once there.

He hadn't eaten much of anything since the night before, but that didn't deter him from drinking whiskey like water, one after the next. How much he'd consumed by the time nine o'clock rolled around was lost in the haze of several rounds too many. When Jimmy finally noticed Alice approaching the bar, he'd long since lost track of the fairly important fact that it was to see him that she had come, even if he'd been aware of it when he'd first arrived and taken his seat.

He managed to raise himself to an almost upright position as he turned to smile at her. "Alice, it's nice to see you. I like your hair that way."

Alice came a little uncertainly up to the bar and stood not far away. Her shiny auburn hair was not in the customary pony tail but fell loose about her shoulders. Neither was Alice dressed in her standard white and yellow uniform, but instead she was wearing a dark blue sleeveless dress that accentuated rather than hid her figure.

"Hey, Jimmy," she said, repeating their customary greeting softly. "Looks like you've been here a while."

"I have, I have," Jimmy agreed readily, smiling at her. "A fine place to be."

Alice stood watching him, and Jimmy felt her eyes searching his face. "Come, come," he said to her. "Sit down, take a load off. You stand all day. Would you like a drink?"

Alice slid cautiously into the seat next to Jimmy, but she did not take her eyes away from him for very long and didn't order anything. When she spoke again, it was in the same soft, gentle tone with which she had greeted him. "Is everything all right, Jimmy?"

"Well, I can't really speak to everything, you know, but I'm all right. How about you? Good day today?"

"Yes, mostly," Alice said. She sat stiffly beside him, still watching him carefully.

Jimmy smiled and nodded. "I'm glad of that."

For a moment or two, nothing else passed between them. Jimmy took another sip from the drink he was nursing. Then, after a while, Alice spoke again as she started to rise. "I think I'd better go home."

Jimmy looked up at her as she stood with her hand resting lightly on the bar. Suddenly, tears formed in his eyes as he smiled. He reached over and gently stroked her hand. Then he turned away from her and sat once more, slumped over the bar with his forehead buried in his open hand.

"Jimmy?" he heard a soft, beautiful voice say, but it sounded far, far away and he didn't want to open his eyes. The light was painful. Life was painful. Everything was painful.

For a long time he sat in darkness. Then, after a while, he felt himself being hoisted up into the air. He opened his eyes and watched curiously as the dark wood floor and a few chairs bounced past him. He heard voices above him and the sound of a car door. After that, he remembered nothing further.

He struggled to get used to the faint light in the room. Gradually, he became aware of his surroundings, and sitting up, realized he was not at home. Coach was sleeping in a recliner not far away, and he was lying in a sofa bed with both a sheet and a thin blanket twisted around him in disarray. Wherever he was, he'd had a hard night. His attention was eventually drawn to a brighter light, shining through an open door on the far side of the room. It looked like a kitchen, and he could smell coffee.

Sitting up quickly was a mistake, but he recovered enough to get up and his head throbbed less as he shuffled as quietly as he could past the lightly snoring older man. The lit room was a small kitchen, and around the corner, sitting with a cup of coffee and a book at a small table against the wall, was Eddie.

Eddie looked up at Jimmy and smiled as he slipped into the seat opposite him. He set the book down gently on the table. "Welcome back to the land of the living."

"Was I gone?"

"You took a timeout, I guess," Eddie answered, still smiling.

Jimmy looked around at the small, neat kitchen. "This your house?"

"It is," Eddie answered.

"How'd I get here?"

"We picked you up."

"We?"

"We," Eddie said. "Big Johnny and I. Alice called and asked us for some help."

"Alice," Jimmy repeated the name as vague details of the previous night and a sinking realization that he'd been supposed to meet her for a drink came flooding back. He rubbed his eyes. "Could I bother you for some of that coffee?"

"You could," Eddie said as he got up and crossed the kitchen floor. "Cream or sugar?"

"Both."

Eddie placed a cup in front of him and returned to his seat. "Everything all right, Jimmy?"

Jimmy took a sip of his coffee. "Everybody seems to be asking me that."

Eddie didn't say anything, and Jimmy looked up. "I didn't mean to sound abrasive."

"Jimmy," Eddie said after a moment. "I'm not really a beat around the bush kinda guy. You don't have to tell me anything you don't want to tell me. Alice called us because she didn't want to leave you at the bar, and she didn't know who else to call. We brought you back here because we didn't know where else to take you. Now that you are here, you can stay for a while if you'd like, or not. It's up to you. I can take you back to your car when you're ready. I have to be at Calvary for the 9:30

service, but if you decide you want to rest easy for a while, we can take you later."

Jimmy thought then of the envelope and the picture. He opened his mouth as though to speak and then stopped himself. He took another sip of coffee. "This is just what I needed, thanks."

"You're more than welcome to it."

Jimmy looked around again. "Hey, I'm sorry for putting you and your family out."

"Coach is all the family I have anymore," Eddie said. "And he didn't mind."

Jimmy regarded his host again in the light of this statement. There was a hint of sadness in Eddie's eyes, but his smile and voice were still warm and inviting.

"Did Alice say anything?" Jimmy asked.

"Not much," Eddie said. "She just asked if Johnny and I could come get you."

"Did she tell you she was supposed to meet me, but that I was already drunk out of my mind when she got there?"

"Not in so many words, but I figured the story went more or less along those lines."

"Well, what she probably didn't tell you, because she probably didn't know, was that I was so wasted, I didn't even remember when she came up to me that we had plans to meet. It didn't even register. Some first date, huh?"

Eddie took a sip of his coffee. "All things considered, probably not the best plan."

Jimmy sort of laughed and nodded. "No, not the best."

"So what happened?"

Jimmy looked up from his careful study of his cup and returned Eddie's even gaze. He picked up the coffee and held it in his hands, enjoying the warmth, then went back to studying the cup. "Thanks for coming to get me. Who knows what the barkeep would have done with me when closing time came. I'd probably be in the Avalon Falls drunk tank, sobering up this morning."

"You're welcome, Jimmy, but you should thank Alice, not me."

"I will. As soon as I get up the nerve to go see her, I'll apologize."

"That would probably be a good idea."

Jimmy finished his coffee and stood from the table. "I'm sure you know this already, but it really wasn't my plan to make a fool of myself last night."

"None of us plan to do that, not usually anyway," Eddie answered. "It just seems to come naturally."

"Yeah," Jimmy said. "I guess sometimes it does."

"You want that ride now?"

"Sure, but you probably need to be getting ready for church."

Eddie shrugged. "Church isn't more important than loving my neighbor, right? Isn't that what it's supposed to be about?"

"I really wouldn't know about that," Jimmy answered, "but it sounds like something I might have heard once or twice in confirmation class."

Eddie rose and picked his car keys up from the kitchen counter. Jimmy poked his head around the corner to check on Coach, who was still snoozing in the recliner. "Did Coach stay up during the night with me?"

"For a while. He wanted to be there in case you needed anything."

"Tell him thanks."

"I will."

Jimmy stepped outside into the early morning air, and Eddie pulled the kitchen door closed behind them.

6

The following Thursday, Jimmy didn't make the basketball game in the park for the first time since early summer. He'd been up and dressed in time, he'd just not gone. He didn't think Eddie or Coach would have made a big deal out of the previous weekend, but he thought maybe he'd give it some time anyway. More to the point, it had occurred to Jimmy that it was Big Johnny's sister he'd treated so shabbily. Jimmy had a sister of his own and suspected that if Big Johnny felt about the situation more or less the same way he would have, well, it wouldn't hurt to give Big Johnny a wide berth.

He gave Alice and Cabot's the same wide berth. In fact, he gave the whole town of Avalon Falls a wide berth. He'd not gone out except to work his shift at the mill and do his late night grocery shopping. It had been strange, not taking Major to the park or eating lunch in town and chewing the fat with Alice over coffee, and he missed the brown bag suppers he'd grown accustomed to. By the second week after the incident, he was willing to admit to himself that he missed these slight exchanges of genuine human warmth more than he would have expected.

So the second Thursday after, he went back to the park to play. Eddie and Coach welcomed him, assigning him to a team as though nothing had ever happened, and since Big Johnny wasn't there, he shook off any feeling of awkwardness and lost himself in the game. That was the beauty of basketball, the beauty of sports in general, Jimmy thought while shaking hands with the others after the game. When you were playing, you could forget everything else and leave it far behind.

As the guys got a drink at the park water fountain and began to make their way across the grass to the van, Coach walked up to Jimmy.

"I'm glad you came back," Coach said, taking Jimmy's hand in a firm grip.

"Thanks," Jimmy said, looking over his shoulder at some of the guys from the program playing with Major. Coach held onto his hand.

"Don't think for a second I judge you for what happened," Coach added with an earnestness that commanded Jimmy's full attention. "My past is strewn with more nights like that then I can remember."

Jimmy met Coach's level gaze. "Yeah?"

"Yeah, so don't punish yourself too much. Shame just feeds the cycle."

"Well, I don't know that I have a cycle. What happened the other night isn't exactly routine for me."

"Good," Coach said. "Keep it that way. Call me or call Eddie if you think you're headed that way again. We'll come get you any time you need it."

Jimmy laughed. "Offering to be my sponsor?"

"I am."

"Like I said, I don't really need one."

"Maybe not, but we all need help from time to time," Coach said. "I'm just sayin' we'd be more than happy to give it. Eddie reached out to me when nobody else would. That's who he is. He wouldn't expect anything in return, and neither do I. I'm just looking to give what I've received."

"Well," Jimmy said, trying to take the offer in the spirit it was given, "I appreciate that, Sam."

"Good," Coach smiled, letting go of Jimmy's hand at last. "I need to get up to the van with the guys. See you next week."

"See you next week."

Eddie walked over when Coach had left and Jimmy was rounding up Major. "It was good to play with you again. We missed you last week."

"I missed playing."

"Well, we're glad to have you. You're not bad for an old guy like me."

"I may not be bad for an old guy, but I'm nothing like you. You toy with us."

"No," Eddie said, smiling, "I pace myself."

Jimmy looked up at the van sitting in the parking lot. He could see Big Johnny's massive form silhouetted in the driver's seat.

"Hey," Jimmy said before Eddie could go. "Let me ask you something."

"Sure."

"Is Big Johnny ticked?"

"Ticked?"

"Yeah, because of what happened with Alice."

Eddie nodded in recognition and shrugged. "I don't think so. Big Johnny is a gentle soul—the most gentle soul I know in fact. I doubt he thinks you meant it personally."

"I didn't, but it was his sister."

"True, but I don't think you need to be worried about him. Alice though, she might be a different story. Have you talked to her yet?"

"Not yet. I will though."

"Good." Eddie shook Jimmy's hand too. "Enjoy the beautiful day."

"You too."

The next day Jimmy headed into town in the early afternoon and pulled up opposite Cabot's on Main Street in his usual place. Though it was late September, the week had been unseasonably warm. Jimmy sat for a few moments in the Bronco with his windows down, looking occasionally at the mountains, and occasionally at the diner in his rearview mirror. Taking a deep breath, he stepped out and walked swiftly across the street and into the diner before he could think twice about it.

Cabot's was busier than usual, with most of the tables and half the counter filled. Jimmy was disappointed. He'd expected to know more or less right away where he stood with Alice by how she reacted. With a largely empty restaurant, general avoidance would have been easy to detect. With a largely full restaurant, what felt like avoidance could be genuine busyness.

Jimmy walked over to the seat at the counter nearest the far wall, both because it had a few open seats beside it and because it meant he'd have to walk right past Alice who was serving pie to some guys sitting near the middle of the counter. As he walked past, Alice looked up at him and nodded.

Jimmy tried to interpret the look as he took his seat. It wasn't a glare. There was nothing overtly hostile about it. At the same time, it wasn't a smile either. There was nothing overtly friendly in it. After what had happened, though, and after his two week absence from Cabot's, Jimmy thought that maybe a strained neutrality was as good as he could have expected. Consequently, when Alice eventually did come over to take his order, he was feeling pretty good about things and greeted her cheerfully with the routine formula.

"Hey, Alice."

Apparently, this was a mistake.

"Hey Alice?" she said frostily, but so quiet no one else in the restaurant could catch exactly what she was saying. "If you'd called me the day after or come to see me on Monday before your shift, if you'd bothered to explain what the hell happened, then maybe I would have accepted a 'Hey Alice' from you, but don't you dare come strolling in here two weeks later and 'Hey Alice' me."

With that she strode away, her head held erect and graceful so that anyone in the place who might have been watching probably wouldn't have guessed at the seething nature of the just concluded exchange. The matter of avoidance was no longer in doubt. Jimmy spent forty-five minutes sitting in his chair, trying his best to be unobtrusive and not attract attention from any of the steadily dwindling number of patrons, especially since he had nothing in front of him to occupy himself with, not even a coffee cup. Finally, when it was a quarter past two and only the old guys in the corner were left in the place aside from him, Alice returned, hands on hips.

"Why are you still here?"

"Because I haven't said what I came to say."

"Well?"

"You're right, I should have come sooner, but I was ashamed. And, if truth be told, the thing that drove me to the bar in the first place still had me down, depressed even."

"What do you mean, 'drove you to the bar?' I thought you were there to see me."

Jimmy nodded, knowing enough to know he had to be careful how he explained this. "I was excited about our date, I was, but I got something in the mail Saturday morning that kind of threw me for a loop. It was unexpected, and it unsettled me so much I ended up wandering around the park in the afternoon before heading over to The Rusty Nail several hours before we were supposed to meet. By the time you got there, I was so far gone, I didn't even remember at first that you were there to see me."

Alice stared hard at him. "You're saying you forgot about me?"

"I'm saying I got so hammered I lost all track of time, myself, you and the world itself, which was the point of getting hammered in the first place, I guess."

Alice examined Jimmy intently. "Let me give you a hint for any future romantic overtures you might make in life," she finally said. "After showing up completely wasted to a date, it probably isn't a good idea to try to smooth things over by saying it wasn't personal because you'd forgotten about the date itself."

"I'm not trying to smooth things over."

"You're not?" Alice asked, crossing her arms as she stared at him.

"No."

"Then what are you doing?"

"I'm trying to apologize."

"What's the difference?"

"I don't know," Jimmy said fiddling with his hands, a mannerism that tended to show up when he felt himself getting worked up. "Maybe this is the difference. Smoothing things over would mean I'm here to say whatever, just so you're not mad at me anymore. Apologizing means owning up to what happened, which means telling you what really happened, even if that means making me look worse than I already did. Apologizing means telling the truth, doesn't it? Otherwise, how is it real?"

Alice was looking at Jimmy intently as he spoke, and even though he paused, she didn't say anything, so he continued. "Look, I asked you to have a drink with me because I like you. And, whether or not I ever get another chance to take you out for that drink or not isn't the important thing right now. The important thing is that not being here for a couple weeks hasn't been easy. I've missed you."

"I've missed you too, Jimmy," Alice replied, tenderly, and Jimmy could see she was close to tears.

The front door opened and both of them turned instinctively at the sound of the jingly bell that rang when it did. Jimmy's attention was immediately held by the crisp brown uniform of the officer who had stepped into the diner. His hair was iron grey and he had a meticulously trimmed mustache. Jimmy scanned and processed the details of the uniform quickly, and he realized this was probably Avalon Falls' top law enforcement official, though he wasn't personally acquainted with the man or the local department's precise organization. His suspicion was confirmed by Alice's forthcoming greeting.

"Good afternoon, Sheriff Anderson."

"Good afternoon Alice," he replied. Sheriff Anderson was walking toward them, and as he came slowly over, he nodded to the men in the corner table. "Elliot. Jack. Robert. Afternoon."

"Afternoon, Sheriff."

Jimmy felt himself tensing as the Sheriff approached. Glancing past the approaching figure, he quickly sized up the young officer waiting just outside the door in the bright afternoon sun. His eyes were naturally drawn to the holster and gun.

Sheriff Anderson stopped next to them, and looking at Jimmy, said simply, "James Wyatt?"

"Yes?"

"Would you come outside with me and talk a minute?"

Jimmy looked at the stony face of the sheriff, which looked a little strained, then glanced past him again at the deputy, who this time was gazing in through the glass door at the scene unfolding within. "Why?"

"I'd like a minute of your time."

"Here'd be fine then."

The sheriff looked from Jimmy to Alice, then back. "Just a minute outside, if you please."

"Look," Jimmy said, none too warmly, "I have to head to the mill for my shift, and I still haven't had any lunch. Now really isn't a good time. Tomorrow, maybe? Or after my shift if you like, but I don't finish until eleven."

"I'm afraid this is time sensitive, Mr. Wyatt."

"What is?" Jimmy said sharply.

"Why don't you sit down, Sheriff? Then you two can just talk here." Alice said. "I'll get you some coffee."

"That won't be necessary, Alice," Sheriff Anderson said motioning ever so slightly to her.

"Mr. Wyatt," the Sheriff said, turning back to Jimmy and continuing, insistently. "You are in no trouble of any kind. I ask you as a professional courtesy to me, to come outside for a moment and hear me out."

Jimmy examined Sheriff Anderson's face. He knew. The words 'professional courtesy' had been carefully chosen and slightly emphasized.

"All right," Jimmy sighed, getting up.

He turned to Alice. "I've said what I came to say. I'll see you later."

"All right, Jimmy," she said, watching him as he moved off with the Sheriff.

Jimmy followed Sheriff Anderson out the door.

"Stay with the car, Greg," the sheriff said to the deputy as they emerged. "Walk with me over here a little, Mr. Wyatt."

"As you please."

They walked in silence down Main Street for a little ways, past several shops, until they came to an empty bench. The sheriff motioned to Jimmy to sit.

"I think I'll stand," Jimmy said.

"Suit yourself," Sheriff Anderson replied. He took out a cigarette, placed it immediately in his mouth and lit it, taking a long even pull.

"How'd you know?" Jimmy asked.

The sheriff shrugged. "Avalon Falls is a small town, Mr. Wyatt. A car with Illinois plates passing through for a day or two would be noticed but wouldn't draw too much attention. When the car is seen around for a week, and the owner gets a job at the mill and rents a house outside town, well, that's a little different.

"There are a bunch of reasons a man might relocate to a town like Avalon Falls, not all of them desirable. It's good to get out ahead of any potential problems. An ounce of prevention and all that."

"You ran my plates?"

"Not personally, but yes, I did."

"Is this Mayberry or Moscow?"

"Neither," Sheriff Anderson replied. "Just a small town struggling to find its way like the rest of the world."

"All right," Jimmy said. "So you checked me out. I've been here almost nine months. Why are you taking me aside now?"

"Because I need your help."

"My help?" Jimmy said, surprised.

"Yes," the sheriff said, dropping the remains of his cigarette on the sidewalk and crushing it under the heel of his well-polished shoe.

"If you looked into me, you know I walked away from all that," Jimmy said. "I don't see how I can help."

"Listen, James—or should I call you Jimmy?" Sheriff Anderson said as he stood. "Do you mind if I call you Jimmy?"

"Jimmy's fine."

"Good," the Sheriff said. "Listen, I'm proud of our department, but I've been doing this for thirty-five years. I know trouble when I see it, and this case is trouble."

"Then get help. You must have some kind of procedure for that."

"Of course we do. Usually I'd get help from Missoula, but they had a double homicide last night, and there isn't going to be any help coming from there anytime soon. Normally I'd be out of luck, but here you are. Maybe it's Providence."

"I don't believe in Providence."

"Call it what you will," the Sheriff said, "you're being here is fortuitous."

"For you, maybe, but my fortune is hardly improved by it," Jimmy said, stepping back from the sheriff and the bench. "I've heard you out. Now I'm heading to the mill."

"I've already called the mill."

"And said what?"

"That you wouldn't be in today, and that I'd explain later."

"You said what?" Jimmy said angrily. "You have your problems, Sheriff, and I have mine. I need the money from my shift."

"You'll get paid."

Jimmy stared at Anderson, still displeased. "You had no right, I don't want to get involved, and you can't force me. That much, I know, even if Big Brother is running town."

"No, I can't force you," Sheriff Anderson said quietly, ignoring the last remark. "But I'm asking you. Take a ride with me to see the body. Please? Even if you just help us with the initial evaluation at the crime scene, I'd be grateful."

Jimmy stood with his arms crossed, staring away from the Sheriff, away from Cabot's, down the nearly deserted Main Street. The piece of the past that had caught up with him in the mail a few weeks ago had been bound to do so sooner or later. This piece of his past, though, he thought he'd buried and left behind. He might not believe in Providence, but something that felt pretty irresistible at the moment was at work, pulling on him mightily.

Jimmy turned back to the Sheriff and said quietly. "All right. I'll see what you've got."

7

"Should I follow you in my car?"

"No," Sheriff Anderson replied, "Drive with us. I'll fill you in on the way."

Jimmy followed the Sheriff to the waiting deputy and vehicle, and he was a little surprised to see the Sheriff slide in beside him in the back. The deputy pulled out of the parking spot with his lights flashing and the siren off. They were on their way.

"Where are we headed?"

"The park."

"The park?" Jimmy asked, incredulous. He'd left the park with Major a little after twelve. It was only two-thirty now.

"Yes," the Sheriff said. "It was called in about ninety minutes ago."

"It didn't take you long to find me."

"Finding you was easy, once I found out Missoula couldn't help and I decided I wanted you found."

Jimmy returned to the original line of questions. "Where in the park?"

"In a portion of the walking track that's more remote and densely wooded."

Jimmy nodded. "As beautiful as it is, it occurred to me when I first jogged the track that it could be trouble."

"You don't need to tell me that," Sheriff Anderson said, disgust evident in his voice. "I told the mayor, the town planner, and anyone who would listen when the park was being developed, that as designed, the walking track was dangerous. I was worried more about sexual assault, though. Never dreamed of this."

Jimmy listened to the Sheriff and wondered what had him so rattled. Surely, even in this sleepy little town, he'd had a dead body before. What was it then about this one?

"Where would you like me to start?" the Sheriff asked.

"How about with why I'm here?" Jimmy said, watching the Sheriff closely. "Murder is serious, of course, but as we've already established, Avalon Falls isn't Mayberry."

"No, it isn't," Sheriff Anderson said. "You're here because of the condition the body was in."

"Go on."

"It's rather unpleasant."

"Fifteen years, Sheriff. I stopped being surprised and squeamish at things unpleasant a long time ago."

Sheriff Anderson sighed and began. "The body was found just off the path, though no real effort was taken to conceal it. Time of death was sometime last night, maybe even early evening. We'll know more shortly. The body was, well, mutilated, I guess."

"You guess?"

"Well, I suppose mutilation is the word, though I usually associate mutilation with being cut in strange or bizarre ways."

"That's not the case?"

"No. Cause of death seems pretty clearly to be blunt force trauma. The victim's face has been smashed into an unrecognizable mess and …"

"And?"

The Sheriff colored. "I'm not a squeamish man either, Mr. Wyatt, but I've not seen anything like this. The victim's pants were down, around his ankles, and he'd been beaten repeatedly… there, so much so that gender determination wasn't immediately obvious."

"Have you ascertained yet if those wounds were postmortem?"

"Yes, we think they were," the Sheriff said, eyeing Jimmy with curiosity. "How'd you know that?"

"I didn't, that's why I asked."

"Why'd you ask?"

"Because the order of events matters. Did you say 'face' before to indicate that the blows to the head were only in the front?"

"Yes. The back of his head is somewhat intact."

"Was the murder weapon recovered?"

"Yes."

"Was it a bat, a metal bar or pole or something else extrinsic to the park?"

"No, it appears to be a branch broken off a nearby tree."

"Broken off? Not just found?"

"It appears so."

"How big was it?" Jimmy asked.

"Pretty sizeable."

"And it was ripped off a tree?"

"Yes."

"Interesting," Jimmy said, turning to look out the window as they approached the park. "Do we know who the victim was?"

"Well, he had a wallet with identification in his pocket, but it's hard to tell if he's really the guy or not."

"Height and weight appear to match?"

"Yes, but if this was some kind of switch, you know, for whatever reason, then that would be the case either way."

"True, but from what you've told me, I wouldn't worry about that."

"Why?"

"All kinds of reasons, but mainly because the nature of the crime feels intensely personal. The blows to the face might make sense if a switch was in play, but why the groin? And why continue well after the man was dead? That would hardly be necessary. And you'd expect better planning, like killing the guy somewhere less risky and dumping the dead body—not ripping off a branch in a public park and doing it right there."

"You think the wallet is the victim's?"

"Almost certainly, but I'll have a good look at the scene before I tell you exactly what I think."

The car pulled into the parking lot, past the deputy who had moved the wooden police barrier to let them through. A small but growing crowd of onlookers was gathered across the street. Jimmy knew from experience that while the park would be virtually impossible to really secure, the policeman at the entrance and emergency vehicles in the lot would keep all but the most determined away.

Jimmy stepped out and followed the Sheriff across the open field toward the walking track. "Gorgeous weather we're having."

"Very," the Sheriff said.

"Sometimes," Jimmy continued, surveying the idyllic park around him. "I would arrive at the scene and think, 'of course a murder happened here, look at the place.' Other times, though, the brutal nature of the crime and the beauty of the location seemed so disjointed and incongruous. Like this. I've come to love this park, Sheriff."

"A lot of people do. When news of what's happened spreads, it will send shockwaves through the community."

They walked along the track, beside the still waters of the little lake and into the wooded section. The September afternoon was hot, and the shade of the tall trees was welcome. The Sheriff had grown quiet, and Jimmy could almost feel the weight the man beside him was carrying. By contrast, Jimmy felt almost nothing.

People killed other people all the time. It was a fact of life, and certainly a fact of his former job. If you wanted to do the job well and survive, you learned to accept it. He'd long since learned to approach a crime scene like a disinterested spectator. It was for the victims—the living ones, that is—and their families to feel grief and pain. It was for the surrounding communities to feel a sense of moral outrage. It was for the local law officers to feel the burden of duty. It was for the perpetrator to feel whatever he felt—guilt, triumph, uncertainty, fear or whatever else it might be. As far as Jimmy was concerned, the less he felt the better.

The sound of voices up ahead told Jimmy they were almost there. They rounded the bend, and he saw the small huddle of figures just off the path. On the ground, a pair of nice hiking boots and a bunched up pair of jeans lay in the grass, attached to a pair of pale white legs that disappeared behind the nearest of the men.

Jimmy stopped and stared, suddenly aware of a flood of memories rushing through him. It had been almost a year, but he felt eerily comfortable with the scene.

"Here we are," Sheriff Anderson said, motioning to Jimmy to proceed.

"Yes," Jimmy said. "Here we are."

8

Jimmy surveyed the photographs laid out neatly on the table. They told a grim tale, which by now was becoming less rather than more clear. He rubbed his eyes, stood, and left the small, stark room behind.

Down the hall was a small, brightly lit kitchen, and Jimmy wandered there, more from the desire to stretch his legs and change the scenery than from any real need. The coffee pot was surprisingly full, and the thought of something like a fresh cup cheered him significantly. The coffee he'd had upon first arriving had been weighed in his scales and found severely wanting, but perhaps the evening shift was better at brewing than the day shift.

He glanced at the large clock above the sink as he took a new Styrofoam cup. It was 10:45, and over at the mill, the rest of his shift would be getting antsy to be away home. He'd not be heading home anytime soon, though. The first twenty-four hours in any investigation were always the most important, and the old adrenaline that had kept his mind ticking and churning away deep into the recesses of so many nights gone by was surging through him.

Sheriff Anderson had headed for home around eight, knowing that his presence couldn't accelerate matters. He'd left instructions to be summoned at any time of day or night if he
should be needed, but as his lead investigator, a man named
Eric Gibbons who'd been in the department for 22 years and
was a decade or so older than Jimmy, was heading up the case,
it seemed unlikely Sheriff Anderson would be needed for anything more than updates. Since the initial flood of information
had come pouring in, it had been some time since there'd been
anything new to tell.

Jimmy leaned back against the sink and sipped his new cup
of coffee, marginally better than the one he'd endured before
it. His first impression of Gibbons had been pretty good. The
man was a competent investigator and didn't appear to be concerned about marking his territory, even though Jimmy was
not only an outsider, but an outsider who wasn't even currently
on the job. He had expected the man to begrudgingly include
him, especially after the Sheriff had left for the night, but Gibbons had appeared to genuinely welcome his help and input.
Though he knew this kind of goodwill was sometimes short-
lived, he was grateful for it nonetheless.

He wandered back down the hall, past the small interrogation room where Sheriff Anderson had set him up after they'd
come back from the scene. In the large, central office, Gibbons, a lean man with a serious five o'clock shadow, sat behind
his desk, his pencil in his mouth and feet up on the desk with
his eyes closed. He looked so comfortable that Jimmy almost
hated to interrupt him, but before he had to decide whether or
not he should just head back to his makeshift office, Gibbons
opened his eyes and looked up.

"Not sleeping," Gibbons said. "Just lost in my thoughts."

"I've been a little lost in mine as well."

"Can I help you with something?"

"Yeah, actually," Jimmy said. "It usually helps me think more clearly to talk through a case like this. I was wondering if you had time to come down and maybe walk through where we are?"

"Sure," Gibbons said, sliding his chair back and standing up. "Can't hurt, can it? I'm stuck."

They walked back down to the small room where Jimmy had spent the late afternoon and evening, and entering, they stood surveying the grisly selection of photographs on the table. "So," Jimmy said after a moment, looking up from the table. "Let's try a chronological approach. Do you mind if I start at the beginning?"

"Whatever you'd prefer."

"OK," Jimmy said, moved around, behind the table. "This guy, Alex Morrison, he's a carpet salesman from Missoula, right?"

"Right."

"And we think he's here on vacation?"

"Yes," Gibbons said, starting to page through the small spiral notebook in his hand. "I confirmed that a little while ago. His manager finally returned my call."

"Oh, good," Jimmy said. "Did he have anything to add?"

"Only that Morrison was touring some sites on the eastern side of the continental divide. He's been on vacation all week, away all that time as far as the manager knew. He was expected back at work on Monday."

"Do we know what had brought him here? Does he know someone in Avalon Falls?"

"That the manager didn't know. He thought Morrison was just here to see the falls."

"Which we assume he was going to do today?"

"I guess so. It would have been a lovely day for it."

"I haven't been."

"Haven't you?" Gibbons asked. "You should. They're spectacular. It's a bit of a drive and a fair hike, so it'd eat up a whole day, but worthwhile, definitely."

"That's what I hear," Jimmy said, turning the conversation back to Alex Morrison. "So as far as we know, he didn't know anyone here and was only passing through. He arrived late afternoon yesterday and checked into his room at the Best Western. He ate at the restaurant there, then headed out for a drink at The Rusty Nail."

Jimmy's own recent excursion to The Rusty Nail flashed through his head, and it occurred to him that Gibbons might be aware of it, given that he appeared to have been a known quantity in the department for a while. He thought maybe he wouldn't ask.

"That's right," Gibbons confirmed, again flipping through his notebook. "The receipt in his pocket says he paid his tab at 9:28."

"And sometime between 9:28 and midnight he got himself beaten to death in the park."

"Yes, the coroner said he'd been dead since at least midnight, probably earlier."

"So what happened between 9:28 and midnight?" Jimmy said, half to himself.

"That's the million dollar question."

"Chronology doesn't tend to answer many questions, but it sometimes helps raise the right ones. This guy rolls into town. Hangs out. Eats dinner. Goes for a drink. He doesn't do anything strange. He's not in a hurry. There aren't any red flags anywhere along the way. Then he turns up dead in the park."

Jimmy paced along the far side of the room beside the table for a few moments, then he stopped and glanced back down at the photographs. "All right, enough about the timeline. Let's turn to the crime scene."

"Yes," Gibbons said, nodding grimly. "The crime scene."

"It tells a strange and convoluted tale."

"Yes it does."

"The murder weapon was a branch, broken off a nearby tree. What does that tell you?" Jimmy looked up at Gibbons.

"It tells me that it was most likely a crime of opportunity."

"Certainly seems to be," Jimmy said, frowning. "Why—if the killer had planned this—why wouldn't he have brought something with him? Why would he leave that crucial element to chance? At the same time, if Morrison didn't know anyone in Avalon Falls, who would kill him in such an intensely personal way?"

Gibbons didn't respond directly to Jimmy's question. He stood, gazing down at the photographs.

"I mean," Jimmy continued, picking up one of the photos, "look at what the guy did to Morrison's face. He beat him past recognition. It's as though he wanted to make sure Morrison couldn't see him finish his work."

"On his groin, you mean?"

"Yes," Jimmy said, meditatively. "The killer's real task, perhaps, was the beating he gave Morrison there. He really went to town, over and over, long after Morrison was dead. That's about as personal as it gets."

"So who did Morrison meet on that path?" Jimmy asked, looking up. "Or who did he go there with? Who would want him not only dead, but disfigured?"

"That," Gibbons said, "is as mystifying as anything else. His co-workers said he was a nice enough guy. In fact, if anything, they suggested he was a little boring. Even his ex-wife didn't really talk badly about him. She indicated more than anything else that he was lazy and apathetic."

"How did she describe the divorce?"

"It wasn't amiable, exactly, just matter-of-fact. She says he was out of work for a couple years, and she basically got tired of supporting him. Talked about him like he was a deadbeat. There were never any kids, and he got the gig selling carpet after she left. He'd worked a variety of sales jobs before that."

"She still lives in Missoula?"

"Yeah, she remarried about 18 months ago and hasn't heard from him more than twice since the wedding. She sounded genuinely sorry to hear he was dead, at least as far as I could tell."

"An important caveat," Jimmy added. "You never can know about ex-wives and ex-husbands. I stopped trusting their crocodile tears years ago."

"Fair enough," Gibbons said, "but she didn't sound overly grieved, you know, like his death had rocked her world. She sounded more sad, like the guy had lost his way a long time ago and his death was more a pity than a tragedy. If it was a put on, it was pretty restrained."

"Hmm," Jimmy said, gazing back down at the photos. He looked up and stepped away from the table. "These pictures are ticking me off."

"Not much sense here," Gibbons said. He lowered his notebook and leaned against the wall behind him.

"Not much? Not any. The pieces don't fit," Jimmy looked up at the man across the table. "Profiling a killer from the evidence at the scene is never exact, but it's usually easier than this. Individuals are individual, of course, but certain patterns recur frequently throughout human nature, hence the basic value of profiling.

"Even so," Jimmy continued, looking back down and surveying the scattered images, "the devil is in the details, often buried in the circumstances that are essentially lost to time. Somehow, somewhere, this crime involves some form of standard profile, but that standard profile has collided with something bizarre that altered the pattern. You know, circumstances alter cases."

"You lost me there," Gibbons said.

"Sorry," Jimmy said. "I was quoting my mentor's favorite phrase about human behavior, 'circumstances alter cases.' He argued that if you know enough about a man or woman, you can build a profile that's so detailed you can almost always predict their behavior, but only almost always. Why? Because some circumstances are themselves so complex you can't account for them in advance. Once the circumstances mix with the complexities of the person, surety is out the window."

"So you're saying profiles are helpful most of the time, but this may not be one of those times."

Jimmy shrugged. "I guess it could be boiled down to that, but what I meant to say is that there's probably a pattern here that makes sense, somewhere, even if it's currently obscured. To find it, though, we'll need to figure out what might have warped that pattern into its current, twisted shape."

"I'd say that sounds good," Gibbons said, "but it sounds pretty abstract."

"Maybe," Jimmy said, starting to pace again. "Humor me. Let's come at this a different way."

"I'll do what I can."

"We've got a couple basic options. Option 1—the killer and Alex Morrison knew each other. That would account for the personal nature of the crime. The killer hated Morrison. Whether he lived here in Avalon Falls or simply followed Morrison from Missoula doesn't matter at this point. He knew Morrison, hated him, and beat his face and groin to bits because he didn't just want to kill him, he wanted to mangle him.

"The problem with this option, though, as we've already noted, is that Morrison doesn't seem to inspire this kind of passionate rage. He's bland. He's the kind of person most of us don't think twice about. Even his ex-wife doesn't get worked up when she thinks about him. So who'd do this to him? What's more, with no obvious connection to Avalon Falls, it looks for the moment like it would have to be an outsider. So who would not only hate Morrison enough to do this but follow him all the way here to do it?"

"The key question."

"It certainly is if option 1 is correct."

"With slight variations, it's the key question whichever option is correct."

"True," Jimmy said, then continued. "Now, obviously, option 2 would be that they didn't know each other, and Morrison provoked the attack. In this option, the personal nature of the killing is explained by some act on Morrison's part that excited the brutality. I would assume, from the whole pants around the ankles thing, that the provocation in this scenario would be some kind of sexual assault. Sexual assault and attempted sexual assault have certainly accounted for some pretty brutal slayings."

"They have."

"But," Jimmy continued without waiting to hear if Gibbons had more to say. "The obvious problems with option 2 are even more glaring than with option 1. First of all, there is nothing whatsoever in our preliminary investigation into Morrison to suggest sexual assault with connection to this guy. What's more, we've been assuming from the murder weapon and how it was obtained, that the killer was a man.

"We have even less to suggest Morrison had a penchant for same sex liaisons than we do to suggest he was given to sexual assault. How likely is it, exactly, that this dull carpet salesman goes away on vacation and then decides to wander the local park with his pants down looking for a guy to assault?"

"Not very."

"No, not very."

"Maybe," Gibbons said, suddenly animated, "he attacked a woman but a man was nearby, maybe a boyfriend or something, and maybe the guy intervened."

"Possible," Jimmy said, nodding, "but that brings me to the other big flaw of option 2. Morrison bore no evident signs of having been in a fight."

"Other than being beaten to death?"

"Sure," Jimmy said, "I mean, there was no skin under his nails, no ripped clothing on the path nearby, just an empty beer can. If he had started to attack anyone, girl or guy, wouldn't there be some evidence of a struggle?"

"There'd be something," Gibbons acknowledged.

"But there isn't anything. He just seems to be there, pulverized. So if he provoked this attack, how'd he do it? What did he do to make his killer so mad that he didn't leave any physical evidence behind?"

"Beats me." They stood, the silence heavy between them, until Gibbons said. "Is there an option 3?"

"Yes, though you might say option 3 is a variation of option 2," Jimmy said. "In option 3, Morrison and his killer don't know each other, but in this scenario, Morrison didn't provoke anything—the psychosis lies in the killer. Morrison would be the innocent victim. You know, the typical 'wrong guy, wrong place' kind of deal."

"That seems to fit best."

"It does, except there are some pretty strange improbabilities."

"Like what?"

"Well, like the fact Morrison had only been here for about half a day. Are we supposed to believe some crazed, psychotic killer has been lingering in Avalon Falls, and he just happened to explode into action during the very brief visit of Mr. Alex Morrison? That's a bit much, isn't it?"

"I don't know."

"I think it is, especially since these guys usually obsess more. They tend to pick their victims, watch them, get to know them, then plan the kill. They don't usually kill in the open with a branch they ripped out of a tree."

"Maybe he picked Morrison a while ago and followed him from Missoula. Couldn't he want us to think it's someone from here, not there, especially if he lives there?"

"I guess, but it doesn't feel right. It starts to feel like option 1, like they knew each other. No, if this guy didn't know Morrison, if he was just looking for someone to kill, and if Morrison fit some internal profile or pressed some unknown trigger,

I doubt he would have followed him here. He'd kill in his own town where it was familiar and felt comfortable. And again, if Morrison was just the guy the killer happened to pick, why him? I mean, what about the obvious sexual overtones? What about Morrison makes him a likely candidate?"

"Well, we haven't had time to gather much info on his relationships since his divorce. Maybe he chose the wrong girlfriend or took the wrong girl home for the night."

"Maybe, but this is a bit extreme for that, though I guess we'll have to take a closer look. Anyway, these are, as I see it, our three choices. And yet, there are two pieces of evidence that I'm not sure how to fit into any of the possibilities."

"Which are?"

"Well, you noticed the blood spatter, right?"

"On the legs you mean?"

"Yeah, the blood spatter from the blows to the head are down his legs and on the inside of the pushed down jeans. If he'd had his jeans up when the first blows were struck, there'd be more blood on the outside."

"The pants were down from the beginning."

"Looks that way. How'd the killer get him to drop his pants, and why? If Morrison provoked the attack in some sort of assault, I can see his pants being down from the start, but I'm not sure it fits with options 1 or 3. Either way, it's pretty weird. If someone threatened me on a dark path in a strange town, whether I knew him or not, he'd have to beat me to death first before he got my pants down, I can assure you of that. I wouldn't be dropping them voluntarily."

"Maybe he was afraid. Maybe our guy had a gun or something."

"Maybe, but that brings me to the second thing. The murder weapon."

"The branch."

"Yeah, the branch. Did you notice it was broken on both ends?"

"I did, but I hadn't thought much about it."

"Well, if he broke it off of the tree, I'd expect the larger end to be broken but the small end to be intact."

"Maybe the small end broke during the beating."

"Could be, one blow too many and it shattered or something. But, I was thinking that the small end would be in his hands, right? Wouldn't it? It would be unlikely to break there, as solid as that branch was. So maybe—and I know I'm speculating here—maybe when he was done he put the big part down on the ground and stepped on it to break the small part off. See what I mean? That way, no fingerprints."

"I doubt we could have gotten any prints off such an irregular surface."

"Yeah, but he might not have known that."

"So if he did break the branch after the fact, how does that figure in?"

"Well, it would indicate presence of mind. Options 2 and 3 indicate at least some loss of control, either from exterior or interior influences. This might push us back toward option 1."

Gibbons leaned against the wall and tilted his head back, closing his eyes. "So I'm not sure how things are any clearer."

"They're not, but maybe what we're looking for is clearer. To make the case for option 1, we need to find someone with a motive to kill Morrison. Someone from Missoula, from here, from anywhere. To make the case for option 2, we need to find something in Morrison's past that would suggest some sexually predatory behavior. To make the case for the last, well, we'll need to get lucky. Those guys don't usually get caught until they've struck more than once, and if the killer isn't from Avalon Falls, we may never know if he strikes again."

"Basically, we don't know what happened and we need more information."

"Yeah," Jimmy said, smiling as he finished his cup of coffee. "Aren't you lucky you have me here to help?"

Gibbons smiled. "Hey, if you weren't here, I'd be sitting behind my desk, staring into space, wondering what I'm missing. At least now I know it isn't just me."

"Now you know."

"Well, I'll get back on the phone first thing in the morning. Do you need one of the guys to give you a ride back to your car?"

Jimmy looked back at the table and the photographs. "Not yet. I'm too wired to sleep right now."

"All right," Gibbons said, opening the door. "Just holler if you need me."

"I will."

Gibbons closed the door behind him, and Jimmy could hear his steps echoing down the hallway. He looked back down at the photos. There was a story here, somewhere. There always was. Unfortunately, Jimmy knew well enough that it wasn't always found in time to save the next victim.

Sometimes, it was never found.

9

Jimmy turned off the engine of the Bronco. It was only 7:30 AM. If Eddie wasn't up, he didn't want to wake him.

He'd left the station about 4:00, but even though his body was telling him it was time to sleep, he hadn't been able to. He'd spent a few restless hours tossing and turning, then finally given up trying. He'd pulled out of his driveway shortly thereafter, still not completely sure where he was headed. Eventually, he'd found himself headed out to Eddie's place, located just a hop, skip and a jump from Calvary Baptist and New Start.

Now that he was here, though, he wasn't sure if he'd been foolish to come. After all, though he'd played ball with Eddie each week for a few months now, and even though he'd spent the night here after the most embarrassing bender of his life, what were those things, really? Why come today? Why did he feel almost drawn here? What could it profit him?

Suddenly, the answer to these questions popped into his head. It was surprisingly simple. Eddie was the closest thing to a friend that Jimmy had. There was also, perhaps, Alice, but that was more complicated. He needed to go somewhere, but the only place he could think to go was here. That simple, plain fact, and Coach's dogged insistence about the kind of person Eddie was, had pulled Jimmy out of his house, away from town, and out here for what exactly, even Jimmy didn't know.

He heard the sound of the screen door swinging open, and he looked up through the windscreen of his Bronco. Eddie, in pajamas and a bathrobe, was shuffling out onto the porch in his slippers, a cup of coffee in his hand. Again Jimmy felt the doubt. It had been silly to come. Eddie couldn't help him with the case, or with the decisions he would have to make at some point if the case dragged on. He leaned back and regarded his steering wheel closely, realizing only then that he was still holding it tightly.

Movement out of the corner of his eye and the sound of gravel crunching under foot told Jimmy that Eddie had come down off his porch. Before long, Eddie leaned against the passenger side door. The window was down, so Eddie's arm and coffee cup lay nicely horizontal along the door. "Good morning, Jimmy."

"Good morning, Eddie," Jimmy said, casting him a brief glance. "Sorry if I woke you."

"You didn't wake me," Eddie said. "At least I don't think you did. I was sort of half awake. You know, thinking I should get up but making excuses to stay in bed."

Jimmy nodded, again studying his steering wheel, but he didn't say anything further. Eddie continued. "Something on your mind?

"Had a strange day yesterday. Couldn't sleep."

"Wanna come in?"

"You're probably busy."

"I'm always busy," Eddie said, laughing. "Loving your neighbor is a messy concept. It tends to disregard our schedules and plans, so I keep my agendas flexible and my plans revisable. Come on, you drove all the way out, come in and have some coffee."

Jimmy swung his door open. The sudden sound of the metallic creak split the morning quiet. Jimmy stepped out onto the gravel driveway and shut the door, then followed Eddie up onto the porch and into the house.

The pull-out sofa wasn't out, but the living room was much like he remembered it. Things were generally neat and tidy, and he followed Eddie through to the kitchen, where he accepted the same seat at the same table, along with a fresh cup of coffee.

"Coach around?"

"Out walking. He likes a quiet morning constitutional before things really get going. New Start keeps him pretty busy most of the day."

"I see," Jimmy said, and they both sat drinking their coffee in the bright, quiet kitchen.

"So," Eddie said after a little while. "Yesterday was a strange day."

"Yeah, I went to talk to Alice…"

"Good."

"It was rough at first, but a little better by the end."

Eddie nodded. "A little patience and persistence goes a long way."

"No doubt, but we didn't get to finish."

"Oh?"

Jimmy took a larger sip of his coffee and sat watching Eddie, who was sitting, nursing his own cup, listening attentively to everything Jimmy said. Everything about Eddie—his tone, look, posture, manner, everything—communicated care and interest. Jimmy wondered if he had looked half as interested as Eddie did now when conducting interviews for his cases. That question stirred up other questions, but he stopped himself from following that trail of thinking any further, and he focused. He was delaying the inevitable, so he plunged ahead.

"Sheriff Anderson interrupted us," Jimmy continued.

"Sheriff Anderson?"

"Someone was murdered in the park, and he wanted my help. I used to be an FBI agent."

"Whoa," Eddie said, looking genuinely surprised for the first time that morning. "I'd heard about the murder, but your former profession is a bit of a shocker. What did you do for the FBI?"

"Behavioral Analysis."

"Behavioral Analysis?"

"Yeah, what you might call profiling."

"Ah," Eddie said, nodding.

Jimmy shrugged. "It's strange, I never lied to you explicitly about what I did before I came here, but I still feel like I deceived you."

"Well," Eddie said, the hint of a smile playing at the corners of his mouth, "don't feel too bad. It isn't as if you deceived me that much."

"What do you mean?"

"What I mean is that you might not have said what you did before, but I never actually believed you were a blue collar lumber mill worker by trade."

"No?"

"No."

"Why not?"

"Well, for one thing, the first time we met, when I talked about New Start, I mentioned *recidivism,* and you didn't ask me what I was talking about or even look confused. That was my first clue that your education was probably pretty good."

"I could have been bluffing."

"Maybe," Eddie said, shrugging, "but I like to think that in my job, I know people pretty well. Even if you'd bluffed me then, I would hope that by now I'd have figured it out."

"You probably would have," Jimmy conceded. "Still, even if you didn't buy me as a mill worker, I feel bad about not telling you."

"That's natural, I think," Eddie said as he moved to the counter to refill his cup. "Friendships are built through small steps of mutual disclosure. To this point, I've done all of the disclosing. Now that word of your past is bound to find its way trickling through the community, of course you feel bad that you haven't already told me."

Jimmy peered across the room at Eddie, leaning against the kitchen counter with the steam from his coffee rising in front of his face. "Are you sure you weren't a profiler in a past life?"

Eddie smiled. "Like I said, in my job, I get to know people pretty well. I guess you could say I am a profiler, just a different kind with different goals in view."

"Maybe I need to be more careful what I say around you."

"Maybe you'll find it's a relief to talk to someone safe, someone you don't have to work so hard to guard you secrets from."

"Maybe."

Eddie walked back to the table and sat down. "You were talking about your strange day. Sheriff Anderson interrupted your talk with Alice to ask for your help with the case. What then?"

"Well, I ended up going with him to the crime scene."

"Sounds like you were reluctant."

"I was," Jimmy said. "I'm not, you know, on the job. I don't profile anymore."

"Is that why you're here?"

"Is what why I'm here?"

"Do you want to talk about yesterday, about the case, or about why you don't profile anymore?"

Jimmy sat quietly. The FBI, Chicago, Nina—it all flashed through his mind. "No. I don't want to talk about why I'm not a profiler anymore."

"The case, then?"

"I can't really talk about that either. I mean, maybe I could—I doubt anyone would care that much if I talked confidentially to you, but I was always careful not to discuss ongoing investigations."

Eddie leaned back in his chair, and Jimmy could feel his penetrating gaze still regarding him closely. He began to wonder again why he'd come.

"Perhaps," Eddie began, hesitating at first, "since you can't discuss the case and you don't want to talk about why you left the FBI, maybe it would help to talk about something else. What about telling me how you became a profiler? Maybe you don't want to talk about working for the FBI at all, but I'd be curious to know how that came about."

Jimmy thought for a moment. The urge to tell at least part of his story, to remove at least a fragment of his anonymity, was almost overwhelming. "I tell you what, Eddie, explain something for me, I'll answer your question for you."

"Sounds fair. What?"

"How'd you get here? I mean, no offense, but you and Avalon Falls don't seem to, you know, go together."

"I was born here."

"In Avalon Falls?" Jimmy asked, surprised. "Was the town, how should I say it, more diverse in those days?"

"No," Eddie said. "Less."

"Less?"

"Less. There were only a handful of black families back then."

"Must have been hard."

"At times, but I got by all right," Eddie said. "Though, some relationships at Calvary got strained when I became a Presbyterian."

Jimmy's eyes grew wide. "You're a Presbyterian?"

"Is that so hard to believe?"

Jimmy leaned back, took a sip of his coffee, considering what he should say. "My work with the FBI took me all over the place, and the Presbyterians I've met have just about all been suburban white folks without any visible inclination to mix racially or socio-economically. What's your story?"

"My story is that I got out of college and didn't know what to do. A friend suggested seminary—even though I didn't really want to be a minister—because I was pretty serious about my faith. So I started taking classes long distance, and somewhere along the way I became convinced that the Presbyterian way of understanding the church and the Bible was right. I didn't set out to become a Presbyterian, I just sort of became one. It took me a long time to admit that, even to myself."

"Fascinating," Jimmy said. "My dad is a Presbyterian, but other than what I've told you, I don't know much about the differences between them and other Protestants. Of course, my dad never went to church that I can remember, so I couldn't say he was a good example of a Presbyterian. I couldn't say he was a good anything, in fact."

"That's a pretty strong statement."

"Just calling it like it is," Jimmy shrugged. "Look, my dad was an abusive pig, but I don't harbor any illusions that only Presbyterians can be messed up. My job took me all over the country, and I saw the very worst of human nature. I learned quickly that murderers come in all shapes, sizes, colors and religious persuasions. Catholics, Presbyterians, Baptists—they can all kill, and they all do."

"Depravity."

"Depravity, sin, evil—whatever. It's universal."

"So," Eddie said, leaning back, "what led you to profiling?"

Jimmy pushed his cup of coffee back and crossed his arms, staring down at the table. "I suppose," he said after a moment, "that if I'm going to tell you this story, I should do it right and start at the beginning. I grew up in Red Lodge."

"Red Lodge?" Eddie said. "Now there's another surprise. I had you pegged for a runaway, a guy coming west to leave something or someone behind. Maybe I was wrong about that. Maybe coming to Avalon Falls was a way to come home without really coming home."

Jimmy avoided Eddie's gaze and continued on with his story. "I didn't dislike life in Montana, or even in a small town like Red Lodge, but I disliked life at my house. My mom and dad were both drunks, but different kinds. My Mom was a weepy, sentimental drunk, and she drank more regularly than my dad. She drank all the time. He was more occasional, but he was a mean drunk. He was mostly a shouter, but every so often he hit her. He never hit us kids, but we lived in pretty constant fear of him.

"I was the youngest of three, and by the time I was in 10th grade, I was the only one at home. My older brother moved to Missoula for school and never came back. My sister got married the summer after she graduated, already pregnant with my nephew. She got married more to get out of the house than anything else, and the marriage was a disaster. It only lasted two years. Her second marriage hasn't been perfect, but it's been more than fifteen years, and they're still married.

"So anyway, all of that left me to endure my last three years of high school at home with them on our own—just the three of us. My mom was a Catholic, and even though we went to Mass pretty regularly for a while when I was little, that stopped when I was in grade school, though I don't remember why. My dad never came, and he didn't go anywhere else, either. In fact, I remember that when he would drink too much, one of the things he'd ridicule my mom about was being religious, even though sometimes he'd proudly refer to himself as a Presbyterian. I was too young to see the disconnect there, but then again, not much about him made sense.

"Anyway, I decided early on I wanted to go far, far away, which is ultimately why I ended up at UCLA."

"UCLA? That's a pretty selective school. I bet it was a big step from Red Lodge."

"It was, and if I'd known as much then as I do now, I probably would have assumed I couldn't get in and not applied. But, I was a good student, and I didn't even consider that I wouldn't get in. I'd grown up hearing about UCLA my whole life, and as soon as I'd realized I had to get away, I just decided that was where I was going to go. I only understood years later how fortunate I was to be accepted."

"Did you grow up hearing about UCLA because your mom or dad had gone there?"

"Oh no, they didn't either one have a college education. My dad was just a huge John Wooden fan. Basketball is probably what he cares about most in the whole world. I was always hearing stories about Lew Alcindor and Bill Walton. My dad didn't seem to like anyone, but these men were gods to him, and they became gods to me."

Jimmy leaned forward and rested his elbows on the table, now staring straight ahead at Eddie. "Don't think I've completely missed the central irony in this part of my story. Yes, even as I was running away from my father, he was shaping my life. I ran to the school I'd learned to love from him."

Eddie watched thoughtfully, and Jimmy looked back down at the table as he continued. "I moved to L.A. with the only things I owned that I cared about, my clothes, my records and tapes and what books I could carry in my Jimmy—I know its tacky, but I drove a GMC Jimmy in high school."

Eddie smiled and nodded but didn't interrupt. "Anyway, I moved to L.A., and I basically worked and studied all the time. I missed my friends in Red Lodge, but I couldn't go back. I took classes in the summer term instead. I had no idea what to major in, so I just took my gen eds and tried different things out until the fall semester of my junior year, when I ended up in a class called 'Human Behavior' in the psych department. The prof, Dr. Roberts, was fantastic. I ate it up. It all fascinated me. I quickly realized that I might not know what I wanted to do, but I knew what I wanted to study.

"So I became a psychology major and took nothing but psych classes from then on out. I was a good student, took lots of summer classes, so I was ready to graduate a semester early at the end of the fall term in '89. But, as Christmas approached in southern California, I was increasingly paralyzed by trying to decide what to do next. I didn't want to go back to Montana, but I didn't know what else to do or where else to go. So when Dr. Roberts—who'd become my advisor—encouraged me to consider staying on and getting a Masters, I thought that sounded pretty good. Spring rolled around and there I was, taking a full load of graduate psych classes.

"All right, jump ahead a year to the fall of 1990. I'm finishing up my first year in the grad psych program at UCLA. Again, Dr. Roberts altered the trajectory of my life. He encouraged me to go to a lecture one Thursday night by a visiting FBI profiler. The lecture was being sponsored jointly by the Law School and the grad psych department. I was supposed to work that night, but I altered my schedule to go and it changed everything. I knew before he was ten minutes into his lecture what I wanted to do. I talked to him after to find out what kinds of things the FBI would be looking for in my application and tailored the rest of my program to fit that bill.

"Of course the guy was recruiter for the FBI, not just a profiler, which I would have realized if I'd thought about it at all before going to the lecture. He was a good friend of Dr. Roberts, and he was there, of course, precisely to draw out guys like me who might be interested in behavioral analysis work. Well, it worked. I applied and was accepted. The next spring I finished my masters, graduated and headed east to start work in the FBI. That's how I became a profiler."

"You've been a profiler ever since?"

"Sort of. The man who recruited me, John Stokes, became my mentor. I trained under him once I got out of the Academy. Shortly after, there was a power struggle of sorts within our unit, and he emerged as its new head. I was a favorite pupil, and before long, I was working cases all over the country. They were always the hardest and highest profile cases. It was exciting, challenging and exhausting. Normal life was impossible. For the most part, I stopped doing that work in 2002, after ten pretty wild years in the field. I took a job at a regional office, but now we're getting too close to those things I've said already I'm not going to talk about."

"Are you sure you don't want to talk about them?"

"I'm sure."

"Well," Eddie said, smiling again as he gestured with his hands, "you can't blame me for asking. It's all so interesting."

"Maybe one day," Jimmy said, "but I wouldn't hold my breath."

"Hey, I'll take it. 'Maybe' leaves me some room for hope." Eddie stroked his cheek for a moment before asking another question. "What about your parents? When was the last time you saw them?"

"My graduation from UCLA. My dad came down mostly to walk the hallowed grounds of the school he adored, and even though I didn't want him to come, I'm glad now that they did. My mom, who had been drinking herself to death for years, died less than a year later."

"I'm sorry to hear that."

"It was hard. With her death, my last real connection to my father was cut. My sister, who still lives in Red Lodge, sees him every so often—when he can be bothered to play grandfather to her kids—but I haven't seen him in fifteen years." Jimmy pushed his chair back from the table and stretched. "I ought to go."

"Heading back to the station?"

"I hadn't decided on that yet."

"Well, I wish I could offer some advice, but I know when I'm out of my depth. If I had a better feel for your experience as a profiler, why you left, and what's brought you to this point, I might be able to give you some direction …"

"Nice try," Jimmy smiled, "but sorry, I've already said more than I intended. I'm going to have to leave it at that."

"I understand. I was mostly teasing," Eddie said. "Mostly, but not completely. I wish I could be of more immediate help with whatever it is you're wrestling with, but I appreciate your desire to keep your own counsel."

"Thanks," Jimmy said as they walked back through house to the front porch. They stood for a moment on the top step, breathing in the cool morning air. Jimmy turned to Eddie and shook his hand firmly. "Thanks for listening."

"That," Eddie replied, "I can always offer you. I was happy to do it."

Jimmy stepped down off the porch and started down the walk to the driveway. He stopped on the far side of the Bronco, hesitating before getting in. "I feel better, you know. Telling you at least that much about my background."

"Good," Eddie said. "I'm glad."

"If we take too many more of these steps of, what did you call it, mutual disclosure? We might just end up friends."

"We just might," Eddie replied. "In fact, we may already be closer to that destination than you think."

"See you later."

"Thursday?"

"Unless I get more involved in the case and it interferes."

"All right, I'll see you then."

Jimmy got in the Bronco and headed down the driveway. For a long time he sat at the road, wondering if he should go home to try to sleep some or head back to the station. Even though both places lay for a long way along the same road, he didn't feel he could turn out without knowing to which destination he was headed. Finally, he pulled out, feeling that he was being drawn, almost inescapably, back to the little stark room with the glaringly bright light and the table covered with pictures.

Those awful, revolting, and yet mysteriously beckoning pictures.

10

Jimmy let Major out of the back of the Bronco. Major stood, panting rhythmically, watching Jimmy's hand and the ball. With a quick throw, the ball flew through the air and Major raced after it, across the open green of the park.

Jimmy looked at the complete absence of cars in the parking lot. It was a beautiful Sunday evening, and yet there was no one. No one playing on the playground. No one lying in the grass. No one strolling by the lake. No one there at all, except for him and Major.

There was no axiom, no truism that Jimmy knew from his years in the Bureau to predict how long it might take for the good people of Avalon Falls to return to using the park as usual. A similar slaying in Central Park might shut down a small portion of the park for several hours, but it wouldn't close entirely and park usage the following day would probably be much like always. Perhaps this was because killings in New York City were hardly news, perhaps because the size of the city gave all such crimes a surreal, "look what happened on T.V." quality, or perhaps because New Yorkers couldn't afford to avoid for long the reprieve Central Park afforded them from the urban madness they inhabited.

Avalon Falls was not New York. It wasn't Chicago. It wasn't even Des Moines. The park was not the only pretty place people could go for a break, brutal slayings were not a dime a dozen, and while the crime might have had a surreal quality for the town's citizens, Jimmy imagined they did not feel like curious but removed spectators. A stranger to their town had been horribly beaten to death in their park. There had been no arrest, so whoever committed the crime was still at large, perhaps far away by now, or perhaps walking toward them along the sunny sidewalk of Main Street, smiling as he came.

Perhaps that was the real difference. In New York City, a murder in a park could feel distant and far removed because the odds that you knew the murderer or his victim were very, very poor. In a town like Avalon Falls, though, if a killer lived in your midst, the odds that you had crossed paths from time to time with him, had once stood behind him in the checkout line at Wal Mart, or perhaps even knew him, were exponentially greater. That uncertainty was itself distressing.

Jimmy walked in the grass, taking the slobbery tennis ball and hoisting it again for his delighted dog. He'd neglected Major these past few days as he buried himself in the case, but nothing had come of it. He'd spent a second frustrating day at the station, to no avail. No one who knew the unfortunate Mr. Morrison could think of any reason why someone would want to kill him. Detective Gibbons had contacted his family, his co-workers, his neighbors and landlord, even his old high school principal. There was nothing anywhere in all the phone calls and all the conversations that raised a red flag or made even a little sense out of the bizarre crime scene.

Consequently, the notion that the murder had been committed by someone who knew Alex Morrison and had a homicidal dislike for him seemed to Jimmy to be increasingly unlikely. Killers, as a general rule, were not any brighter than the general population, and Jimmy didn't have the highest regard for the intellectual prowess of the average citizen. If Morrison had died for some past misdeed, the killer had done a brilliant job of hiding the offense that had caused it.

Of course, there was always the possibility that Alex Morrison had secrets. Many people, the bright and the not-so-bright alike had those. Perhaps the offense that had brought about Morrison's demise was unknown to everyone else who knew him, because the offended party was likewise unknown.

It was certainly possible, Jimmy conceded as he strolled down the gently sloping hill, just not likely. There was nothing in Morrison's phone records, his bank account or computer files that hinted at a hidden life. Consequently, Jimmy had essentially dismissed this possibility and directed his thinking toward the other options. He now felt quite sure that either Alex Morrison had provoked this attack with a relative stranger, or the killer had singled Morrison out to die, for some reason known—for now at least—only to his own twisted mind.

While Jimmy liked to think the case was becoming clearer, this wasn't good news. With no past connection to link the murderer and his victim, there remained only the physical evidence, both on the body and at the crime scene, and the possibility of a witness to point him in the right direction. As of yet, neither the body nor the crime scene had revealed anything of use, and no witness had come forward. Nor was one likely, given the location and time frame for the slaying. The clock was ticking. With the approach of nightfall, they would hit the 72 hour mark. All trails had grown cold.

Jimmy stopped in the middle of the park. Major waited before him, but Jimmy's attention had turned to the walking trail as it moved along the peaceful lake to the place where it disappeared in the wood, now dark with shadows as the sun started to sink behind the glorious mountains to the west.

Major dropped the tennis ball in the grass and nuzzled Jimmy's hand in an attempt to regain his master's full attention. Jimmy looked down at the dog and smiled, but his gaze quickly returned to the path. He'd been back to the crime scene yesterday, and he hadn't seen anything new or of note that he hadn't considered Friday, so he didn't know what good it would do to go back. Even so, the woods beckoned to him, and he started back down the hill with Major following close behind, his ball once more gripped tightly in his teeth.

Though the evening was warm for this time of year, Jimmy felt a distinct chill as he entered the wood. A breeze rustled the trees, sending a few autumn leaves fluttering to the ground on the path. He pulled the light fleece he was wearing tight and zipped it about half way up. He looked down at Major, trotting along happily, impervious to this slight shift in temperature, and the dog, oblivious, moved briskly forward beside him as they went deeper and deeper into the shadowy wood. Finally, he rounded the bend and came upon the yellow police tape strung across the path and tied between two trees. He ducked underneath and walked quietly to the spot where Alex Morrison had been beaten beyond recognition three nights before.

He squatted on the portion of the path just beside where Morrison's body had been found and gazed at the ground. Even in the dusky light, the dark patches where Morrison's blood had soaked the earth and the undergrowth crushed beneath him was still discernible. He was not religious, but he had come over the years to understand what people meant when they described places where blood had been shed as *hallowed*. He could feel it, could sense that it would simply be wrong—and not simply because of the remote possibility of new forensic discovery—to trample upon these broken vines and trudge across this blood-stained soil.

Instinctively, he reached over and stroked Major's soft fur as he stood obediently beside him. The dog also seemed fascinated by the crime scene and the dark patches. He wondered, given the dog's superior senses and instinct for such things, if the scent of death still lingered, heavy in the air. If he had not stopped and loitered here, would Major, passing by, have had an idea of what had transpired? Would the visible and invisible signposts of a life lost in this place have called out to him, bidding him come and see?

There was nothing in Major's demeanor that betrayed an eagerness to investigate the site more closely, and Jimmy was glad. Though this long after the murder the crime scene would have no secrets left to reveal that would be admissible in a court of law, he still wanted to leave the spot more or less as he had found it when he left.

His mind quickly strayed from Major, back to the ghost in the grass. The unanswered and perhaps unanswerable questions that the murder presented competed for his attention. What had happened here to spark such passionate brutality? What had Morrison done or failed to do? What had led him here in the first place? What had he come seeking, only to find such a gruesome death?

Jimmy stood and walked a few steps further down the path to the portion of the undergrowth where the lone piece of physical evidence other than the body and the murder weapon had been found. A single, mostly empty can of Coors Light had been discovered, lying half obscured in some leaves. Morrison's fingerprints had been on the can, and given its proximity to the body, it seemed reasonable to suppose it had been tossed aside or knocked from his hand at the time of the attack.

Had Morrison come here for an evening stroll, beer in hand? He'd already had a few drinks at The Rusty Nail. Had this last drink pushed him over the proverbial edge? Had he found someone on this path, and had a repressed sexual urge of some kind taken control of him? Had a sexual predator awoken in him in this place, only to meet with something even more savage?

Perhaps that wasn't the case at all. Perhaps the alcohol had not propelled but impaired him. Perhaps it had not spurred on his will to harm but disabled his ability to defend. Had Morrison stumbled upon something going on or someone he'd not been meant to see? Had he walked unwittingly into someone else's nightmarish reality? Maybe the lack of defensive wounds, the absence of any sign of a struggle, had been due to his intoxication and inability to recognize or react to what was happening.

In either of those cases, the alcohol would have served as an unwitting aid to Morrison's death, and it was of course possible that neither scenario accurately described what had transpired. Perhaps Morrison had met someone at the motel, at The Rusty Nail, or somewhere else entirely and come here to share a drink in private. Had he walked here with the killer as they sipped their beers together? Had he walked here with the killer's wife or girlfriend? If he had come with someone else, why was only the one can found? Had the killer left the murder weapon behind but remembered to recycle his beer can?

It did not seem likely to Jimmy that the killer's state of mind and subsequent actions could be attributed, at least entirely, to alcohol. Yes, he'd seen some bizarre and brutal things done by those under the influence, but the clearly directed and sustained intensity of this attack would be very unusual for a man in a drunken rage. That made the killing all the more chilling. The victim might well have been drunk, or close to it, but the killer had most likely acted with a cold and frightening sobriety, without the ill effects from alcohol to spur him on.

Jimmy turned away from the side of the path where the body was found, where the ground sloped upward from the small park and manmade lake, ultimately rising up and over a ridge to a service road beyond. This hill had been carefully examined for physical evidence, as had the service road, and they had yielded, like the rest of the investigation, nothing of significance. The other side of the path to which he now turned was also wooded, but it sloped downward toward the lake. Here, Jimmy had noticed, the trees were thinner and the view of the water clearer than any other place he had seen along the path. He stood for a moment, looking down at the tranquil water as it lapped the smooth pebbles of the shore. A large rock lay just up from the water's edge, and on a whim, Jimmy stepped off the path and started down through the trees.

Emerging from the edge of the wood, he scanned the beautiful lake. To his left, he could see where the woods ended and the shore led up to the open fields of the park. To his right, he could see the shore bend around in a rounded curve with the trees thick beside it, and he knew that just up from that shore all the way around ran the jogging trail. He moved around the large rock and sat down, facing the lake.

Major walked down to the water's edge and dropped the tennis ball, which bounced and rolled until it came to rest, just barely above the waterline. Jimmy didn't worry or move to retrieve it. He knew Major's reflexes were keen. He wouldn't let the water wash his beloved ball away. Major leaned down and lapped up the cold water, and the sound of his drinking echoed in the solemn stillness.

There were no answers here, only questions. Jimmy had known this before he came, but he had come anyway, unable to turn away. The park, the path, the hallowed ground—they had called to him and he had come. An exercise in futility, though, was all it had been. He had not been willing to admit what deep down he already knew. The case was dead, as dead as Alex Morrison. He knew it in his bones. Unless the killer killed again and provided more information for making a profile or this time left useful physical evidence behind, unless by some miracle a witness came forward, unless some deus ex machina provided answers from above, there was nothing further he could do.

He would, of course, assist Gibson as he went through all the formalities of completing the investigation, but he already knew how this ended. He had been down this road before. He knew all to well when a trail was warm and when a trail was cold, and this trail, literally and figuratively, was cold.

Suddenly, Major, who had laid down beside the lake, looking out over the water, sprang up and whipped across the pebbled shore, back to the edge of the wood. There he stood, looking intently up through trees. Jimmy rose quickly and turned to peer up at the pathway above, but he couldn't see anything that would have excited Major. Major was excited, though, and he moved laterally along the tree-line, staring up the hill. Jimmy felt the hair on the back of his neck stand on end. He couldn't see anything or anyone, but he had the definite feeling he was being watched.

It had been foolish to come here alone. Killers often returned to the scene of their crime, for many different reasons. Jimmy knew that well. What's more, he was unarmed. The image of his .38 lying in the drawer of his bedside table mocked him as he strained in the failing light to scan the woods both above and below the path.

A cracking sound, like a breaking branch, echoed from somewhere above the path. Major barked, looked up at Jimmy for the briefest of seconds and then leapt into the woods, tearing up through the trees. Jimmy hesitated, still startled by this turn of events and uncertain about what his best move was, then he too leapt into the wood and followed Major as quickly as he was able.

He tried to balance speed with caution, not knowing what or who Major was chasing. He reasoned with himself as he ran. Even if the killer had returned, there was no reason to assume the man was armed. He'd not used a gun on Morrison. At the same time, however, a sturdy branch had proven more than adequate for his purpose before, and Jimmy didn't want to be on the receiving end of blows like those that had disfigured the Missoula carpet salesman.

He paused when he reached the path, looking quickly both left and right. The police tape was unbroken, and he could see nothing in either direction that suggested trouble. He looked up the hill and saw a flash of grey and white, far up the slope as Major ran on, and this time he didn't hesitate but plunged off the path, back into the woods.

The further up he went, the steeper the slope became, and it grew harder to keep Major in view while also sparing a glance here and there to survey the broader horizon. He did, though, at one point, think he saw a flash of something larger than a dog moving between trees much further up the slope, near the very top in fact, but he was unable to catch sight of it again, whatever it had been. He gathered that had anyone or anything been up there at all, it or he had moved over the ridge and out of view. Major disappeared over the top of the hill as well, and Jimmy pressed on.

A moment later he crested the ridge and found himself looking down through ten to fifteen yards of trees at the service road. He heard Major bark in the distance and started down the hill. The first step he took turned out to be a poor one, as the rock on which he unwittingly stepped, covered as it was by leaves, gave way beneath him. He fell backwards, flat on his back, hitting his head soundly upon another stone. He grunted as he bounced hard and slid further down the hill, whacking his shin sharply on a nearby tree trunk as he came at last to a stop. He grabbed his leg, tears rising unbidden to his eyes, but he bit his tongue and managed to keep from calling out. If Morrison's killer was in these woods, he certainly didn't want to draw his attention now.

He started to sit up and pain shot through his head. He leaned back down, wincing as he massaged his shin. He took a deep breath in an attempt to calm himself. He could feel his heart racing. He closed his eyes, and the image of the canopy of leaves above him remained vivid in his mind's eye. When he felt his body calming down and the immediacy of his pain subsiding, he opened his eyes and rolled back onto his side. His leg and head were both aching, but he managed to slide awkwardly down the rest of the hill until he reached the side of the service road.

He looked around, only to see Major trotting back down the road toward him from wherever he had gone in the meantime. The dog came loping along, gazing at him as though he'd been out romping in the park.

Jimmy sat down as Major approached. The dog stopped not far from his face, and Jimmy stroked his fur while he felt gingerly along the back of his scalp with his other hand. A sizable bump was already forming, but to his surprise, there was only a little blood on his fingers.

During all this, Major looked calmly on, and Jimmy sighed, frustrated. "People and animals are all around us every time we come here, but you don't run after them. Why now? Why today? Do you even know what you were chasing? Did you see it?"

The dog didn't move, though his eyes darted from Jimmy back up the hill they'd just descended, toward the ridge. Jimmy realized that with the hunt now over, Major was probably anxious to return to the lake and retrieve his beloved tennis ball.

"A killer, a possum, a tennis ball—are they all the same to you?" Jimmy said at last, standing with some effort, his head throbbing. "We'll go back and get your ball, but I really wish you could tell me what on Earth just happened."

11

"Yes, Mrs. Colson, I did hear you," Sheriff Anderson said, holding the phone and standing with his back to Jimmy and Gibbons, who were waiting patiently as he tried to calm the obviously agitated Mrs. Colson.

"I understand that you saw Mr. Janssen disappear around back behind his house with an axe," the Sheriff repeated for at least the third time, only this time he hastened to add before the excitable Mrs. Colson could chime in once more, "he was probably just going to chop some wood."

From the length and volume of Mrs. Colson's reply and the sheer number of 'uh huh's' that the Sheriff felt obliged to contribute on his end, Jimmy could tell that Mrs. Colson didn't find this wood-chopping theory terribly convincing.

"Mrs. Colson," Sheriff Anderson said, when at last he had opportunity to speak, "Mr. Janssen has lived in Avalon Falls, across the street from you, for over twenty years. I hardly think, without any actual evidence, that a search warrant for either his house or shed is justified at this point—"

The sudden silence on the other end of the phone and the Sheriff's slightly surprised look as he glanced down at the receiver before setting it back down in its cradle told Jimmy that

Mrs. Colson hadn't quite agreed with the Sheriff's assessment of the situation. Unsolved crimes tended to breed suspicion, and in a small town like Avalon Falls, it could get ugly.

Sheriff Anderson sat back down in his high-backed leather chair, behind the large, dark wood desk in his otherwise modest office. He leaned back with his hands touching at the fingertips of all five fingers, just below his chin. He appeared deep in thought, and Jimmy didn't know if it was the phone call or Jimmy's experience in the park that had the Sheriff thinking.

"It could have been almost anything, or anyone," Sheriff Anderson said after a moment.

"Could have been," Jimmy replied.

The Sheriff looked at him and his mouth twitched to the side. Jimmy wondered what it was that the Sheriff wanted to say that he wasn't saying.

"Look," Jimmy said after another moment of silence. "You may think that I'm wasting your time, and that's entirely possible. I can't prove it was the killer, but nevertheless, I think it was. He was there. He was watching me. If I'm right, then that all but proves he's a member of this community. I don't know why he was there and now that he knows he was discovered he almost certainly won't come back, but I think we should keep watch at the park, teams of two around the clock, just in case. It's a long shot, but it's the best we have right now."

"You want me to dedicate a patrol to the park because your dog chased something you never saw through the woods?"

"Yes," Jimmy said, "and because you brought me into this investigation because of my experience, and this is what I'm asking you to do."

"I wanted your expertise in behavioral analysis," the Sheriff replied. "I'm not sure the two are connected."

"You know what, Sheriff?" Jimmy said as he stood up. "You're right. I'm way out of bounds here. You've clearly got the case well under control, an arrest is plainly imminent, and listening to me would just be a waste of your time."

Jimmy turned toward the door, but Sheriff Anderson quickly rose before he got very far. "Don't be like that, Mr. Wyatt. I didn't say I wouldn't consider it. I'm just not sure what to do. It seems like a stretch to think he would come back, if he was even what you and your dog chased tonight."

Jimmy turned back from the door and wearily took his seat again on the couch, as the Sheriff sat down again too. "It is a stretch, a big stretch, and I wouldn't hold my breath that it will yield any results."

"Then why?"

"Why?" Jimmy said, looking up and turning from one man to the other in rapid succession while he talked, his hands gesturing in the air, punctuating the points he was making. "I'll tell you why. Because this investigation is over. It's finished. Unless—and this is the point—unless the killer either does something really stupid, like come back to the park again, or we get really lucky.

"When all the good options are gone, Sheriff, you either try the ones that aren't so good, or you give up and call it a day. In another life, that was my call. Not any more. This is your case, so do what you want to do. I'm just calling it like I see it."

"I appreciate your candor," Sheriff Anderson said as he leaned back. His fingers tapped each other rhythmically as he stared into space. After a while he sat forward and swiveled to look at his lead detective. "What do you think?"

Gibbons shrugged. "It's a long shot, but Jimmy's right. We never had much of a trail in this case, and now we basically have none."

Sheriff Anderson put his hands behind his head and gazed up at his ceiling. "What I hear both of you saying is that a shot in the dark is all we have left."

"Something like that," Jimmy agreed, nodding slowly.

"Well, I'm not big on taking shots in the dark. When a case has you beat, it has you beat. We might as well admit it now and save ourselves the wasted time."

"Like I said, that's your call."

"And if it was yours?"

"I've told you what I'd do," Jimmy said, "but then again, it was me out there in the woods tonight. I'm the one that feels in my gut that our guy was there, just an hour ago. Maybe, just maybe, he was there for something that's important enough to him that it'll draw him back. So if it were up to me, I'd take this particular shot in the dark."

"You are most earnest, Mr. Wyatt," Sheriff Anderson said "I'm persuaded enough to say I'll think about it."

"Fair enough."

"Was there anything else?"

"Yes, actually," Jimmy said. "I wanted to tell you that I have a .38 at my house, and for as long as I'm going to be working this case for you, I want to be able to carry it. I was caught off guard tonight, and should I find myself in such a place again, I'd like to be prepared."

"That's a lot to ask," Sheriff Anderson replied. "There's enough red tape surrounding the use of a firearm by one of my officers, I hate to think what all would be required if you used your weapon."

"I understand, but I'm asking all the same. I assure you it would remain holstered unless absolutely necessary. In all my years with the Bureau, I only drew my weapon twice, and I never fired it."

"You are doing me a big favor by helping, so I will grant you your request. This arrangement will remain unofficial and private, however, and should you draw or use your weapon in anything remotely like an inappropriate way, I will not protect or aid you. You will be on your own. Is that understood?"

"Perfectly."

"Very well then, I will let you know what I decide about the park."

Jimmy rose and stepped to the door, but he halted there and turned back to face Gibbons and the Sheriff. "There is one more thing, Sheriff."

The Sheriff looked up at him but did not speak.

"Another shot in the dark, as it were."

"Another one?"

"Yes," Jimmy hesitated. He'd been internally conflicted over whether or not to raise this last point, but he felt he needed to. "Look, I don't want to step on anyone's toes, but as long as we're reaching here, I think someone should go out and interview the guys in the New Start program."

Sheriff Anderson peered at Jimmy. "Do you have any particular reason why you'd like to do that?"

"None beyond the obvious. You have a cluster of convicted criminals here in town. It would seem like doing our due diligence to at least drop by and have a chat. I don't have access to their records, so I don't know if any of them are good candidates for this or not."

"I do have access, and I don't think there's much point to it," the Sheriff replied.

"So that's a no?"

"Not necessarily, but there were some folks around here with some strong objections when New Start first got started. It took time for Eddie and his boys to build a trust with the community, but now they've got it. If we go up there to investigate without cause and word gets round, it could do some real damage."

"Let me go," Jimmy said. "I'm not a member of your department. I've been up there a few times already, and I'll be discreet."

Sheriff Anderson's mouth twitched to the side again, and Jimmy could tell he was wrestling with this one.

"Look, unlike monitoring the park, saying yes to this requires almost nothing from you."

"Almost nothing?"

"A phone call from you in the morning to say I'm coming and to prepare the way would be all I ask."

Sheriff Anderson frowned. "You'd go tomorrow?"

"Why not?"

"And be discreet?"

"Absolutely."

"I'll call," Sheriff Anderson said, "but I'll be clear that this is an unofficial visit and that we have no specific interest in any of the boys."

"I'm not as comfortable with the second part of that message as I am with the first."

"Be that as it may," the sheriff said, "I'll be clear."

"I assume you have files on each of them here?"

"I do."

"Could I take a peek? It would help me keep things brief and to the point if I knew a little more than I do now before I head out there."

"That's fair," Sheriff Anderson said, getting up and coming around from behind his desk. "I'll see that you have a chance to see all we have on them tonight, and you'll see that you are careful in how you go about your business tomorrow."

"Deal. And you'll think about the park?"

"I'll think about the park."

A few hours later, Jimmy stepped out the front door of the station. He felt the brisk, cool night air and shivered. The street light right in front of the building flickered out momentarily, then popped back on with a loud fluorescent buzz. Jimmy jogged down the steps and headed out into the small parking lot. He slowed down as he looked up at his Bronco and saw the figure leaning against the driver's side door. Even though that side of the vehicle lay mostly in shadow, he knew who it was.

"Alice?"

"Hey," she said. She looked cold despite the puffy blue jacket she wore over her yellow waitress outfit. Her arms were crossed as she hugged herself tightly, but she lifted one hand up enough to give an anemic wave as she greeted him.

"What are you doing here?"

"I was just headed past, coming from work, and I saw your car. I pulled in and saw Major in the back seat. I've been keeping him company, haven't I boy?"

She turned and peered through the cracked front window at the dog who stood on the back seat, watching her with his tongue wagging. "Well, I'm sure he appreciated it," Jimmy said. "How long have you been here?"

"Oh, a little while."

Jimmy stopped beside her, puzzled. "Why, Alice?"

Alice shrugged. "We didn't finish the other day, and I got tired of waiting for you to come back."

"I've been a little busy," Jimmy said, wondering how to explain what had been going on.

"I know," Alice said. "And I would have waited patiently, but I saw your car and thought I'd drop by and see if maybe I could catch you."

"You look cold."

"I'm all right, but if you'd been much longer, I would have had to leave a message for you with Major and go."

Jimmy glanced at the panting dog and smiled, then turned back to Alice. "I'm glad it didn't come to that. He never gives me my messages."

"That's between the two of you," Alice replied. "Do you have a minute?"

"Sure, do you want to go somewhere warm?"

"No, just walk me back to my car."

Jimmy looked at the blue Subaru parked next to his Bronco with one empty space between them. "Your car is right there."

"I know. Does that mean I don't get treated like a lady, because I parked too close to merit an escort?"

"Not at all," Jimmy said, raising his hands in mock defense. They walked across the intervening space. She'd backed her car in, so they didn't need to walk around to the far side to reach her driver's side door.

"Look," Alice said as they stopped by her car. "I don't want to make a big deal out of this, but I wanted to let you off the hook."

"Off the hook?"

"Don't be dense, I'm talking about the disaster that was supposed to be our date. You came to apologize, and I gave you a hard time."

"I deserved it."

"You did, but that isn't my point. If we hadn't been interrupted, we might have resolved things and reached an understanding."

"And what might that have been?"

"Well, in summary form, it might have included understanding that you were the first guy in a long time that I'd agreed to see, socially, and that you blew it—majorly. It might have also included understanding that I was pretty sure, right up until you walked back into Cabot's, that there'd be no second chance. But, and you need to hear me when I say this was big for me, when I talked to you, I realized that maybe, just maybe, I wasn't ready to give up on you yet."

"I'm glad of that," Jimmy said, reaching out to take her arm in his hand.

Alice moved away, avoiding him, and Jimmy pulled his hand back in surprise.

"I need to know you're hearing me," Alice said. "Trust me when I tell you this, coming here and talking to you? This is a big deal for me. I wanted you to know that I miss having you around the restaurant. I know you're busy with the case, but you're welcome to come back whenever you have time, all right?"

"You know about the case?"

"Of course, murder is big news in Avalon Falls."

"No, I don't mean the case itself, I mean about me."

"You can't be serious," Alice frowned, "Of course I know. I'm like the town shrink, you know that. People plop down at my lunch counter and tell me everything. It was only a matter of time."

"Are you mad?"

"Mad?"

"Because I didn't tell you myself."

"No, Jimmy, I'm not mad. We've talked a lot, but not about each other."

"I guess not."

"Now, that doesn't mean I don't want to know more about you, but I've always assumed you'd tell me about yourself when you're ready."

"Should I assume the same?"

"Yeah, you should. When I'm ready, you'll know."

"Fair enough."

Alice opened the door to her car. "Good night, Jimmy."

"Good night, Alice."

She waved as she pulled out. Jimmy waved back, watching her go.

12

Eddie was waiting at the side door of the church when Jimmy pulled in. The New Start building was set about fifty yards back from Calvary Baptist and off to one side, but a gravel path led from the church parking lot, so Eddie had directed Jimmy to park there when they'd spoken briefly by phone, earlier that morning.

Jimmy looked down at the handle of his .38, protruding slightly from underneath his seat. He pushed it all the way under and out of sight with his heel, then stepped out of the car and locked his door.

Eddie, meanwhile, had not moved from the doorway. He stood, an impassive expression on his face as Jimmy approached. "Good morning, Eddie."

"Before we walk over, I want to know something," Eddie said, looking Jimmy in the eye. "Is this about the other day? Some kind of getting back at me because you told me more about yourself than you'd intended?"

"Come on, Eddie—"

"No, don't act like it's ridiculous," Eddie said. "Even though it was obvious you wanted to talk about stuff, even needed to, it was equally clear that part of you didn't want to. Well, maybe you begrudged doing it more than I thought. Here you are, come to interrogate my boys, when even Sheriff Anderson doesn't think it's necessary."

"Hold on a minute," Jimmy said, anger rising. "First of all, I'm not here to interrogate anyone. Second of all, this has nothing at all to do with the other day."

"No?"

"No, it doesn't. You're right. I was reluctant to talk about things, but I'm not angry with you because you did me a favor."

"Then why are you doing this?"

"Because it's the job."

"Not according to Sheriff Anderson."

Jimmy clenched his fist and took a deep breath. He had no official jurisdiction here and needed to watch his tone as well as his words. "What did he say to you?"

"He basically apologized for this and told me that he didn't think coming out was necessary, that the boys aren't suspects. He said he'd told you the same."

"The Sheriff told me he'd be clear when he talked to you that we had no specific interest in the boys," Jimmy said, his tone a bit caustic despite his best efforts to restrain it. "I didn't expect his clarity to be quite so undermining. I'll have to remember to thank him later."

"That doesn't explain why you're here if he doesn't think it's necessary and if none of the boys are suspects."

"Eddie, you're a smart man. This isn't that hard to understand. I'm sure you don't always see eye to eye with everyone who works, you know, in your same field—corrections, the penal system, rehab, or however you'd refer to it. It can't be that much of a stretch for you to imagine that two law enforcement officers might disagree over how to proceed in a case, especially one this difficult."

Eddie didn't say anything, and Jimmy added, less stridently. "Anyway, the disagreement between the Sheriff and I isn't even that big. There's no definitive link between the murder and New Start…"

"Then why?"

"Because a man is dead, Eddie," Jimmy said. "He's dead and the trail is all but cold. We've got very little to go on, and I can't let the fact that I know you and the boys interfere with doing my job. If this were my case, if the Bureau had flown me in here, and New Start was a computer file or manila folder in the Sheriff's Department, I'd have been here already."

Jimmy realized he'd been gesturing pretty emphatically, so he shoved his hands in his pockets and stood, staring across the distance between the church and the New Start building. Eddie glanced down at his watch. "It's after ten. I told Coach and Big Johnny we'd be over. I don't want this to be any more disruptive than it has to be."

"Neither do I."

Eddie started across the parking lot toward the gravel pathway and Jimmy walked with him. "It would help me, before we get over there, to ask you a few questions."

"Like what?"

"Like what is the overnight procedure? How are the boys secured? Things like that."

"Curfew is ten o'clock on weeknights, midnight on weekends unless there's a special event. There's always someone there overnight with the guys. Big Johnny takes Monday to Wednesday, and Coach takes Thursday to Saturday. They alternate Sundays. I stay on occasion, when necessary."

"So Coach was there this past Thursday?"

"Yes."

"And the building is secured at night? The external doors are locked and only Coach or Big Johnny can open them, or something like that?"

"Look, if you're trying to establish that we're not a prison, you've got us. That's one of the reasons why the program works. I don't doubt that our guys could have gotten out. They could, but they didn't. They know that violating curfew is a strike, and three strikes means going back into the system. Three strikes means serving time."

"Not to quibble with you on this point, but I'm not sure how much of a deterrent getting a 'strike' would be to someone intent on murder."

Eddie stopped a short distance away from the building, perhaps wanting to make sure their conversation was not being heard within. "Look Eddie," Jimmy continued, "I'm not criticizing your program—I'm really not. Your mission is laudable and your track record exemplary, but these are things I need to know. I'm sure your system works great for guys that fit your program's profile, but mistakes can be made. Sometimes the wrong people end up in programs like this. That's why I'm here."

Eddie didn't offer a reply. He just stood, gazing at the New Start building. Jimmy got more specific. "I've seen their files. We both know one of these guys isn't like the others."

That got Eddie's attention. "Hey, there's nothing in his record to suggest he'd do anything like this."

"I'm not saying there is," Jimmy said. He'd known this would touch a nerve. "But he is the most recent addition to the program and has the most serious offenses in his file. Are you going to tell me he isn't some kind of experiment to see how New Start does with more serious offenders?"

Eddie seemed to chew on that for a moment, but in the end he just said, "No, I'm not going to tell you that, but he didn't do it."

"I'm not saying he did, but you know what I'm saying, right?" Jimmy waited, but he realized he wasn't going to get any overt validation, so he just moved on. "Do the guys stay in one big room, like a barracks or something?"

"No, they sleep in quads. Each quad has a pair of bunk beds."

"And Coach and Big Johnny? Where do they spend the night?"

"I can show you when we go in, but there's a single by the door that connects the dorm area to the rest of the facility. It's opposite the bathroom. They do a room check at lights out to make sure everyone is in, then they read for a while or do some paperwork before turning in."

Jimmy nodded. "When we go in, a quick tour of the facility with you would be great. I want to see it, of course, but as importantly, I want the guys to see us interacting calmly. Seeing us relaxed will help them relax. Then, if you'd put me somewhere private, where I can talk to them one at a time, that would be perfect."

"That can be arranged."

"Good, and one other thing, I want to start with Adam."

"Why Adam?"

"He's a bit older, and he strikes me as though he's someone who won't be paranoid about being asked to go first. Start with him, then the rest of his quad, then the other. Just don't bring Nathan last."

"Why not?"

Jimmy shrugged. "I don't know if he knows his record is different then the others, but I don't want him thinking he's being singled out in any way."

Eddie nodded that he understood, then turned and led them into the building. Inside, the New Start building was as nondescript as it was outside. There was a large lounge, like a big open living room with a T.V., some chairs and couches and a table. Most of the guys were in the living room, as was Big Johnny, his massive frame sitting in an arm chair near the door. He looked up and nodded at Jimmy when they walked in. Some of the boys said, "hey" when Jimmy called out a general greeting, but most just looked up at him and then turned back to the T.V.

Jimmy and Eddie walked past a small business office on the way to a kitchen, which opened onto the eating area, comprised of two long tables sitting side by side. Coach and a handful of the guys were playing Texas Hold 'Em with plastic chips at one of them. Jimmy got a similar, half-hearted response when he greeted this group.

As they moved toward the back of the building, they came to the sleeping area. A long hallway led past the small single bedroom on the right and the bathroom on the left. Beyond were the quads Eddie had mentioned, though Jimmy noted there were three of them, even though there were only eight guys in the program. They were empty save for the furniture: bunk beds, all neatly made, a pair of desks and one comfortable chair.

At the end of the hall, on the left, was one other room. It was smaller than the quads, had a couple of metal folding chairs facing a wall with a small table against it and a cross hanging above it. Two pictures hung on either side of the cross, and for a moment, Jimmy found himself absorbed by the images.

On the left there was a picture of a man on his knees, head down with one hand grasping at the back of his head. Though his face was hidden from view, he seemed to be in the clutches of great distress. His free hand, though, was reaching up above his own prostrate form only to be clasped between the hands of another figure, standing erect and upright. This other figure was pictured only from the shoulders down. The blue sky behind this standing figure was strikingly blue and bright, and the colors of the clothes were likewise vivid. From the style of clothing the two men wore and the title of the picture, "The Leper," Jimmy figured it was meant to portray a biblical scene of some sort.

The other picture, though also immediately recognizable as a Bible scene, had a very different feel. An immense table lay covered to overflowing with food, and a large gathering was feasting uproariously. Food was held midair in hand, between plate and mouth, and cups filled with wine were raised in celebration. In the center of the picture, in the middle of the long side of the table, an elderly figure sat, his arms around two younger men, reclining on either side of him. His arms were around both, but he was turned toward the one on his right, the figure who alone in all the picture had his face downcast. The older man was leaning in as though to kiss his forehead, or perhaps whisper something over the din.

Jimmy was captivated. The elderly man had a look on his face of something very much like happiness, though happiness wasn't quite the word. Maybe the word was serenity, or maybe it was joy. Beneath the picture ran a caption in small letters, and Jimmy leaned in to read it. "*We had to celebrate and be glad, because this brother of yours was dead and is alive again; he was lost and is found."*

"A Chapel?" Jimmy asked, returning to a more upright position.

"We call it the Prayer Room," Eddie replied. "It's never used for anything official. It's just a quiet place, a peaceful refuge."

"And the door at the end of this hallway? It's an external door."

"Required by the fire code for a residence like this as a second exit," Eddie said, catching Jimmy's implication. "It's always locked. The only way out is to push the emergency release bar, and doing that would trigger the fire alarm, which is fairly loud and hard to miss."

Jimmy nodded. "All right then, I guess I'm ready to start the interviews. Where would you like me?"

"We'll go to the office."

Jimmy was seated beside the desk in the office when Adam came in a few minutes later. He had moved the rolling chair from behind the desk to the side. He wanted to appear less formal when the boys came in and set them at ease.

Adam was pretty laid back and flashed his characteristically easy smile as he entered, using his hand to slide his brown hair, long in front though not on the sides or in the back, out of his eyes. Jimmy had found him to be a pretty bright guy, though his education had ended after high school. This was a shame, Jimmy thought. Adam could have gone a long way with a college education behind him.

"Should I sit down, Jimmy?"

"Please do," Jimmy smiled as he looked up at Adam. He had a pad of paper and pen in hand. Adam glanced at them as he sat.

"So you're FBI."

"Was," Jimmy said. "Not any more."

"But you're here to ask questions about the guy from the park."

"Yes, but that's more as a favor to Sheriff Anderson."

Adam's eyebrows slipped up a notch. "The same Sheriff Anderson who told Eddie he didn't think you should ask us questions?"

Jimmy tried to hold onto his smile. The Sheriff's helpful little call at work again. He didn't need this, and there would be words when he got back to the station.

"I meant that my help with the case is not official FBI business. It is more of a favor to Sheriff Anderson—even if the Sheriff doesn't always show his gratitude as fully as he might. Now, perhaps we could begin."

"Sure," Adam said, adjusting himself in the seat and crossing his arms as he slid down a bit. His posture wasn't uneasy, exactly, but Jimmy sensed a tightening, some defensiveness rising to the surface.

"How often do you and the guys slip out of here at night, Adam?"

"What?" Adam said, surprised by the question. Jimmy noted his surprise as he looked down at his pad, taking in Adam's shift in posture. Jimmy looked back up, gesturing slightly with both pen and pad as he spoke.

"You know, eight guys staying together in a place like this. Nothing between them and an occasional night out but a door with a deadbolt easily unlocked from within and a single watchman, a kindly senior citizen half the time."

"Kindly, sure, but Coach is harder to sneak past than Big Johnny."

"Yeah?"

"Yeah, Big Johnny sleeps like the dead."

"Fair enough," Jimmy conceded, "but you do know who it's easier to sneak past."

"Sure," Adam said, looking at Jimmy, warily. "We all do."

"So I repeat my question. How often?"

"Not often," Adam said quietly, "and definitely not Thursday."

"Definitely not?"

"Definitely not."

Jimmy smiled again. "For now, let's leave Thursday out of it. Why not often?"

"Because it isn't worth it. We've got it pretty good here, and we know it."

"Got it good because it's easy time?"

"I haven't been to jail, so I don't know what it's like on the inside. I don't know that any time is easy time. What I meant is, we've got it good here because Eddie and Coach and Big Johnny actually care about us. No matter how skeptical we are when we first get here, we all get that eventually, and we like it."

"Then why sneak out at all?"

"Because we can, though not everybody does. I did it twice during the first six months I was here, but I haven't been out in more than a year and I'm not going out again. I'm finished in January, and I don't want to screw it up."

"Do you have any of these strikes Eddie talks about?"

"One."

"Then you can afford another, why not sneak out."

"Because they'd be disappointed. I'd let Eddie down."

"It matters that much?"

"Yeah," Adam said, "it does."

Jimmy nodded, then looked down, doodling in the note-book. He rarely wrote much when doing an interview. Usually that came later. He'd rather pretend to write and observe the reaction of whoever he was interviewing when they didn't think he was looking. "Well, what about the others. How do you know they don't sneak out much?"

"Guys don't usually hide it when they're going somewhere."

"But they could, right? I mean if—and I'm saying if—if someone wanted to get out without anyone knowing it, they could, couldn't they?"

"I suppose, but it would be hard. The bunks creak. The floors creak. The doors creak. You'd have to get out and back in, all without being caught by one of us. Chances aren't good."

"No one said anything about going out on Thursday?"

"No, and usually they'd say something before or after or both. If one or more of the guys had gone out Thursday night, they'd have said something Friday morning for sure."

"Maybe they didn't say anything because of the murder."

"But we didn't even know about that Friday morning. Eddie told us at supper time. There was no reason not to admit being out."

"Maybe," Jimmy said, but then he leaned in toward Adam. "Of course, if someone had been out, and again I'm just saying if, and if they'd been a party to what happened, they would have known long before supper, and they wouldn't have told you Friday morning, would they?"

Adam didn't reply.

"Would they?"

Adam stared at Jimmy. Jimmy leaned back and returned Adam's calm gaze. Neither said anything for a moment, until

Adam finally spoke. "You're cold, man. I had trouble seeing you as FBI when they said it, but I believe it now."

"Cold?"

"Yeah, cold."

"Why cold?"

"You know. You hang with us, play ball with us, but here you are, saying this stuff."

"What I just said, Adam, was for your benefit, not mine. I already know the truth of what I'm trying to tell you."

"What truth? That you think one of us did this?"

"No, that's not what I'm trying to tell you."

"Then what are you telling me."

"Listen, maybe you think because God or fate or the courts or whatever has brought the eight of you here for a time, and maybe because you wouldn't do anything to abuse the relative freedom you enjoy, maybe you think the other guys feel the same. But how do you know? How do you really know? If there is something I learned when I was an FBI agent, Adam, it is that anyone is capable of anything. We could all be a murderer, if the situation was right."

"Even you?"

"Absolutely, even me," Jimmy said emphatically, leaning forward again, staring Adam in the eye. "Don't doubt it for a moment."

"Cold," Adam said again.

Jimmy leaned back and smiled warmly, seeking to diffuse the tension. "Look, despite what you or anyone else here might think, I didn't come to throw accusations around. I'm not saying you or anybody else from New Start snuck out on Thursday night. I did come to look for the truth, and if I'm going to look for the truth, I need to establish the truth. I don't believe for a second that eight guys in their late teens and early twenties could live in a place like this without occasionally taking advantage of the, shall we say, rather minimal security. So I appreciate your candor in confirming that."

"I didn't lie about that, and I didn't lie about Thursday. I didn't need to. Nobody was out."

"All right," Jimmy said. "I hear you. You can go."

Adam looked uncertain. "That's it?"

"That's it."

"You're not going to ask me stuff about my past or why I'm here or anything?"

"Nope, we're done, unless you want me to ask about those things."

"No," Adam said, shaking his head and rising to his feet. "That's all right."

"Thanks for your help," Jimmy said, smiling as warmly as he could.

"Sure," Adam said, and he slipped out the door.

It was almost twelve-thirty when Jimmy finished and Eddie escorted him from the New Start building, back along the gravel path to the parking lot. When he'd emerged from the office, he'd found himself alone in the building with Eddie.

"You're not going to ask me about how it went?" Jimmy said as they walked.

"I know how it went," Eddie replied.

"Because the guys reported to you when they left me?"

"Because I know none of them were involved in this."

"Oh, right," Jimmy said.

"You disagree?"

"Actually," Jimmy said, "to be completely candid, not really. Not at this point. I lack your certainty, of course, but I'm not sold on any of your guys, either."

"Nathan checked out."

"Sure, as much as any of them did."

"So what now?" Eddie said, looking over at Jimmy for the first time since they'd left the New Start building.

"Not sure," Jimmy replied. "In the short run, my next step is to go have a little chat with the Sheriff about the benefits of teamwork."

"So sounds like you think you're done here."

"Am I not?" Jimmy said, stopping where he was, standing face to face with Eddie.

"Well, let me put it this way. What brought you here?"

"You know why I'm here."

"Yes, to interview the New Start guys. But why? You said that if you didn't know me or them, if you'd been sent here by the FBI, that you would already have been here. Why?"

"What's this about?" Jimmy frowned. "You know why."

"I think I do, but I wanted to hear it from you."

"Because eight young men with criminal records, convicted of a wide range of crimes, live here together under this roof. That kind of thing usually draws attention in matters like these."

"So for the record, it was these boys' past that drew you, not anything in their present behavior or situation."

"More or less."

"Again for the record, before I go on, I want to say that what you've just acknowledged is the very reason I didn't want you to come and do what you've done. As I've told you, I work very hard to convince these guys that they are not what they did. Society labels criminals with their crime, making their offense their identity. For example, someone convicted of stealing is not a person who stole but a thief.

"I try to counteract that, to convince them that their past is not their future; their offense is not their destiny. They tend to be skeptical of this, with good reason, since the rest of the world sends the opposite message, but I work hard to convince them anyway. In just two short hours, you've done a lot to undo that work."

"Well, I'm sorry about that, but I did what I believed was right in the pursuit of justice."

"I don't doubt that you did. What I'm trying to show you now is that you're hypocritical."

"How so?"

"By your own admission, it is merely the fact that these boys were convicted of a crime in the past that brought you here."

"So?"

"So you haven't questioned every other past offender in Avalon Falls, have you?"

"No," Jimmy scoffed, "but that's hardly the same thing. Here they live together in a tight knit community. It's the grouping of these boys that attracted my attention more than their particular records. Such groups often educate and encourage criminals and their activities. You know that, running a program like this."

"I do."

"So you see that your point isn't exactly valid. Some ex-con settled in the outskirts of Avalon Falls, or even in the heart of town, isn't necessarily of interest the way a program like this would be."

"I wasn't talking about anyone like that. I was talking about the fact that if your intent was to interview everyone here who has a criminal record, you're not yet finished."

Jimmy stood on the gravel path and looked back at the New Start building. He looked back at Eddie, finally getting it. "I'm not?"

"No, you're not."

Jimmy sighed and rubbed his forehead with his hand. "All right, I'll play along. How many have I missed?"

"Three."

13

Jimmy frowned skeptically at Eddie. "Three?"

"Three."

"All of you?"

"All of us."

"O.K.," Jimmy said, suddenly laughing to himself and throwing his hands up in the air. "You got me. I had no idea that apparently, you, the church man, Big Johnny, the gentle giant, and Coach, the geriatric, are all dangerous criminals. You brought it up of your own accord, though, so I assume you aren't terribly worried that I'll discover anything too incriminating by following up on this information."

"No, I'm not, and I wasn't concerned about the boys. I'm trying to make a point that you're using a double standard."

"Well, I don't want to do that," Jimmy said. He motioned back toward the New Start building. "Should I go back to the office and interview the three of you publicly so you can display my fairness to your boys, or do you just want to give me the highlights and summarize your past offenses? I'm sure they're most grievous."

"I don't mind telling you about my past, and both Big Johnny's story and Coach's were public enough at the time. Most folks around Avalon Falls already know."

"Well then, by all means, enlighten me."

"Why don't we go into the church and sit down," Eddie said, motioning to the side door where he'd been standing when Jimmy pulled in.

Jimmy glanced over at the Calvary Baptist building, hesitating. "I'm not really a church guy. I'm fine here."

"Look, I'd like to sit down, and the pews are nicely padded. We'll just step in and have a seat in the sanctuary. I won't try to convert you—I promise."

Jimmy shrugged. "Lead on."

The sanctuary of Calvary Baptist was like any of a number of similar, small protestant churches that Jimmy had been in over the years to interview witnesses, suspects or even check out a crime scene. The light wood pews had mauve seat pads that matched the faded carpet. The front of the sanctuary had a large table in matching wood, inscribed with the words, "Do This In Remembrance Of Me." Twin pulpits, also matching the wood of the table and pews stood on either side of the front. The one on the left as Jimmy looked toward the front had purple fabric draped over the top, hanging down with a symbol like a cross inserted through a crown. The table and pulpits were raised just a couple of steps higher than the rest of the room.

In the back, a small balcony with a couple more rows of pews sat above the entrance to the rear of the sanctuary. Aqua blue stained glass that harkened back to the 70s let in shafts of heavily filtered daylight. Jimmy surveyed these surroundings casually as he sat down, while Eddie turned on the lights and took a seat beside him in the front row.

"And now," Jimmy said as Eddie sat down. "Time for more of my sermon?"

"No," Eddie said, "I've sermonized enough with you for one day. Now I'm going to tell you three stories, or parts of them anyway. The application of these stories, I'll leave up to you."

"I'm all ears."

"I was arrested for shoplifting twice during my junior year of high school."

"Shoplifting?" Jimmy replied. "And here I was thinking that you were going to relay some story of past involvement in petty crime. I had no idea you were such a dangerous man."

Eddie looked quietly at Jimmy for a moment. "I admit that I didn't set an especially friendly tone when I greeted you this morning. I apologize for that. Even so, as a courtesy between friends, I'd appreciate a little less sarcasm."

"You're right," Jimmy conceded, feeling as he did so, genuinely sorry. "Go on."

"The first time, or at least the first time I was caught, the store manager called my dad and they worked things out privately. I was forced to apologize, which I did, begrudgingly. I was also made to promise never to shoplift again. I didn't keep that promise, obviously. I just worked at getting better at it. I got quite good, to tell the truth, and I kept right on going.

"When I was caught the second time, it was, ironically, in the same store where I'd been caught the first time. Again, the manager called my dad, but my dad told him to call the police. He did, and I was picked up from the store and taken away in hand-cuffs. I don't know what conversation passed between my father and the police, but I was left at the station overnight, alone in a cell. Ask Sheriff Anderson if you like. He was in the department then, a sergeant at the time, I believe.

"I had just turned seventeen, and even though I tried to look tough through it all, when they turned out the lights and I lay back on my bunk in that cell, I was scared, really scared. They brought a guy in and put him in the cell next to me. He reeked of alcohol, and he groaned all night, even though he barely moved. My dad picked me up the next day, and neither of us said anything all the way home. I was furious at him for leaving me there, and I know he was disappointed in me for breaking my promise.

"About a month later I had a trial, and the store manager and my dad testified at the trial that I was a repeat offender and had failed to learn any lesson from being let off lightly the first time. The judge fined me, sentenced me to a hundred community service hours and placed me on probation, where any violation in the next year would send me immediately to a juvenile detention center, where I would serve my sentence until I was 18 and old enough to be transferred to an adult facility.

"I got the point. I never shoplifted again. As an aside, I worked off most of my community service hours volunteering for the athletic department of the high school, largely under Coach's supervision. He knew me from the team, and while he was always the first to give me grief if I messed up on the court, he never said a word about what had happened. He seemed to understand intuitively that I'd already gotten the message and didn't need further reproach. I always appreciated that."

"So Coach was your coach, way back when?"

"Yeah, he was."

"Do you want to tell me about him, or is there more about you?"

"No, that's it in a nutshell. You're right. My offenses weren't—by most standards—especially grievous, but I never said they were. My point is that they weren't predictive of my future either. They didn't define me or become my destiny."

"I thought you were going to leave the application-making process to me?"

"Sorry," Eddie smiled. "No more sermons."

"I understand."

"Let's talk about Big Johnny before we talk about Coach."

"All right, Big Johnny. I can't imagine what he's guilty of."

"Well, that's why I want to talk about him next. I feel bad letting you think all three of us were actually guilty of committing crimes."

Jimmy frowned again. "You lied to me?"

"I didn't lie, as such. I said we'd all been *convicted*," Eddie corrected him. "As it turned out, Big Johnny's conviction was later shown to be wrongful, and he was released from prison."

"Prison? What was he convicted of?"

"Murder."

Jimmy looked wide-eyed at Eddie. "Murder? Someone convicted Big Johnny of murder?"

"Has Alice said nothing of this to you?"

Jimmy shook his head. "No, I mean, I think she started to once, a while back, when I mentioned how huge Johnny was after meeting him. She got upset, though, and didn't. It's not come up again."

"It's not something either of them discuss easily or often," Eddie said. "It's a really tragic story."

"I guess so. How much time did he serve?"

"About 8 years."

Jimmy sat stunned, slowly shaking his head.

"I'll go ahead and start at the beginning. Johnny, as you've noticed, is not especially aggressive."

"That's a bit of an understatement."

"Yeah. He's always been fairly quiet, even shy and retiring, which can be misunderstood. He has also always been big, but it wasn't until he went to prison that he became so muscular. Before that he was just, you know, big. Not obese, but big and kind of flabby. Not an athlete at all.

"Anyway, he finished high school and started at a community college outside Missoula. He got a job at a hospital there as an orderly and shared an apartment with another kid from Avalon Falls who was finishing up his Associate's at the same school. After his first year, though, this other kid finished and moved on, and Johnny needed a roommate. Another orderly from the hospital named Darren Kester moved in with him. Johnny was 19 at the time. Kester was 23.

"Anyway, as you'll have guessed by now, Kester was the guy who committed the crime. It attracted a lot of attention because it was fairly brutal. Kester raped and killed a ten year old girl from the neighborhood."

"Oh, no." Jimmy slid his hand slowly down his face and closed his eyes. "He went to prison as a pedophile rapist?"

"Yeah, and with your background, I don't need to spell out for you how things went for him."

"He didn't have a chance."

"None."

"What happened? What detective or DA could possibly have thought Big Johnny did it?"

"It mystified all of us from the beginning. All I know is that evidence led to Kester pretty quickly, and Kester, apparently, tried to minimize the damage by saying that he'd been in on the raping, but that Johnny did the killing. Hardly any of Johnny's neighbors or teachers at the community college really knew him, and everyone the police interviewed there confirmed that he was quiet and kept to himself. I think by the time they talked to anyone here, they'd already convinced themselves he was some kind of introverted serial killer.

"At any rate, both men were prosecuted successfully—Kester is still in prison, by the way. A zealous prosecutor named Daniel Collins, who was in the process of becoming the Missoula District Attorney, handled the case. Does that name ring a bell?"

"Vaguely."

"Well, he's well known in Montana because he ran a campaign for congress about six years ago. During the campaign someone dug up evidence of a number of ethical violations from his days as the District Attorney and before. The short term consequence of this was that he dropped out of the race. The long-term consequence was that several of his cases were re-opened and some dozen or more convictions thrown out. Apparently, on a number of occasions physical evidence had been falsified, juries tampered with and so forth.

"In Johnny's case, all the physical evidence pointed to Kester, and nothing but Kester's very dubious word pointed to Johnny. In fact, the testimony of a witness that established an alibi for Johnny at the time of the crime had been completely buried and withheld from Johnny's less than adequate defense. The case against him was dismissed about four years ago. He was immediately released and came back to Avalon Falls. What more could be done? Johnny was nineteen when first arrested, twenty-one when sentenced, and twenty-nine when finally set free. He'd lost ten years of his life, and nothing could repay him for that."

"Ten years in hell."

"I can't even imagine. I visited him periodically throughout the whole time, and still, I can't imagine. He only occasionally talked about what it was like, about what went on, and even then I know he hid the full horror of it from me. He quickly realized that no one was going to help him in there, so he took to the weight room as a matter of survival. In about 18 months, he was big enough that most people left him alone. He would say that by the start of his third year, he was untouchable. Nobody messed with Big Johnny. Still, he kept lifting. He lifted and lifted and lifted. Even when he got out, he lifted all the time. I still work with him on it, but it's like an addiction. It's part of him. It's part of what being inside did to him."

"Is that why he helps with New Start? Is he your living warning sign?"

"That's part of it. You can imagine the effect his story has on guys in our program."

"I can. Does he talk to the guys about what it was like?"

"Enough. It's something to see and hear. These days, I just sit and watch the boys when Big Johnny tells his story to the new guys. But, that's not the only reason why he works with us. Like I said, he was always withdrawn, and when he came home, he had, shall we say, trust issues."

"Yeah, I guess so."

"I just happened to be someone he still trusted, and it all seemed to come together. He started working for me as a transitional thing, and now I can't imagine New Start without him."

"Man," Jimmy said. "I wonder if I should talk to Alice about this."

"I can't help you with that one."

"What happened to the prosecutor, Collins?"

"His case never went to trial. He made some kind of deal and served two years. He's already out."

"Two years?" Jimmy scoffed, rolling his eyes. "That's about right. The ones who really deserve it never seem to get it. Probably well off, right?"

"I think so."

"Always," Jimmy said. "In America, money is everything."

"Hopefully not everything."

"Close enough, most of the time."

"Well, we can't afford to waste too much energy being angry about all that. Big Johnny has come a long way in the last four years. In fact, when one of our guys graduated this past spring, a kid named Brent, Johnny said something pretty amazing. He'd really helped Brent a lot, and he knew it. He told me that without prison and everything that happened there, he wouldn't have been able to have the same impact, that maybe even things like what happened to him, happen for a reason."

Jimmy shook his head. "Sorry, Eddie. I never bought that whole 'everything is part of God's plan' idea. If a mere man put someone through all that just to help a few petty criminals rehabilitate, we'd call him a monster. So why do people say this kind of stuff about God and think it lets him off the hook?"

"I hear you," Eddie said, "and I agree. If it really boiled down to that, if it was just that simple, you'd be right. But, I don't think it is that simple. Perhaps this is something we can take up another time?"

"Perhaps," Jimmy said, without meaning it. He just wanted to change the subject. "What about Coach?"

"Ahh, Coach," Eddie said, nodding his head thoughtfully. "Another sad story, but not without its upside, though I'll spare you the details of how I think God has used these hard things in Coach's life and the lives of others."

"I'm much obliged."

"Coach was a legend in Avalon Falls," Eddie started. "Still is, really, but the legend is tarnished now, though by and large I think he's been forgiven by the community."

"Did he wrong the whole community?"

"In a way. As a coach and a teacher, he was the keeper of a public trust, which he violated. Anyway, some background. Coach was twenty-eight when he took over the varsity basketball team at Avalon High, and he was an overnight success. Though we were a small school, we were always competitive while he was at the helm. We were great some years. We were good some years. We were even mediocre some years, but we were never bad. Finishing the year a few games under .500 was the worst it ever got during Coach's 30 years, no matter what the talent level was."

"So you're saying he was a good coach."

"The best."

"Well, what happened?"

"It was a close game, some fourteen years ago this coming winter, right about the time Big Johnny was coming under investigation in Missoula. Strange how those roads intersect, you know? I remember thinking at the time about how when it rains it pours. Anyway, it was an important game, and we were playing poorly. Just awful. Very uncharacteristic. Bad decisions, sloppy play, silly fouls—all the things that drove Coach crazy.

"Anyway, he called a timeout with a few minutes left. I remember it like it was yesterday. I was sitting in the stands, not twenty feet away. I turned to say something to the guy next to me, another alum, and I heard it. Whack! It echoed across that gym. It still echoes through my head, through this whole town. I turned and saw the boy's face, blood pouring down, just everywhere."

"What happened?"

"Coach hit the kid with his clipboard. The metal clip part struck the boy along his eyebrow and split it wide open. The boy bled like a stuck pig."

"Why'd he do it?"

"Why? Lot's of reasons, I think. Because the boy rolled his eyes when Coach started to tell him off for a stupid foul. Because Coach's marriage was breaking up, even though no one knew that at the time but Coach. Because Coach had started seeking comfort, more than was usual anyway, from a bottle. Because Coach was three sheets to the wind before the game even started, and not for the first time as several of the boys admitted during the follow-up investigation. Because Coach had finally reached his breaking point, and the boy was there, right in front of him to absorb all that fury and frustration."

"And the consequences?"

"He lost everything. He was fired, both as a teacher and a coach. His wife finally left after a year of threatening to go. He was prosecuted and convicted for assault. The judge was lenient, and since he had no prior record he was given probation and released, provided he got into a program and got cleaned up. That's how he ended up here, actually. He came to live with Martha and me, and his rehab started right away."

Eddie paused, and Jimmy stirred at the mention of "Martha." He looked at Eddie with eyebrows ever so slightly raised. Eddie understood the look. "Yes, I was married. Martha died of breast cancer 9 years ago. That part of my past I do not frequently discuss and won't now, except to say Martha was the best woman I ever knew.

"Knowing how much Coach had meant to me, she insisted that we take him in. He lived with us while he sobered up. It started as a temporary arrangement, but it worked really well and he never left. He helped me get New Start up and running, and by the time Martha died, we were the only family the other had. He's been with me ever since and will be until one or both of us are in the ground, I would imagine."

"Frightening, isn't it?" Jimmy mused after contemplating Coach's story for a while. "Thirty years of hard work, all undone in a second. A single lapse of judgment; a single swing of the arm. So quick, so fast, so final. Impossible to call back."

"I'm not sure I'd say undone," Eddie said. "The boys who'd learned from Coach and benefited from his years of teaching and coaching didn't suddenly cease to know the lessons they'd learned. I know what you mean, though, and yes, it's a little frightening. A good lesson to learn vicariously, rather than through your own experience."

"Which makes Coach another valuable asset to your program."

"Just so."

"So that's it, huh? The shocking tale of the 'New Start 3.' Turning your own experiences with the law into an effective intervention into the lives of other young men."

"Something like that."

"And yes," Jimmy quickly added. "I haven't forgotten the point. Despite what you all did, or in Johnny's case, what was done to him, you haven't let your past become your destiny."

"That's right."

"Message received," Jimmy said, standing up.

"Time to be heading out, is it?"

"Past time. I need to report back to the station and have my little chat with Sheriff Anderson."

"May I ask if any of your conversations today produced anything you thought might be noteworthy?"

"The only one I really had any concerns about was Nathan, for obvious reasons. His profile showed a real if not yet homicidal penchant for violence, suggesting he could possibly be someone of interest. Don't worry, I didn't find anything in any of the conversations to justify pursuing this matter further with you or your boys at this time."

"Good, I'm glad to hear it."

They stepped outside and walked over to Jimmy's Bronco. He hesitated at his door, fumbling in his pocket a moment for the keys. When he had finally unlocked it, he said, "Well, I'm off."

"All right, Jimmy," Eddie said. "I hope you catch a break. I really do."

"With the case?"

"With the case. With life. With anything."

And with that, Eddie turned and headed back to New Start.

14

Jimmy sat at the end of the lunch counter at Cabot's, turned sideways on the stool with his back against the wall. He looked out the big window at Main Street and the world beyond. It was one of those really stormy days when rain fell down in sheets, sending water scudding along the pavement. Jimmy gripped his coffee, held tightly in the palm of his hand, and sipped slowly.

He liked the feel of the wall against his back. It comforted him, reminding him of UCLA, where he'd always taken a seat on the right side of the room so he could sit sideways in his desk with his back against the wall. He leaned his head back and rested it too, closing his eyes and enjoying the quiet.

"Is the pervert gone?"

Jimmy opened his eyes to see Elliot, one of the codgers from the corner table, standing next to the stool, peering at him.

"The pervert?"

"Yeah," Elliot said. "What else would you call a guy who bashed another guy's family jewels? Who the hell did you think I was talking about?"

Jimmy sighed. "I don't know who he is, so I can't say if he's gone."

Elliot shrugged. Jimmy's matter-of-fact assessment seemed oddly satisfactory. Elliot shuffled back toward the corner table and stopping midway, turned and looked over his shoulder. "If he tries that business with me, though, I'll blow his head off, I'll tell you that much."

Jimmy was just leaning back against the wall again when Alice reappeared from the back. She looked at him and smiled. "Must be nice."

"What?"

"Not having anywhere to be, apparently." She grinned. "Did the Sheriff tell you not to come back?"

"No," Jimmy said, sitting forward a little bit and shaking his head. "I'll go back in a while. I was just taking my time."

"Well…" Alice said, leaning in over the counter and motioning to him to lean in as well.

Jimmy leaned forward, looking curiously at Alice. "I have one piece of Banana Cream Pie left. Do you want it?" she whispered.

"Absolutely," he whispered in reply.

She stood back up and slipped quietly from the room. In a moment she returned with the pie, covered gloriously with an absurd amount of whipped cream.

"Just how you like it," she said as she put it down.

"Looks fantastic."

She leaned on the counter again. "So still working the case then?"

"You could say that," Jimmy said before shoveling a forkful of pie into his mouth.

"What do you mean?"

"Mmm, perfect," Jimmy mumbled, swallowing the soft, silky mouthful. "Even better than usual."

"Thanks."

Jimmy sipped his coffee. "Working is a generous term. There's not much left we can do. Not like things are, anyway."

"It just feels so … wrong," Alice said, "you know, thinking about someone getting away with this. When you watch a crime show on T.V., they always get the guy who did it—or almost always, anyway."

"Yeah," Jimmy said, scoffing a bit. "But sadly, there was no rare microfiber left behind in a footprint at the scene that is only manufactured in three plants in the world, one of which just happens to be right outside of Avalon Falls, which would then take us to the only employee of that plant with a pair of size 12 New Balance tennis shoes who was also seen at the park on the night in question so we'd have enough for a search warrant and then find the shoes with matching microfibers and blood spatter, conveniently still in the culprit's closet so we could wrap the case up and be home in time to see the next episode of *CSI:Avalon Falls.*"

"Sorry," Alice said with mock sincerity. "Did I touch a nerve?"

Jimmy smiled as he wolfed down another bite. Eventually he answered. "No, but like *ER* was hard to watch for a nurse I once dated, crime dramas tend to annoy me."

"Too far-fetched?"

"Sometimes, but mostly, they bother me because real investigation and forensics requires hours and hours of fairly tedious work. Those shows suggest that policemen and FBI agents run around waving their guns or having shoot outs, when in fact, I hardly ever drew my weapon when I was on the job. Mostly, I just spent a lot of hours plowing on ahead."

"So you're saying you're not Jack Bauer?"

"No, I'm not."

"Good," Alice added, "because he's had some really bad luck, don't you think?"

Jimmy laughed and almost choked, then raised his hand to cover his mouth as a flake of pie crust flew out and landed on the counter. Alice laughed too as she pulled a rag out of one of her big pockets and wiped the flake off the counter. "Sorry about that, I didn't mean to make you spit up your dessert."

"Quite all right," Jimmy said, regaining his composure and sipping his coffee.

"Now," Alice said, "About this nurse ex-girlfriend?"

"What about her?"

"I don't know," Alice shrugged. "You never talk about people from your past, so I thought maybe she was important."

"Nope," Jimmy said. "Only dated her a couple of months, and that was more than ten years ago."

"Disaster?"

"No, just didn't go anywhere."

Alice nodded and didn't press the matter further. "Do you think your work in the Sheriff's department has a future, or will you be going back to work at the mill?"

"Back to the mill, at some point," Jimmy answered, pushing the plate with pie crumbs and a smear of whipped cream away from him. "I just don't know when. That's up to the Sheriff. Whenever he gets fed up with me, I suppose."

"Fed up with you?" Alice looked mischievous. "Have you been difficult?"

"Well, I wouldn't say difficult, but the Sheriff and I haven't seen eye to eye on everything, and none of my ideas have led anywhere exactly."

"No? Like what? Can you tell me?"

"Sure, if you promise to keep it to yourself."

"Absolutely."

"This past Sunday I was at the park with Major and thought I saw someone near the crime scene."

"You think it was him?" Alice said, wide-eyed.

"Maybe. Anyway, Sheriff put a couple deputies on the park for the next 72 hours at my suggestion, but nothing came of it."

"That's not your fault," Alice said, a little defensively. "It was worth a try, wasn't it?"

"That's what I thought, but whenever I push for an acknowledged long shot and miss, I feel like I lose a bit of credibility. That's just how it works. Then there was the New Start fiasco on Monday."

"Yeah," Alice said, her smile slipping a bit. "I heard about that."

"Your brother told you?"

"He did."

"What did he tell you?"

"Just that you were out, interviewing the guys. Eddie was a little upset about it, and that made Johnny upset. He looks up to Eddie so."

Jimmy looked at Alice for a moment. This was the time, and he knew it. "I know about Johnny, about what happened to him, and about what Eddie has meant to him."

"Yeah," Alice said, her lips trembling as she reached for the empty plate on the counter.

Jimmy reached out and stopped her, taking her hand and holding it gently. "I'm sorry, Alice. I can't imagine how hard all that was for you."

"It was a nightmare," she said, withdrawing her hand from the counter as Jimmy let it go to wipe tears from her face. "Still is. Johnny is just so ... so ... "

Jimmy searched for something to say. "Eddie thinks Johnny's made some good progress, I think."

"Eddie looks for the good in everyone and everything. Johnny's made progress, all right. He speaks some and doesn't lift weights for three hours everyday. Maybe just two hours, most days. I guess you could call that progress."

Jimmy didn't say anything further. What could he say? He knew better than most what kind of hell Johnny must have been through, so he could imagine better than most how helpless Alice must have felt for more than a decade, unable to stop or mend it. He wasn't about to cheapen her suffering with further weak attempts at consolation.

Alice cleared away his plate and returned a moment later with the coffee pot to refill his cup. "How'd you find out? Eddie?"

"Yeah, Eddie told me."

"Why?"

"He thought I needed to learn a lesson about, well, about judging someone based on their past, I guess."

"How does Johnny come into that?"

"Indirectly, admittedly. Eddie was annoyed because I went out to New Start to interview the guys, just because they had previous records. So to prove his point that it was a bad reason, he gave me some grief for not interviewing himself, Coach and Johnny for their records."

"Eddie has a record?" Alice looked surprised.

Jimmy was taken aback. "Shoplifting. When he was in high school. I thought it was general knowledge."

She shrugged. "I might have known, at some point, but if I did, I've since forgotten."

"Well," Jimmy said nonchalantly, "I guess he isn't too shy about it being known. Still, if you don't mind not mentioning that I told you …"

"I won't," Alice said, frowning at him. "What do you think I'll do? Go 'hey Eddie, done any shoplifting lately?'"

"No, I don't know, I just don't want to give him more reason to be annoyed with me."

"I doubt he's still annoyed. Eddie's not one to hold a grudge. Have you spoken to him since?"

"Not yet."

Alice nodded and leaned closer to Jimmy on the counter. "I'm not upset that you know about Johnny. In fact, I'm relieved. I've been meaning to tell you, ever since I acted so weird when you first mentioned him."

"Hardly weird, given the facts."

"Thanks, but I've wanted to tell you," Alice hesitated, standing across the counter from Jimmy. "It's just, I feel like I still don't know how to talk about it."

"Well, I don't plan on discussing it with anyone, and I don't expect you to talk about it if you don't want to. I just wanted you to know that I know."

"Thanks."

"Got any plans this weekend?" Alice said, redirecting the conversation.

"No, you?"

"Yeah, I'm taking Ellen and Ethan to get Halloween costumes."

"Halloween?" Jimmy said. "But it's only just turned October."

"I know, but Ethan especially is still young enough to get really excited about Halloween. He likes wearing his costume now and again during all the lead up to the actual holiday."

"Any idea what he'll want to be?"

"Something from Star Wars probably, or maybe a pirate. He'll look at other things, but when it comes right down to it, it'll be one of those two things."

"Star Wars," Jimmy shook his head. "Amazing how that whole thing is still going."

"Going strong," Alice said. "Lego toys, light sabers and video games—anything Star Wars goes over very well with Ethan."

"Well, I guess that makes for some easy decisions at Christmas time."

"That's true. He's not too hard to buy for yet. Ellen, on the other hand, is getting more complicated."

"How old is she?"

"Thirteen."

"Ahh," Jimmy nodded. "A teenager in the house."

"Yes, but it isn't so bad. More complicated, perhaps, but not bad. We get along pretty well still."

"Good," Jimmy said. "Well, I should probably be heading back to the department."

"Yeah, you've squandered quite enough time loafing around here."

Jimmy smiled and gave her a deferential nod as he rose. "I may have loafed as long as I'm allowed, but it hasn't been nearly as long as I would like."

Alice took the cash from his hand with a subdued but pleased smile and walked to the cash register.

15

Jimmy walked into the Sheriff's Department, almost drenched to the skin by the walk from the parking lot, and he was immediately struck by the hum of activity. On the far side of the room, a slim man in a flannel shirt with a creased baseball cap with a Broncos logo appeared to be giving a statement to a uniformed deputy while another hovered ominously nearby. A third deputy, not in uniform and likely called in for whatever was going on, was on the phone not far away, talking in emphatic but hushed tones. The normally calm and sedentary administrative assistant, Sandy, who usually greeted him upon his arrival from her desk by the door, barely noticed him as she hustled from the filing cabinet in the corner over to the Sheriff's office. The door opened and she disappeared inside.

Jimmy peered through the open blinds of the office as a folder was placed in Sheriff Anderson's hands. The Sheriff set the file on his desk, not allowing the brief interruption to derail his conversation with Detective Gibbons. Meanwhile, Sandy re-emerged and bustled past him, managing a quick but slightly breathless and wheezy "Hi, Jimmy," on her way down the hall to the kitchen in the back of the station.

Jimmy started drifting closer to the Sheriff's door, looking again at the man seated across the room. He was thin, gaunt even, with a mop of stringy, dark but heavily greying hair falling shoulder-length below his cap. His face was grizzled by a several day growth that was going to be a pretty poor excuse for a beard if allowed to continue for all the bare patches in it.

Whatever the man was saying to the officer behind the desk, he was gesticulating freely and with animation, and Jimmy could see gaps in his yellowing teeth. Jimmy thought him about fifty, though he inwardly handicapped his guess at about five years in either direction. He was usually more sure of himself, but some wore years more heavily than others.

He turned back toward the Sheriff's office and noticed that he had been spotted, for the Sheriff was already almost at the door. It swung open, but the Sheriff did not emerge. Instead, with a furtive, silent movement, Jimmy was waved inside. Jimmy walked swiftly inside as the Sheriff shut the door behind him.

"We'd given up waiting," Sheriff Anderson said. "Gibbons was getting ready to start without you."

"Sheriff, Detective Gibbons," Jimmy said, almost casually, nodding to each of them in turn. "Given up waiting for me for what?"

"Don't be daft, man," Sheriff Anderson said impatiently. "Can't you see we've got a suspect?"

"In the Morrison case?"

"What else?"

Jimmy glanced over his shoulder again at the man at the desk. "Just like that? Two hours ago we're at a total loss, a dead end, then I go out for lunch and a break to clear my head, and you crack the case?"

"No one said it was cracked," Gibbons said quietly. "He's a suspect is all."

"All right, fill me in."

"Sheriff Anderson can give you the basics. I'm going to move him down to the questioning room and Mirandize him. You can join me when you're ready, if you'd like."

Gibbons slipped out of the office, and both Jimmy and the Sheriff watched as the deputies, in response to Gibbons' directions, began to move the visibly unhappy man down the hall. His hands were cuffed, and echoes of his voice slipped through the Sheriff's otherwise fairly solid walls. "I didn't do nothin.' You can't do this."

In a moment, though, the whole scene disappeared from view. Jimmy turned back to Sheriff Anderson, raising his eyebrows and motioning expressively with his hands. "Well? What's the deal with that guy?"

"His name is Dyson Beck. He came in about an hour ago to register."

"Register?" Jimmy said, cocking his head and locking eyes with the Sheriff. "You mean he's a sex offender?"

"Yup," Sheriff Anderson nodded.

Jimmy stared, wide-eyed. "How long has he been here?"

"A month."

"A month," Jimmy whistled. "And he's just now registering?"

"Yeah, well, he just got a job. There's some ambiguity in the statute. Since he's only just started working here, he can argue that he's within his week of taking up residence. Up until he got work, he could technically have been considered a tourist."

"Yeah, right."

"You know how it is. We don't write the laws."

"I know. We just have to figure out what they actually mean as opposed to what they're supposed to do."

"You're preaching to the choir."

"So what's his rap sheet say?"

"Take a look." Sheriff Anderson reached beyond the file folder just deposited on his desk and picked up a few pieces of paper stapled together and handed them to Jimmy. "Here's the print out. We're still checking up on a few things."

Jimmy took the sheets in his hand and scanned them rapidly. He lowered it as he looked up at the Sheriff, frowning. "This is it?"

"As far as I know. Isn't it enough?"

Jimmy looked back down. "Two exposure convictions, both involving minors, along with allegations of child molestation that never went to trial?"

"That's right."

Jimmy handed it back, still frowning. "Do you mind if I sit in with Gibbons?"

"Not at all, that's why we waited."

Jimmy slipped out of the office and walked past Sandy, who was whispering at her desk to one of the deputies. They both grew quiet as he approached, acknowledged him as he walked by. He walked past them and down the hall toward the questioning room, which had only a little over a week ago been his makeshift office.

Jimmy entered the room quietly. Gibbons was sitting on the far side of the table so Beck had his back to the door. Even so, Beck didn't look around when he heard the door open, and Jimmy slipped past the table to the far side and pulled out a chair to the far wall so he could sit a little back from the interview. Dyson Beck looked over at him with disinterest before his eyes flickered back to Detective Gibbons. Gibbons, for his part, was writing something down in his notebook and had not looked up either during Jimmy's entrance.

"All right, Mr. Beck," Gibbons said, looking up. "As I said, I'll get your previous employer's number and your most recent permanent address from your registration, but I'd like to talk to you some more about your time in Avalon Falls."

"What for?" Beck said, gruffly. "I already told you I haven't done anything. You got no cause to question me, or handcuff me. I'll sue."

"You're a convicted sex offender who's been in this town for a month even though the law requires you to register within the week…"

"I only got a job and a real place this week." Beck's voice was loud and defiant, echoing in the small room.

"Which is the only reason you're not already in jail. Even so, your choice to defer registering is, at best, questionable. I'm quite sure a judge would be willing to grant us a fair bit of latitude, so sue away."

"Of course a judge would give you latitude," Beck sneered. "It's fixed, the whole deal. I ain't ever done nothin' wrong."

"Really," Gibbons said, looking up from his notebook and staring at Dyson Beck. "I'm not sure the family of that boy in Helena would agree."

"Shoot, what do you know about it? David was my friend. I'm a friendly guy. I like kids. We were buddies is all. Besides, that never even went to trial. What about innocent until proven guilty? Or doesn't that apply when it's a so-called sex offender you're talking about?"

"Oh, it still applies," Gibbons said. "But so do all the other rules, and it's usually the sex offender who doesn't bother with them."

Beck had nothing to say to this, so he sat their scowling while Gibbons set his notebook down on the table. "Look, what I'm most interested in, is hearing from you about what you were up to last Thursday night."

Beck jerked forward, gazing angrily across the table. "I thought that was why you was dragging me through all this song and dance. I've heard the whispers about the way that guy died. Once you pigs started hanging all over me, I figured you was gonna try to pin that thing on me, just because you can't catch the guy that really did it. What a joke."

Gibbons waited until Beck had finished his rant and continued. "So how about it? Where were you last Thursday?"

"Home."

"At your motel room?"

"Yeah."

"Alone?"

"Yeah."

"All night?"

"No, not all night. I had a few drinks at the bar down the street."

Jimmy suddenly felt his interest growing in this conversation. Morrison had been drinking at The Rusty Nail, which wasn't down the street from the Best Western where he'd been staying, but it was close enough. If Beck had been in the same bar and had a room at the same motel, there might be more to this then he'd first thought.

Gibbons had been writing, but he stopped and asked. "When you say the bar down the street, you mean Connelly's?"

"Yeah, that's where I've spend most of my evenings here."

Jimmy's excitement dissipated. Connelly's was nowhere near the Best Western, which meant Beck was staying somewhere else.

"Then why did you say you were in your motel room?"

"I thought you meant after that."

"How late were you at Connelly's?"

"Until about 11:00 or so."

"Anybody see you?"

"Sure, everybody. I sat at the bar for a couple hours, talking to the barkeep and a few other fellas. Ask 'em."

"We will," Gibbons said, scribbling. "Afterwards you went straight home?"

"I did."

Gibbons kept writing, and then he stood up. "All right then, Mr. Beck. I'm going to take care of a few things. I'll be right back."

Gibbons glanced at Jimmy on his way past and Jimmy gave an almost imperceptible nod. The door opened and closed, leaving Jimmy alone with Dyson Beck.

Beck, for his part, sat with his head sagging down a bit, the bill of his cap almost shielding Jimmy from seeing his dark, staring eyes, which seemed now to be focused on the table in front of him. The whole time he'd been questioned by Gibbons, Beck had never once looked at Jimmy. Jimmy kept still, observing. He didn't say a word.

At last, after several moments of silence, Beck raised his head and looked over at Jimmy. Their eyes met, and Beck scrutinized him like a disapproving grocer might examine a rotting orange. Finally, Beck spoke. "So what are you, the junior detective?"

Jimmy didn't answer. He kept his steady and dispassionate gaze on Beck, who shifted a little in his seat. "Here to earn your badge? Learning how to be real police, are you?"

Still, Jimmy said nothing, and now he could see irritation in Beck's features as a flash of anger swept across his face. "What are you, a retard?"

Jimmy leaned forward, keeping his eyes fixed on Beck. "I don't really work here. You could say I'm the guy they call when they need a little help."

For the first time since he'd entered the room, Beck looked uncertain, and perhaps a little scared. He glanced back down at the table, and Jimmy leaned back. A moment later, the door opened again, and Jimmy rose, walked over and motioned to Gibbons to remain outside the room with him in the hall.

"What's up?" Gibbons asked as they walked a few steps away from the room, leaving the armed deputy at the door.

"He's not our guy."

"Even if his story checks out and he was at Connelly's until eleven—and Greg's going by to check now—he could have gotten from there to the park in time."

"He's not our guy," Jimmy said again, more emphatically.

"He's all we've got."

"Then we've got nothing, cause I'm telling you, he's not our guy."

"How can you be so sure?"

"Because it doesn't fit. I mean, let's assume for a moment that the allegations about Beck molesting that kid are true …"

"With these guys, where there's smoke there's fire."

"Very often, but that's not the point right now, because we're going to take the worst case scenario. We'll presume guilt. Even so, all his offenses involve children. Little boys, not grown men. Not only that, the allegations are only three years old. From fondling children to annihilating grown men is a huge leap in three years. For Pete's sake, it took him more than three years to move from exposure to molestation. I'm telling you, none of it fits. He's a creep and a perv, I agree, but he's not our guy."

"He may not be."

"He isn't," Jimmy reiterated. "O.K., granted, he's got the whole white trash look going on, but he's not stupid. That's clear. So if he's our guy, why come register today? If he's our guy, why do this a week *after* the murder?"

"He has to."

"Come on, Eric. Don't give me that. You know that half these guys never register when they move. It's almost impossible to keep track of them, and we both know that among sex offenders, Dyson Beck would hardly be seen as a top priority. Guys like him could move to a town like this, never register, and go undiscovered for years. If Beck had killed Morrison last Thursday, I don't think he'd still be here, but even if he did stick around, he wouldn't come walking into the station to flaunt his past in front of us."

"He wouldn't be the first criminal either stupid enough or arrogant enough or both to play games with the people trying to catch him."

"No, he wouldn't, but we both know that's not Beck's profile. He's no Hannibal Lector. He's a lecher, sure, but he's not a deranged mastermind. Besides, not only does he not fit the psych profile, he doesn't even fit the physical profile. Look at him. Beck couldn't obliterate Morrison like that. No way. He's not our guy."

"So what are you saying I should do?"

"Let him go. Don't waste your time."

"I can't do that," Gibbons said, shaking his head. "If we're wrong, and we let him go without checking? If he killed again? No. I can't let him go yet."

"All right," Jimmy said, "but it's a waste of time."

"And posting deputies at the park? Interviewing the guys at New Start? What was that?"

Jimmy looked down. There was no malice in Gibbons' voice, just frustration. He nodded without looking back up. Jimmy knew he was right and said so. "No, you're right, of course. You've got to do it."

When he did look back up Gibbons was watching him carefully. "What's going on here, Jimmy? Why so keen to cut this guy loose?"

Jimmy shrugged. "I don't know. For a moment there, I guess, I thought maybe we had something, but we don't. I know this guy, and he's not the one."

"You know Dyson Beck?"

"No, not Beck. I know his type. I've known too many Becks in my life, and I don't really care to know any more. Mind if I skip out on the rest?"

"Of course not," Gibbons said, moving back to the door. "I'll let you know if I get anything useful."

The door closed behind Gibbons, and Jimmy turned to walk back down the hall, saying softly to no one in particular. "You won't."

16

Jimmy sat on a picnic table in the park. The wind was cold and he was glad he'd brought his heavy jacket. He had a sweatshirt on underneath as well, and his track suit pants were lined and cozy. Major was weary from fetching the tennis ball, and he was lying beside the table, staring at nothing in particular. A lot like Jimmy.

He'd been hesitant to come today after his time at New Start the previous Monday. In the end, he'd decided to come out, thinking that ten days was enough time. Much more might make it difficult to come back at all. He didn't think the New Start guys would hold it against him, though he couldn't be sure. It was Eddie who worried him. Alice had reassured him that Eddie wasn't like that, and maybe he wasn't, but not holding a grudge about it didn't mean things wouldn't change in other ways.

At any rate, he wouldn't find out today what kind of welcome he'd receive from Eddie, Coach and the New Start boys, because they weren't here. The basketball court had been empty the entire time he'd been at the park, and Jimmy glanced over now at the unused blacktop. It had occurred to him once or twice as the fall had progressed that the weekly basketball plan might not be a year round routine, but he'd never thought to ask. Now he didn't know if the regular game was on hiatus or simply canceled for today. At least finding out would give Jimmy a pretense to call Eddie and break the ice. He might even drive out over the weekend and drop by. Maybe.

The sound of a car door shutting grabbed his attention. He peered over his shoulder at the parking area, where a silver sedan was sitting about six or seven spaces away from his Bronco. A woman in bright pink jogging gear with a headband on to keep her ears warm was already moving briskly across the grass toward the running track. Jimmy tensed. While there were signs all over town that the jogging track was open again for public use—and had been since the previous Saturday—it was still strange to see someone actually doing it.

Sooner or later people were going to start returning to their routines. He'd seen it often enough. With things like this, the public seemed to have only so much ability to live with chaos and crisis. Eventually they were drawn inexorably back to the patterns of life they'd kept before their ordered lives were shattered by the intrusion of what Jimmy thought of as the deep ugliness of man.

Still, he watched the woman reach the track and head toward the wood and thought about what had happened on that track two weeks before. Was it running through her mind? As she slipped out of sight, into the trees, did she take a deep breath and did she wonder if somewhere up ahead, waiting for her, the murderer was lurking? Did these things flash through her mind and did she fight to push them away, calling them "improbable" and "irrational?"

For a moment he considered going after her, but he quickly dismissed the idea. He hadn't recognized the jogger, and being followed through the woods by a stranger and his big dog would freak her out if she wasn't freaking out already. Besides, he couldn't post himself here everyday or ensure the safety of everyone who used the track. The powers that be in Avalon Falls would have to decide for themselves whether or not Morrison's death was sufficient reason to re-route the jogging track, clear it or close it. If they didn't, if they left it as is, despite what had happened here, then it was not his place to try to contravene their wishes.

An hour later he walked in through the front door of Cabot's. Almost every seat was taken as the lunch hour was in full swing. Two seats in the middle of the lunch counter were open, though, and he walked over to one of them and dropped his keys on the counter as he sat down. He removed his coat and set it down on the open seat beside him.

He'd barely had a chance to sit when Alice appeared, a pot of coffee in her hand and a cup and saucer in the other. She deftly set the saucer down and popped the cup on it one-handed, and soon it was full and steaming. "You're earlier than usual today, Jimmy."

"True," he said. "It's kind of a weird day."

"Yeah?"

He nodded, sipping the coffee. "You're busy. I'll tell you later, when things settle down a bit."

"You have time to wait?"

"Plenty."

She shook her head, smirking. "I tell you, it must be nice."

"Don't start that again," he said, grinning. "Just get me a hot roast beef sandwich. I'm really hungry today."

"Fries?"

"Fries."

"All right, I'll put your order in," she said, moving down the line to refill a few other cups.

Jimmy ate his lunch and downed several more cups of coffee before things had settled down enough for Alice to be able to linger a while. She stopped in front of him and paused to try to reinsert a few loose strands of hair into her pony tail.

"You should leave them out. They look nice."

"Thanks, but they bother me." She gave up on the attempted repair, pulled the pony tail holder off and started over. The brief glimpse of her pretty auburn hair down about her shoulders reminded him vaguely of the still hazy night when she'd met him at The Rusty Nail. He looked down to avoid blushing as she spoke to him. "So what's weird about today?"

"Well," Jimmy said, "my short-lived career, moonlighting as an officer of the law here in Avalon Falls is over."

"Really?" Alice said.

"It's back to the mill for me."

"Tonight?"

Jimmy nodded.

"When did you find out?"

"I talked to Sheriff Anderson about it yesterday. He agreed with me that as things were, there wasn't a whole lot of reason for the department to keep paying for my services. I might as well go back to the mill."

Alice appeared puzzled. "Are you saying you approached the Sheriff about this?"

"I did."

"It was your idea to go back to the mill?"

"It was."

"But why? I would have thought, you know, given your background, that working with the Sheriff would be a big step up from the mill."

"Yes and no," he shrugged. "Sheriff Anderson came to me when the case was fresh and the details unknown, primarily to help build a profile. I did that. The case isn't fresh anymore, and we're none of us holding out much hope that we're going to catch this guy, not unless …"

His voice dwindled away, and Alice picked up the dropped thread. "Unless what?"

"Unless he kills again," Jimmy finished his thought, looking up at her.

They were both quiet and Alice refilled his cup again. When she was finished, she asked in a hushed tone, barely more audible than a whisper. "Do you think he will?"

"Well, I can't find much reason to think the killer knew the victim personally, despite how much the crime looked like it might be personal. I just don't think they knew each other."

"I don't know what that means," Alice said, looking puzzled. "How does that relate to whether he'll do it again?"

Jimmy sighed. "If he didn't know him, his motivation was internal, not external. He had to, don't you see? To do what this guy did? And not know the victim? He'll do it again."

Alice was silent. "Maybe he didn't like it. Maybe, you know, now that he's done it once, maybe he'll stop."

"Anything's possible, I guess," Jimmy said, "but more likely, whatever inner compulsion drove him to this, it'll be easier for him to give in to it and do it again next time. The monster's out of the box, and once it's out, it doesn't usually go back in."

"That's pretty scary."

"Yeah, it should be. Look Alice, you can't live in constant fear. Nobody can—not and be sane. But be careful. I saw a lady at the park today, headed for the jogging track. It's probably fine, you know, but I'd stay away until you know this guy is caught."

"Did you warn her?"

"No, but I hung around until she'd completed her loop and went back to her car before I left."

"Such a softie, under that aloof demeanor," Alice said, smiling.

"That's me," Jimmy said.

"I don't normally use the park much," Alice said. "It shouldn't be too hard to avoid."

"That's fine, but don't limit your thinking to that. I know you have to close up sometimes, but don't do it alone. Don't be out after dark alone at all unless you have to. I'll be back on nights at the mill now, so I can't help during the week, but I can make sure you get home on weekends if you like."

Alice smiled as she leaned on the counter. "You'd do that for me?"

"I would."

The smile passed, though, and she stood back up. "I guess I'll need to rethink all my normal routines, won't I?"

"You will. We all should."

"Why hasn't anything been said by the Sheriff, or in the paper? Shouldn't a warning or something be issued?"

"The most Sheriff Anderson could do, would be to say 'be careful.' If he was stronger than that, there'd probably be panic, and the mayor and others would be all over him for unnecessarily exacerbating a bad situation. When things like this happen, civil authorities just want it to go away as soon as possible.

Of course they want the person responsible caught—in fact, the Sheriff has been feeling the heat to nab somebody—but at the end of the day, what they want most is for things to return to the status quo.

"So in the absence of an actual arrest and conviction, what's needed is a return to normalcy. Spreading the word that this probably isn't over won't help that. Besides, it's possible the guy isn't from here and the next time he kills, it will be somewhere else entirely."

"Oh," Alice said, perking up, "that would be good, wouldn't it?"

"For us, sure."

"What do you mean?"

"If he kills elsewhere, that killing and this one might never be linked. Sometimes we only get a guy like this because we have enough cracks at different crime scenes to put the pieces together."

"If that's so, then I guess we don't know if this is his first time."

"No," Jimmy agreed. "We don't. We looked, of course. We couldn't find a really similar case in the last few years that was a close approximate to this one. So we think it's his first, but we don't know."

Alice stood, arms crossed, shaking her head. "It's all so surreal."

"I wish I had better news, but I've seen too much of this to be optimistic."

He stood up, put on his coat and picked up his keys. "I'm serious about locking up at night. If you're ever stuck here alone on a night I'm not working, let me know."

"I will," Alice said.

"Good, because I'll be mad if I find out you haven't. I mean that."

"We wouldn't want that," she grinned, moving down the counter to the register.

"No, you wouldn't," Jimmy said, trailing a little behind her, watching her walk, looking back toward him over her shoulder.

She rung him out. "I'm sorry, but I didn't know you'd be at the mill tonight. I don't have anything prepared for you. I could see what's in the back, though."

"Don't worry about it."

"Are you working tomorrow night?"

"I am," Jimmy said. "Back on my normal schedule."

"All right then, I'll have something for you."

"Good," Jimmy said. "I'll look forward to it."

He stepped out into the cold, waved at Alice through the front window and started across the street to his car. He glanced up and down the picturesque street. He'd not wanted to worry her, but he'd needed to do it. If anything, he'd not come on strong enough.

The killer was out there somewhere, and if he was still in Avalon Falls, there was cause to be afraid.

17

A sense of normalcy returned to Jimmy's life more quickly than he'd expected. At his first shift back at the mill, he was something of a curiosity, since awareness of not only what he'd been doing these past few weeks but of his now even more intriguing background prompted an unusual degree of attention. As he sat in front of his locker, before the shift, several others gathered round. But, when it became apparent that no sensational details of either the case or his past were going to be forthcoming, most drifted away before it was time to head to the floor.

During their dinner break, a few of the others attempted to bring up the subject of the case. He spoke as candidly as he was able, but there wasn't much he could say about a technically open investigation. By the end of the night, the subject had run its course. His fellow workers begrudgingly conceded that Jimmy didn't know that much more than they did about what had happened, though Jimmy had the sneaking suspicion that at least some of them thought deep down that he knew but wasn't telling.

After that night, Jimmy returned to being one worker among many on the second shift. He'd neither gone out of the way to make close friends during the three quarters of a year he'd worked there before the murder, nor had he abstained completely from it. Being naturally pretty affable despite his reserved approach to the job, he'd become a quiet but accepted member of the shift. He was welcomed back as much the same, and by his second week, his time working the case for the sheriff seemed surreal and far removed, even to Jimmy.

What's more, a call to Eddie on the weekend after his return to the mill made two things clear. The first was that the basketball games on Thursday morning were finished until spring. Sometimes, Eddie said, there were occasional breaks in the wintry weather before April or May, and on these occasions an impromptu game might break out, but usually winter took Avalon Falls in its grip and held on tight until at least then. So the New Start winter routine revolved around floor hockey, not basketball, which was played in the unfinished basement of the New Start building—a big, open room with four pillars strategically placed in the least desirable places imaginable, so they could be as difficult as possible to negotiate when the flow of the game moved their direction.

The second thing his call revealed was that Alice and Coach had both been right when they'd told Jimmy that Eddie wasn't the type to hold a grudge. There'd been no trace of the irritation and frustration that had been evident when Jimmy had gone out to New Start. In fact, if anything, Eddie went out of his way to make sure Jimmy knew that both he and the guys would be disappointed if Jimmy didn't drop by from time to time to join in the floor hockey games, even though Jimmy made it clear that whatever limited prowess he might possess in basketball, he had even less when it came to hockey. All the same, Eddie insisted Jimmy must come by and play, and Jimmy took Eddie up on the offer. He was every bit as bad as advertised, much to his own chagrin, having secretly harbored the suspicion he might pleasantly surprise himself.

October passed and most of November too, and before Jimmy knew it, he was driving to Cabot's after playing floor hockey at New Start on the Thursday before Thanksgiving. Though he wasn't very good, he found himself oddly down about the fact that there would be no game the next week because of the holiday. He parked and hustled across Main Street, trying not to think about the icy wind that penetrated his coat and chilled him to the bone.

The diner was warm, and Jimmy pulled the door closed and just stood for a second, soaking in the heat. From Red Lodge to Chicago, and now Avalon Falls, he'd spent much of his life in very cold climates. Of course, his time at UCLA had been dramatically different, as were his early years in the Bureau, though his cases often took him to wintry places around the country. Even so, he'd always fancied himself tougher than most when it came to the cold. However, even if it was true, he had to admit that there were levels of cold that just didn't seem to be intended for human beings to endure. He'd tried to imagine, on several occasions, how early settlers had lived in places like Chicago and Avalon Falls, but it defied all comprehension. Even with advances in climate controlling technology, such places were still barely inhabitable.

As Alice walked past him with her tray on her way back from serving some of her customers, all ruminations about life in their frigid corner of the world slipped away from him. She smiled at him pleasantly as she passed, and he caught a tantalizing hint of her fragrant hair. It was a different scent than that with which he'd been accustomed, and though he'd liked the old one, he approved of the change.

After lunch, he found himself lingering longer than was probably prudent. It was a trend that had been increasing of late. He'd gone from getting to the mill long before his shift—in part so he'd have plenty of time to clock in and get ready before it was time to take the floor, but also in part because he had no where else to be—to rushing in at just about the last possible moment. He wasn't the kind to be late, prizing punctuality in professional obligations more highly than his normally relaxed manner might indicate, but he had flirted with tardiness on more than one occasion when coming from Cabot's over the last month. He glanced down at his watch and realized that again today he would be cutting it close.

"Well, I need to head out," he said to Alice, who was cleaning the counter a few seats down from him while they talked.

"All right," she said, "but not before I get your dinner."

She walked briskly into the kitchen while he put on his coat and moved to the end of the counter, where he placed money for his lunch beside the register.

"Here you go," Alice said, reappearing.

"Thanks," Jimmy said, catching another whiff of Alice's new scent. He almost found himself closing his eyes and taking a deeper breath, but he restrained himself and instead merely said. "I like the smell of your new shampoo."

"You noticed," she smiled.

"I did."

She didn't say anything further about it, but Jimmy could see she was pleased. He was just turning to go when she added. "Jimmy, what are you doing for Thanksgiving?"

The question caught him off guard, so he said the simple, unadorned truth. "Nothing."

"Then you must come celebrate it with us."

"Sure," Jimmy said, seeing in this invitation, perhaps, a chance to redeem himself for his shameful showing on their one, now legendary date. "When should I come by?"

"We eat late, often about 2:00, though sometimes later, but you can come by as early as you like. Anytime before then is fine."

"Sounds good. Think about what you'd like me to bring."

"Nothing, just yourself."

Jimmy smiled as he stood at the door, bracing for the winter cold. "I can't come empty handed. Think about it."

She smiled and waved as he stepped out of the diner, and Jimmy gave a quick wave in return before he jogged across the street to the Bronco.

The more Jimmy thought about his Thanksgiving invitation, the slower the week seemed to go. He was a little nervous about his reception from Alice's kids, but not a lot. They'd been through the diner enough while he was there that he felt pretty comfortable with them. Ellen was thirteen and in seventh grade. Her long hair was brown with traces of auburn that reminded Jimmy of Alice. She was friendly enough, as was her younger brother, Ethan, who was ten. Even so, Jimmy realized that coming to their house as an invited guest on Thanksgiving fundamentally put him in a different category than just another friendly customer at Cabot's. His welcome in that capacity, regardless of how they normally treated him, was certainly not assured.

Still, he was looking forward to it all the same, and his eagerness made the time seem to crawl. His shifts seemed to stretch on longer than usual, and his nights were more broken and less restful. In fact, by the Tuesday before Thanksgiving, he began to suspect that his anticipation and its side effects were beginning to take a larger toll on him than he'd suspected. He felt somehow off, and almost all night he tossed and turned restlessly. The sun rose on Wednesday morning, and Jimmy, lying listlessly in his bed, couldn't deny it any longer. There was more going on inside him than nervous anticipation.

He was sick.

All attempts to cure himself that morning, whether by brewing a good strong pot of coffee or by taking it easy, failed utterly. He let Major out to relieve himself, but other than that, he barely moved off of his couch. The T.V. was on, but he couldn't concentrate long enough to watch. He lay staring at nothing in particular, wondering what was happening to him and how long it would last.

The time came around when normally he would be heading out to Cabot's to eat before his shift, but he didn't move. Perhaps, he thought, if he just rested a little more, he could still make his shift. Perhaps, whatever was happening would pass, if only he were patient and lay very still. It didn't pass, and for the first time since coming to Avalon Falls and taking his job at the Mill, he called in sick.

If he'd harbored hopes that skipping his shift and continuing to take it easy might bring a change for the better, he began to despair of this as nighttime rolled around and he felt, if possible, even more miserable than before. When he rose to use the bathroom a little before nine o'clock, his legs actually buckled because he felt so weak. He honestly wondered if they'd support him all the way across the room, and he began to think that he might not be able to go to Alice's for Thanksgiving after all.

When he was finished in the bathroom, he bypassed the living room, his couch and his T.V. and made his way to his bedroom. He flopped down on his bed, still clothed in jeans and a sweater, and crawled under his covers. He couldn't miss

Thanksgiving with Alice. It would look too suspicious after the last time. She'd start to wonder if he was trying to avoid getting to know her outside of Cabot's. He simply had to be better in the morning.

His lamp was on and he could hear the T.V. from the other room. Even so, he couldn't be bothered rolling over to try to reach the lamp and turn it off, and getting up to go turn off the T.V. felt unimaginable, like one of the twelve tasks of Hercules. He simply put up with the light and the noise. If he'd had the strength, though, he would have crawled out of bed to go find more covers. Despite his clothes and thick down comforter, he was freezing, shivering almost uncontrollably. His teeth chattered when he didn't have the will to stop them, and he scrunched up into a ball to try to preserve even a modicum of warmth.

He must have slipped off to sleep, because he found himself once more in the disturbing world of his bad dreams, except this time they felt even darker and somehow, more real than before. The line between his dreams and real life was thin, and he'd find himself lying in his bed, staring up at his ceiling or over at his closet door, suddenly aware he was no longer asleep. It was like coming up for air after having been submerged in a cold, dark lake. He would bob to the surface of his consciousness, tread water for while and then sink, inexorably back down below.

The Chicago apartment was dark and cold, so very cold. The windows must have been open it was so drafty and cold. He shivered and wrapped his arms tightly around himself as he walked down the long dark hallway. His breath puffed out in visible clouds of mist as he exhaled the frigid air. He paused at the closed door at the end of the hall.

He trembled as he placed his hand on the doorknob. He hadn't been in this room in so long. So very long. He'd been avoiding it, but he had to go in. He had to look inside, just one more time.

He turned the knob and opened the door. The room was just as cold as the rest of the apartment, perhaps even colder. Orange tinted artificial light filtered in through the window from the streetlight in the back alley. By the window sat a rocker, and in the rocker was the figure of a woman with her back to the door. Wispy brown hair hung down, and while she sat erect, she was completely immobile. The rocker didn't budge, not at all. She wasn't moving a muscle.

There was no other furniture in the room, but on the area rug in the center of the floor an infant sat, also with its back to him. The baby was only wearing a diaper, and Jimmy felt a pang of worry about the child being in such a cold room with no more clothing or protection than that. Like the figure in the chair, the infant sat erect, chubby legs crossed in front but not moving, not at all. It was most unnatural. No shifting to maintain balance. No motion. No activity at all.

Jimmy held still at the door. He was rooted to the spot, unable to enter the room and unable to walk away. He gazed from one wax-like figure to the other, absorbed completely. Then, at last, there was movement in the room. The head of the woman in the chair began to sink sideways, and he caught a glimpse of her skeletal face. It made him gasp. He looked to the hand on the end of the rocker, and it too was rigid and bony, not living flesh at all. Before his eyes the bones crumbled into dust and the body sank into a pile in the chair. Only a heap of clothes and splayed brown hair remained.

Jimmy, though, was not watching as the body finished collapsing, for the figure of the infant on the floor had also changed. A crack, like a crack in a porcelain doll, had started to run up the back of the child, who seemed now a sickly shade of grey. The crack increased and spread and dust spread out like a cloud across the floor as the body of the child also collapsed into a fragmented heap. Then, as the dusty cloud settled, half a dozen large, awful-looking spiders emerged, scurrying out from the diaper and beginning to spread out across the floor. Seeing the hairy creatures on the move, some in his direction, seemed to shake Jimmy out of his lethargy, and he pulled the door shut with a bang.

This time, when he awoke, he forced himself to slide, inch by inch, toward the edge of the bed. He dropped to the floor with a thud. For a moment, he lay there immobile, feeling as weak as a child. After what seemed like a long time, though, he lifted himself up and crawled out of the bedroom. He wasn't sure how long it took him to get to the bathroom. All he knew was that the tiles were impossibly cold. He struggled to the toilet, raised the seat and threw up.

The rest of the night passed interminably, a relentless procession of feverish dreams and long periods of shivering wakefulness where coherent thought was impossible. Scattered images and random notions came and went, most forgotten as soon as they had come and gone, but chief among them was the persistent thought that he had to go to Cabot's. He wasn't sure why, because he wasn't hungry. The thought of food was repugnant. Still, he felt oddly certain that he needed to go see Alice.

At one point Jimmy woke, facing his exterior wall and noticed that it was day. It wasn't the half-light of morning but the full light of day. What time it was more specifically than that he had no idea. His clock was on the other side of his bed and he didn't feel inclined to try to check it. He gazed out his window. He'd not drawn the curtain fully, and through the crack where daylight filtered in he could see broad grey sky behind the barren branches of the trees that surrounded his little cabin. His mouth was dry. He felt a deep longing for water, but he couldn't think how he could obtain some without great effort. He swallowed painfully. For a while he lay looking out the window, but eventually, he drifted off to sleep.

He must have slept longer this time, because when he woke next, the sun was low in the sky and a brilliant sunset sent red rays through his window and painted his bed and wall. His body ached all over, but he tried to move away from the bright light shining directly in his eyes.

"Relax," a gentle voice said quietly from beside him, and much to his surprise, a cool damp flannel was laid upon his burning forehead. "Can I get you anything?"

Despite the admonition to relax, he rolled over so he could see Alice, though at first she was just a beautiful silhouette, hovering like an angelic presence above him. He blinked his eyes and mustered what strength he had to say, "Water."

"Got some right here. I'm just going to tilt your head up a bit."

Her slender fingers slid underneath his head, through his damp hair. She took a firm but gentle grip, lifting him from his pillow. With her other hand she placed the glass to his lips, and he drank as greedily as he could. The system was imperfect and water slurped out and ran down both sides of his chin, but even those twin cool streams felt welcome to his skin. It was a wetness wholly other than the sweat of his feverish tossings, refreshing and clean.

When he'd drained most of the glass, Alice lowered his head back onto the pillow and set the glass down. She took the flannel with her out of the room, and he heard the sink run in the kitchen, then shut off. She came back with it and gently dabbed his whole face. When she was finished, she put the cloth back on his forehead. "How do you feel?"

"Awful."

"You look it," she said with a smile. "You really do go to extremes to avoid me."

"Sorry," he offered weakly, and Alice's smile immediately slipped from her face, replaced by a look of embarrassment.

"I'm sorry, Jimmy," she said. "That was in poor taste. I know you would have come if you'd been able."

She started to stroke his hair softly, and for several moments he lay with his eyes closed, thinking this must also be a dream. Like the others, just good. Then, as though to check and make sure, he opened his eyes. She was still there.

"How did you know I was sick?"

"The short version is that Avalon Falls is a small town," she smiled. "When you missed lunch on Wednesday and didn't show today, I called Eddie. He called someone from Calvary who works at the mill, and without too much effort we found out you'd called in sick yesterday. Since you hadn't called me or been seen by anyone since Tuesday, and knowing you lived out here all on your own, I was worried. So Johnny stayed with the kids, and Eddie brought me out."

"Eddie's here?"

"He is. When we saw the state you were in, he went off to the pharmacy to get some things. He got back a little while ago and is waiting in the living room. We hadn't decided yet if we were going to take you to the hospital or not."

Jimmy shook his head faintly. "I'll be all right."

"Maybe," Alice said. "If you don't go, then one of us will stay. Probably Eddie."

"There's no need."

"Maybe," she said again. "But one of us is staying, all the same."

She left the room and was gone for a few moments, then she returned with another glass of water and a couple of pills in her hand. "These will help," she said as she tilted his head up again. He took the pills from her hand in his mouth and swallowed them with minimal difficulty.

She moved around his bed to the curtains which she closed completely, before coming back around and turning off the lamp. "Try to sleep."

"Been trying for ages."

"Try some more."

She moved across the dark room to his door where she paused, her hand on the doorknob, silhouetted in the hallway light. "I'm glad we came out. No one should have to be alone at times like this."

"Agreed."

"Now go to sleep. After he's run me home, Eddie will be back," she said, pulling the door closed.

Jimmy lay there, listening as the front door opened and closed. The house was silent, and though he still felt weak, even the memory of Alice's presence seemed to break the spell that his nightmarish dreams had cast upon him. He lay in the peaceful dark, thinking about her soft fingers slipping gently through his hair. Closing his eyes, he felt tears on his cheeks for the first time in years.

18

The morning after Thanksgiving, Jimmy woke to the strong and pleasing aroma of fresh coffee. He could tell that the fever had broken, and though he still felt weak and ached all over, he also felt hungry. He couldn't remember how long exactly he had been without food, but it had been too long.

Jimmy slid to the edge of the bed and gingerly swung his legs over. He felt his weakness, especially as he stood, using his hand to steady himself as the blood rushed to his head. He shuffled across the floor and opened the door to the narrow hallway.

The kitchen was bright, and light as well as the welcome coffee aroma spilled out into the rest of the small house. Ahead, in the living room, a lamp was on beside his couch, and he could see Major lying on the rug in the middle of the room. The wooden hallway floor creaked underfoot, and Major's head perked up and the dog came padding toward him.

"Hey boy," Jimmy said, kneeling down to stroke the dog's soft coat. "I'm all right now."

"Morning, Jimmy," Eddie said, appearing in the doorway to the kitchen and leaning against the casement. "Good to see you up and about."

"Good to be up and about," Jimmy said, rising to his feet and taking Eddie's outstretched hand for a shake. "I'm sorry. I'm sure it already smells of dog."

"That's all right, I'll be having a good wash anyway," Eddie smiled. "You've been pretty sick. A thorough scrub is in order."

"It's still fairly dark out," Jimmy said, looking out through the window over his kitchen sink at the barely visible grey morning light. "What time is it?"

"A little before six," Eddie said. "Want some coffee and breakfast? I was about to make some eggs. It's about the only thing you have in the fridge to eat."

"Yeah," Jimmy said, thinking of his mostly empty fridge. Last he'd looked, there'd only been a few cans of soda and beer, half a serving of spaghetti, butter and a dozen eggs. "It's a little sparse."

"A little," Eddie said, laughter in his eyes. "Sit, you've had a rough time of it the last few days."

"Thanks," Jimmy said, thinking about protesting that Eddie didn't need to make him breakfast but deciding against it. He was famished and didn't see the sense in the obligatory ritual of polite protest when Eddie would insist anyway.

"Did you manage to get any sleep on my couch?" he asked instead. "It's not terribly comfortable for sleeping, I'm afraid."

"A little," Eddie replied, setting a coffee cup in front of Jimmy.

"Sorry about all this," Jimmy said after taking a sip. "Coming out here wasn't what you had in mind for Thanksgiving, I'm sure."

"Don't worry about it," Eddie said, getting another coffee mug down and cracking an egg into it. "I had a nice lunch with the New Start guys, and a nap in front of the Lions game, so most of the items on my 'to do' list had been checked off already when Alice called. Besides, your place is a great little retreat. The phone hasn't rung once, and I've been able to read without interruption. Pretty relaxing, really."

"Well, I owe you one. More than one, really." Jimmy said.

"You don't owe me anything. This is what friends do."

"I'm not so sure," Jimmy said. "Maybe it's what friends should do, but I'm not sure how often friends really do it."

Eddie scrambled the eggs, and Jimmy sipped his coffee. Major settled in on the floor beside the fridge, his rhythmic panting and the sizzling of the skillet the only sounds in the quiet house. When the eggs were ready, Eddie piled them on a plate and handed it to Jimmy.

"Aren't you going to have some?" Jimmy asked.

"Are you kidding?" Eddie said as he refilled his mug. "I'm still full from gorging myself yesterday. I may never eat again."

"I'm starving," Jimmy said, shoveling a forkful into his mouth.

"I bet you are," Eddie said. "When did you eat last?"

Jimmy chewed, thinking. "After my shift, late Tuesday night."

Eddie sat down on the other side of the tiny two-seat table and leaned against the wall. "No wonder you're starved."

They sat in silence while Jimmy ate, and when he'd finished all the eggs on the plate, he sat back and leaned against the wall like Eddie was. "I can make some more if you'd like."

"No thanks," Jimmy said. "That was just what I needed, though."

"Not a problem. Glad to help."

"Eddie, what do you think dreams are all about?" Jimmy set his cup down and looked across the table.

Eddie turned toward Jimmy and the table more. "What do you mean?"

"I was taught that dreams were an activity of the subconscious and nothing more. Maybe a processing of the events of your day, maybe beyond that, a coded glimpse at your life as a whole or your conscience or your past. I was just wondering, you know, since you're religious, if you see them differently—like visions from God or something."

"To be honest, Jimmy, I can't say I've considered the question much, so I wouldn't take my thoughts about it too seriously." Eddie drummed his fingers on the table, then he continued. "I think that dreams probably are a product of the subconscious mind, most of the time. Perhaps a recycling of recent events, or maybe a window into what's on your mind, what it's working on, even when your body's resting. I'm not saying God couldn't use dreams to communicate with us—He certainly did in the Bible. I just don't think that's the norm. Why do you ask?"

Jimmy looked down at his coffee, thinking about the haunting image of the infant crumbling into dust, falling to pieces before his very eyes. He'd seen that image many times before with slight variations. The spiders scurrying out of the diaper—those had been new this time.

"I have such terrible dreams," he said quietly, emotion swelling inside him so that he had to work to hold back the tears that had so recently flowed. Then, as though he'd only just remembered Eddie was there, he looked up and over at his friend, feeling embarrassed that he'd spoken the words out loud.

"I guess," Eddie replied quietly, "given the work you do, or did, that isn't too surprising."

Jimmy shook his head, slowly. "No, I don't mean those. I've had those too. Still do, sometimes. These are different. Worse."

"Would it help to talk about them?"

"I doubt it," Jimmy said, shaking his head. "It was probably just the fever and the sickness, not sleeping well and everything. I'll be fine."

Eddie washed up, despite Jimmy's protests that he leave the dishes in the sink. Then, after a brief, polite but vigorous dispute about whether or not Jimmy should even consider working his shift at the mill that night, Eddie took Jimmy's hints and excused himself, leaving with Jimmy's profuse thanks for all he'd done. Jimmy listened as Eddie's car crunched over his gravel driveway, then walked back to the kitchen for another cup of coffee.

Jimmy didn't end up working that night, and he did little other than sleep and watch T.V. over the weekend, though he did go to the grocery store to buy some actual food. It was earlier than he normally shopped, and there were a good bit more people moving up and down the aisles than he was used to. Jimmy was surprised by how much this agitated him, and he couldn't chalk it all up to the fact he wasn't feeling well, even though he was still a bit wobbly on his feet.

He was almost through shopping, but the frozen food section was a bit crowded and a sudden feeling of nausea led him to roll his cart away from the aisle, and he gripped the handle tightly as he leaned on it ever so slightly for support. Just then, the leering face of Dyson Beck appeared smirking beside him in the same greasy Broncos hat.

"You don't look so good," Beck said, and Jimmy winced as the foul cigarette-breath that reeked from Beck's mouth made his nausea worse.

Jimmy started to roll his cart away but Beck grabbed the side and held it fast. He locked his eyes on Jimmy's, a wicked gleam evident there under the bright grocery store lights. He leaned in even closer.

"I love shopping in the evening," Beck whispered. "After school, but before bedtime—by far the best time of day."

He glanced around the store, and Jimmy couldn't help but follow his gaze, noting as though for the first time the large number of parents who had kids with them in the store. "Maybe," Beck added, having turned back to Jimmy, once more studying him carefully. "Maybe you love it too. Maybe we ain't so different."

"Get off my cart," Jimmy said viciously, jerking the cart away. Nausea or no, he wasn't going to spend another minute in Beck's presence.

"Bye-bye, now," Beck said, laughing as Jimmy pushed his cart away, going around the frozen food aisle all together and accelerating with every step. It was time to go. Now.

The incident bothered him all night, and Beck even showed up in his dreams. Jimmy was working a case, trying to solve a difficult crime, but no matter where he went or what he did, Beck simply followed him, whispering infuriating things in his ears, lurid and dreadful things, and Jimmy was so distracted that he couldn't think straight.

He woke Saturday, though, feeling much better, and on Sunday night, he cooked a casserole and ate food prepared by his own hands rather than simply heated from a can. As he rifled through his cabinets to find a container suitable for storing the leftovers, he thought about how long it had been since he'd bothered.

On Monday, he headed to Cabot's to eat lunch and see Alice before heading to the mill. She was glad to see him, and though she was always conscientious about her work, it seemed to him that perhaps her care for some of the other customers suffered while she was taking extra vigilant care of him. No one appeared to object, though, so he relaxed and enjoyed her attentions. In fact, some of the regulars, including the guys from the corner table, went out of their way to welcome him back, and he suspected that news of his illness had preceded him.

He was sitting at the lunch counter, enjoying a piece of Alice's outstanding peach cobbler, when the door opened and he turned to see Eric Gibbons entering. The detective was stubbly bearded as usual, and when he saw Jimmy sitting at the counter, he smiled slightly and wandered over toward him.

"Eric," Jimmy said. "What brings you here?"

"A cup of decent coffee for one thing," Eric said. "You know how awful the department's coffee is."

"Don't remind me."

"Mind if I sit?" Gibbons said, motioning to the seat beside Jimmy. Then looking from Jimmy to Alice, who was hovering nearby, he added, "I'm not interrupting anything, am I?"

"Not at all," Jimmy said. "By all means, sit."

"Thanks," Gibbons said, walking over to the coat hooks on the back wall and hanging up his coat before returning and sitting down.

"Can I get you anything to eat?" Alice asked.

"I wish," Gibbons said, "but I don't have time right now. A quick cup of coffee and then I've got to get back out."

"Department business?" Jimmy asked.

"Yeah, but nothing very exciting," Eric answered.

Alice returned with the coffee and set it down, then with a discreet glance and smile for Jimmy, moved around the lunch counter to check on the few lunch customers who remained.

"So how've you been, Jimmy?" Eric asked as he stirred a heaping spoonful of sugar into his coffee.

"All right," Jimmy said. "Got a little sick last week, but I'm feeling better now, back on my feet."

"Cold?"

"Flu maybe," Jimmy said, "though I guess it's technically a bit early for flu season. It certainly felt like the flu."

Gibbons drank his coffee, staring at nothing in particular on the other side of the lunch counter. They sat quietly side by side. When he turned back toward Jimmy, Jimmy knew a change of subject was coming before Gibbons ever said a word.

"Let me ask you something, Jimmy."

It wasn't phrased like a question, but it was a question, so Jimmy answered it. "Go for it."

"When you worked for the FBI, you must have had plenty of cases where you came up empty, right?"

"Sure, plenty."

"I mean, you had cases where guys got away with some pretty seriously messed up stuff."

"No question."

Gibbons nodded and sipped his coffee, but Jimmy knew his mind was elsewhere. The mangled body of Alex Morrison was probably hovering before him. In fact, it was probably never far away. While the satisfaction Jimmy felt when he helped to catch a killer grew proportionately with the perceived severity of the crime, it also felt proportionately awful when he failed—the worse the crime the worse he felt. Jimmy had gathered that Morrison's murder was the worst that anyone in the Avalon Falls' Sheriff's Department had seen, so Gibbons' question was not hard for Jimmy to understand.

"A few years before I moved to the Chicago office," Jimmy said, turning sideways and leaning his elbow on the counter, "my team caught the case of a serial killer, commonly referred to as 'the Mailman.'"

"I remember reading about the case," Gibbons said.

"He killed five women in five different cities in the span of sixteen months," Jimmy continued. "It was one of only two cases I worked like that, only with this one, we never did figure out a geographical pattern for the killings. So toward the end of his spree, there were a lot of attempts to communicate with law enforcement departments nationwide, both to warn them and to seek help with the case."

"Why was he called the Mailman?"

"His first victim was a woman from Houston. The Mailman cut off a chunk of her hair, a fact which the investigating detectives duly noted, assuming it was a standard trophy for the killer. Some five months later an envelope arrived at the precinct where the investigating officers worked, with nothing inside it but the hair. Less than a week later, the second victim was killed.

"At the time, the detectives in Houston didn't know about the second woman, because she died in Portland, Oregon, and other than the missing chunk of hair and other less than unique similarities, there was nothing obvious to connect the two crimes. Another four months passed, and then the tuft of hair arrived at the Portland precinct that had been the center of operations for that investigation, and eventually someone put two and two together and called us in. By that point, though, he'd already killed his third victim, a woman from Indianapolis. I was there, in Indianapolis, working on a profile when the envelope arrived with the chunk of hair he'd taken from her."

"Hence the Mailman."

"That's right, by the time he'd earned his nickname, though, three women were dead, and we knew a fourth was soon to follow. It was a dark day. The clock was ticking for someone, but we had no idea where he was or who he was or how to stop it. As it turned out, she was from Pittsburgh, and we moved our investigation there as soon as we were reasonably sure she'd been killed by the Mailman. It was during that investigation that the term 'Mailman' first surfaced in the press. The connection to the fifth victim was never seriously in doubt. Her body was found with a letter opener jammed through her throat—a letter opener that said 'I love the USPS' on it, only it didn't say 'love,' it just the heart symbol, you know."

"Oh, that's nasty."

"Yeah, it was. Some thought that it might be a copycat, because the letter opener represented a serious departure from his routine, but there were too many clear connections in the profile, things a copycat wouldn't have known about."

"I'm assuming you're telling me about this guy because you didn't catch him."

"Nope. The Mailman was never caught."

"So what happened?"

"I don't know. Five murders in sixteen months, then nothing. Time passed, and the local detectives in San Diego—where the fifth body had been found—waited and waited, but the chunk of hair taken from their victim never came back. It got to be that the whole precinct all but ground to a halt each day when the mail came. A few murders that year around the country bore some resemblance to the original five, but none turned out to be connected. It's been years, now, and as far as I know, no one knows why he stopped. He wasn't caught—at least, not for those crimes. The cases are unsolved, and barring something unforeseen, they'll remain that way."

"Like ours."

Jimmy nodded in agreement. "Like ours."

"Maybe the Mailman just stopped, you know, fed up or afraid of being caught or something. Maybe our guy will too."

Jimmy shrugged. "It's possible."

"But not probable."

Jimmy shook his head. "No, not probable."

Eric drained his cup and stood up, stretching as he rose.

"Gibbons, you were gracious to me as an investigator, even though I'm no longer FBI. Let me get your coffee."

"You don't need to do that, Jimmy."

"I know, but I'd like to."

"Thanks," Gibbons said, shaking Jimmy's outstretched hand. "Good luck to you."

"And to you."

Gibbons retrieved his coat and headed back out into the cold afternoon. Jimmy motioned to Alice, who was at the far end of the counter, to come over. "One more cup before I go?"

"You got it," Alice said, heading for the pot, and Jimmy sat back down and stared into the bottom of his empty cup, contemplating the ghosts of cases past.

19

December in Avalon Falls was colder this year than it had been the year before, or at least it seemed that way to Jimmy. The first anniversary of his arrival in the town came and went, observed by Jimmy at Cabot's, where he ordered two pieces of banana cream pie and only told Alice after she'd brought it what it was in honor of and that a piece was for her.

As much as he tried to make the occasion a happy one, he found himself slipping into a dark place that night after his shift at the mill. He sat drinking on his couch, drinking to drive away memories that would not leave, drinking to find comfort that would not come.

He walked to his front door, turned the handle and swung it open. The frigid air hit him in the face like a hammer, and he stood there, absorbing it, while Major dashed out onto the small front porch and turned around to look at Jimmy as though confused about whether he should be inside or out. At last Jimmy moved to close the door, and Major darted back into the warmth, and both owner and dog sat by the hearth and let the crackling fire warm them.

Jimmy closed his eyes and saw the streetlights in the alley and the falling snow. Sergeant waited at the foot of the stairs as he descended and walked out through the gate. The dumpster was empty and the vase flew up in an arc and shattered on the metallic floor. That vase. That beautiful, stupid vase.

The night passed and Jimmy weathered the storm, literally and figuratively. A foot of snow was dumped on Avalon Falls before dawn, and the local school was closed for two days. Jimmy didn't try to go anywhere during the first day; he just worked on digging himself out in time to forge his way through the snow to work. He'd bought the Bronco for days like this, and it served him well. The second day, he did manage to get into town, and he found Cabot's chock full of people, including more kids than usual, like Ellen and Ethan. It was the first time Jimmy had seen them since he'd missed Thanksgiving, and if their attitude toward him had changed because of that invitation, Jimmy couldn't tell. They were friendly enough, though their attention was directed mostly toward some of their school friends who were also there.

Christmas decorations went up all over town, and things got busy all of a sudden. Not for Jimmy so much, but for Alice, and Jimmy felt the ripple effects. The diner was generally busy, both kids had school Christmas programs looming, and the holidays had her stressed out. Jimmy hinted at taking Alice out for dinner to give her a break, and while the suggestion brought a grateful smile to Alice's face, she suggested that they do it after the holidays, "when things had settled down."

As Christmas came and went, though, Alice seemed to relax, and a few days before the New Year, she asked Jimmy what he was doing for New Year's Eve.

"Going out to New Start," Jimmy replied. "Why?"

"Oh," she said, "I just thought you might want to come spend it with us."

"I'd love to, but I told Eddie and Coach I'd come out."

"What about New Year's Day? Johnny's coming over, and we'll eat and play games and maybe watch a couple movies. Johnny's not a huge football fan, but if you want to watch a game, I'm sure he'd be in to it, too."

"I've usually watched bowl games on New Year's, I guess, but I don't really care about them much—especially now that the ones that matter come later in the week. I'd love to come and do whatever you guys are doing."

"All right then," Alice smiled. "That's settled. Come in the afternoon, whenever you like, and stay for dinner. It's a family tradition to watch *The Wizard of Oz* after dinner. It's Johnny's favorite movie, but if you don't want to stay for that, you don't have to."

"I'd love to. I haven't seen it in years."

So the New Year approached and Jimmy found his social calendar booked. With plans to be out for two consecutive nights at two different places with different people, he couldn't deny that he was becoming a part of this small town's community. Whatever had brought him here, and whatever he'd promised himself about staying disconnected, it was what it was.

As he pulled into the parking lot of Calvary Baptist Church, he heard the DJ on the radio station mention that temperatures were hovering around fifteen below, and he shuddered at the thought of opening his door. The Bronco was warm and cozy, and the path winding back to the New Start building seemed long and desolate. He took a deep breath, swung the door open and plunged out into the cold. He threw the door shut with a slam and jogged in a straight line, ignoring the path's curves and running across the crunching snow still covering the ground from snowfalls earlier in the month. Reaching the door, he rapped on it loudly while stomping his feet to shake off the snow.

The door opened, and he looked up to see Johnny blotting out the light from the inside like a cloud covering the sun and casting a great shadow down upon the earth. It occurred to Jimmy as he shook Johnny's outstretched hand while stepping quickly inside that the big fella would have made a formidable bouncer if he wasn't so gentle.

"Hello, Jimmy," Johnny said as he shut the door.

"Hey, Johnny," Jimmy replied. "It's cold out tonight."

Jimmy shivered and held his coat tight, even as Johnny closed the door.

"You'd better come on in, away from the door then," Eddie said, walking over to shake Jimmy's hand as well. "You're just in time to get in the game."

"Oh yeah?" Jimmy said. "What game is that?"

"The boys have a big poker game ready to go, but they held off in case you wanted in."

"Sure, I love poker," Jimmy said, and he followed Eddie through to the big table, where most of the guys sat, listening to music on the radio and fiddling with piles of plastic poker chips on the table in front of them.

"Hey, Jimmy."

"Finally."

"Yeah, now we can get started."

"So what'll it be?" Nathan, the wrestler, asked as the greetings settled down. "Are we dealing you in?"

"Sure," Jimmy said, taking off his jacket. "Are we playing dealer's choice?"

Jimmy was met by several blank stares and some of the guys exchanged confused glances. "We're playing poker, Jimmy," one of them said.

"I figured that part out," Jimmy laughed, "I'm trying to figure out what kind. Are you playing that the dealer calls the game?"

"The dealer deals, that's what the dealer does."

"I think I can help with the confusion," Eddie said, chuckling as he interrupted and both Jimmy and the boys looked to him for help. "The boys are playing Texas Hold 'Em, Jimmy, and that's pretty much all they play. They're of that generation that may not fully realize that other forms of the game exist."

"Ahh," Jimmy said, realization dawning. He raised his hands and gestured his decline. "Thanks guys, but I'm not much of a Texas Hold 'Em player. Now, if you get the urge for some five card draw, guts or baseball, just let me know."

"It's a bit cold out for baseball, Jimmy."

"My, my," Jimmy sighed and shook his head. "This is a sad state of affairs."

So the game began, and Jimmy stood not far away, watching with Eddie for a while. The game was interesting enough, but Jimmy couldn't quite grasp why they'd play the same form of poker over and over and over, when there were so many other variations. After a while, he drifted out to the living room where the rest of the guys were watching the end of some ridiculous movie about a plane that can fly itself and goes haywire.

"Well, it's no *Top Gun*," Jimmy said.

"What's that?" one of them asked.

"Some old movie with George Clooney, I think," another one replied.

"Tom Cruise," Jimmy corrected him.

"Whoever," he replied. "I only saw the cover graphic once when Netflix tried to recommend it for me. No thanks."

It was now a little past 11 o'clock, and the guys started talking about some musician he'd never heard of and a movie he had but had no interest in, so Jimmy excused himself. After using the bathroom, he glanced down the hall past the guys' bedrooms at the only door around that wasn't open. It was the door to the Prayer Room. Jimmy thought about the two pictures he'd seen there and walked down to take another look.

A diminutive lamp sat on the small table against the opposite wall, and it was on, a small orb of light radiating outward, illuminating the cross hanging from the wall above and the two pictures on either side of it. Jimmy stepped into the room, and only then did he notice Coach sitting in the corner with his arms crossed, facing the pictures but with his eyes closed. Another folding chair was near the door, and he gently pushed the door but didn't close it all the way as he sat down quietly. Coach hadn't moved, so Jimmy couldn't tell if he was sleeping, meditating or what, but the sound of light and rhythmic breathing suggested perhaps the former.

Jimmy turned his attention to the pictures on the wall. Again, his eyes went first to the left and the picture of the man on his face with his hand clasping his head. Whoever the artist was, he'd done a brilliant job catching a posture of despair, even though he hadn't shown the man's face. The hand reaching up to hold onto the man above was like the hand of a sailor sinking beneath the waves, reaching up for a lifeline in a storm.

Again, though, his attention was pulled away to the other picture of the riotous feast. What were they celebrating? What did it mean that this man's brother was "dead" but was now "alive?" It was just the kind of annoying riddle one found in the Bible and other religious books. He'd never understood them, not that he'd thought about them much.

Movement from the corner caught his eye, and he turned to see Coach adjusting himself in his seat and squinting as though he was just then opening his eyes to the light for the first time in a while. Coach saw Jimmy and smiled, not a broad laughing smile but a contented smile that spoke of having found something long sought after and much longed for.

"Hello Jimmy," Coach said simply. "I must have dozed off there. I didn't hear you come in."

"Sorry if I disturbed you."

"Not at all. What time is it?"

"A little after 11."

"Oh good, then I haven't been out too long."

"Slipped down here to find some peace and quiet?"

"That's right, a little chance to think and reflect," Coach said, still smiling his contented smile. He glanced at the pictures before them and then back at Jimmy. "Eddie told me that he told you my story."

"He did," Jimmy said. "Hope that was all right with you."

"Oh sure," Coach said, reaching over and patting Jimmy firmly on the thigh a few times and making a face that suggested it was nothing. "I tell every guy who comes to New Start, and it was only lack of a good opportunity that had spared you from my version, which is no doubt longer and much more boring."

Coach grinned and Jimmy laughed. "Well, maybe one day you can tell me your version."

"Maybe," Coach said, growing serious again. "You know, Jimmy, I was like the Prodigal Son myself. I could go into detail about this and that from my past, but what it boils down to is that I lost my way."

Jimmy had a vague recollection of the story of the Prodigal Son from somewhere way back, when he was dragged to church by his mother. A kid running away from home, as he recalled, but being unsure of the finer details and hesitant to betray his ignorance, he decided not to ask Coach about it. He nodded his head knowingly instead.

"Those were dark times, Jimmy," Coach said gravely. "I almost despaired of life itself. I lost Irene and the basketball team, the two great loves of my life. If it wasn't for Eddie, who knows what would have happened."

"What was he like, back then?"

"Like he is now, I guess, only younger."

"And as a player?" Jimmy asked. "He told me about the trouble he got into in high school."

"Oh, he wasn't a bad kid, even then," Coach said. "You could see he was going to be somebody special."

"How?"

"I don't know how much you know about Eddie, but he was the Montana Player of the Year during his senior season. Probably should have been his junior year too."

"Really?"

"Really," Coach said, emphatically. "He took us to the only state championship in school history. He was something to watch, he was."

Coach shook his head, a distant look in his eye as he lost the thread of what he was saying and stared for a moment off into space. "The point I was making, though, was that Eddie wasn't just a talented kid, he was a hard worker. I got to school early every day, but Eddie got there earlier. Bob Ferguson, the janitor, would let him in the building, put on the gym lights and just let him play. No one was worried about liability back then, and Bob wanted the state title as much as anyone else did.

"Some mornings I'd work with him, but usually I'd just stand outside the open door and watch. He'd start at the top of the key, take a stutter step, dribble to the elbow and take the jump shot. He'd get the ball, go back to the top of the key, stutter step and go to the other elbow and take the shot. Back and forth, over and over, again and again. He was lightning off that first step, and he almost never missed. He was something else. I never would have guessed back then that one day he'd give me something even more important than that state trophy."

"A place to stay?"

"A place to stay," Coach agreed, "but more than that. He gave me hope, and hope is worth everything you have and more. He gave me hope and a new start."

"A 'New Start,' huh," Jimmy said, motioning to the room around them.

"The irony isn't lost on me," Coach smiled. "That's why every New Year's Eve, I spend a little time down here, thinking about all I have to be thankful for. Thinking about the blessing of new beginnings."

Coach looked intently at Jimmy, and suddenly Jimmy felt self-conscious. He looked back to the picture of the revelry and feasting.

"It's never too late you know," Coach said. "You can make a new start any time."

"I know," Jimmy said, looking back. "That's one reason why I came to Avalon Falls. You know, to start over."

Coach nodded. "I'm talking about changing more than addresses, though, more than changing jobs or careers or anything like that. I'm talking about the real thing, the clean slate, the fresh beginning."

They sat for a moment in the lamplight, and then Coach stood and put his hand gently on Jimmy's shoulder. "Come, let's join the others, it'll be midnight soon."

20

The wooden porch planks creaked under Jimmy's feet as he waited at Alice's front door. A dull grey sky stretched as far as the eye could see, and it was every bit as cold as the previous night. Even so, Jimmy hesitated for a second before knocking, and drawing a short breath of the near-arctic air, he raised his gloved hand and rapped lightly on the screen door.

A pair of feet came thundering down the entry hallway, and a moment later, Ethan threw the inside door open and looked up at Jimmy with a grin. He pushed the storm door open and Jimmy stepped into the warm interior gratefully.

"Hello Mr. Wyatt," Ethan said. "Happy New Year."

"Happy New Year, Ethan," Jimmy replied. "You can call me Jimmy, you know."

"Mom said I should call you Mr. Wyatt," Ethan said, looking around nervously.

"Mr. Wyatt it is then," Jimmy stooped down. "I wouldn't want to make your mom mad."

"C'mon," Ethan said, starting to retreat down the hall, "we're watching a funny show Mom taped last night."

The funny show turned out to be one of those made-for-T.V. specials highlighting the funniest commercials of the previous year. Jimmy had seen about half of them before and some of them didn't strike him as all that amusing, but they were most of them pretty entertaining. More important, Ethan and Ellen laughed a lot, and he found that relaxing. Any nervousness that his presence would inhibit their behavior disappeared.

When he'd entered the room, he'd found Ethan sprawling out on the floor beside Ellen, who was lying on her stomach on a big cushion. Alice was alone on the couch, and Big Johnny was on a hefty-sized recliner in the corner. The only place left open to him was on the couch beside Alice, so he'd taken the seat, enjoying the warm smile he received from Alice but also well aware of the sideways glance Johnny gave them. When he met Johnny's glance with a friendly smile, Johnny nodded and turned back to the T.V.

When the tape of commercials was over, Johnny got on the floor and "wrestled" with both his nephew and his niece, though in this case the wrestling consisted mainly of letting them jump on him. They were like fleas buzzing around a dog. He let them take him down and roll him over, again and again, but from time to time, he'd grip one or both of them suddenly and lift them straight up into the air as effortlessly as Jimmy might lift a mug for a toast. They'd shriek with evident delight, and then he'd lower them back down and they'd jump on him once more.

He watched the goings on for a while, but when Alice slipped out to the kitchen, he excused himself and followed her. "Need any help?"

"Not really," Alice said, setting a large Pyrex dish on the kitchen counter from one of her cabinets. "But I'd love some anyway."

"Good," Jimmy said, standing to attention. "What can I do?"

"Can you peel potatoes?"

"Ooh," Jimmy said, sucking air in through his teeth as he shook his head a bit. "I'm not really much of a peeler. I start out OK, but I'm impatient and I leave little bits of skin here and there. Others have found my peeling skills less than satisfactory."

"Others, huh?" Alice said, giving Jimmy a curious glance.

"Yes, vague, indefinite, certain personages from my distant past," Jimmy said, motioning as though to indicate a person or object left far behind in the dim recesses of time.

"Well, never mind," Alice said waving Jimmy over to take a seat at the table where a bag of potatoes lay waiting. "You'll be more careful today, I'm sure."

"Yes, of course, I've long desired a chance to improve my peeling ability."

"Fancy that," Alice smiled, approvingly "Here one is."

"Here one is."

They sat, working on dinner, and the kids and Johnny interrupted occasionally, usually for a glass of water or some such, but for the most part, the two of them were left alone to work and talk. Their conversation covered a lot of ground, from the mundane, like updates on life at the mill, to the ridiculous, specifically how old Jimmy had felt on the drive home from his evening at New Start.

"They didn't even know Tom Cruise was the star of *Top Gun,*" Jimmy said, as though the mere mention of this startling reality to Alice conveyed all that was necessary.

"Kelly McGillis was so beautiful, wasn't she?" Alice said.

"I don't know," Jimmy shrugged, a little distracted by the irrelevant change of subject. "She never did much for me."

"Oh," Alice said, frowning as she whisked some doughy concoction vigorously on the far side of the kitchen. "She was gorgeous."

"Anyway," Jimmy persevered, "I felt like Grandpa Simpson talking about *Matlock*."

"Why, they're all just a few years removed from high school. They're only kids."

"I know, but it's hard to think I'm that far removed from my youth. You know?"

"I have two kids, Jimmy," Alice said, "one of which is already a teenager, so I've been coming to grips with my loss of my youth for some time now."

Jimmy set the peeler down and placed the last potato in the big pot of water that Alice had provided. "Can I ask you something, Alice?"

"Of course."

"Ethan and Ellen's father ... you never talk about him."

Alice set the mixing bowl down. "That's because I don't have anything to say about him. Didn't your mother teach you that if you didn't have anything nice to say, not to say anything at all? Mine did."

"That's fine," Jimmy said, backing off rapidly. He'd been prepared for the possibility he might get a response like this. "I was just curious, that's all."

Alice wiped her hands on her apron. She walked over and picked up the pot of potatoes, setting it on the range. "The story is simple. He was a jerk I knew from high school. It was the classic story of the girl who sets out to 'save' the boy. I had this vision of just how wonderful he could be. Turns out, he didn't really want to be wonderful.

"He was an OTR driver, and one time, he just didn't come home. I got a postcard from Topeka a week after he left, saying he couldn't do the family thing anymore. That was the last I heard from him."

"How old were the kids?"

"Ethan was a baby. Ellen was four."

"Does she remember him?"

"Not much. A few scattered images is all."

Alice opened the stove and checked the food cooking within, then adjusted the temperature controls. Jimmy watched. "I'm sorry, Alice."

"Hey, there's no need to be sorry. I'd wanted him gone for a long time."

"Still, it must've been hard to raise Ethan and Ellen alone."

"I wasn't alone. I had my mom to help until she passed away, and Mrs. Gregory next door has been a lifesaver. So I haven't really been alone."

"All the same," Jimmy said, persisting gently. "I'm sorry."

She leaned against the counter and looked at him, sitting at the table, leaning on his elbows. "Thanks."

"When is dinner going to be ready?" Ethan whined from the door. "I'm starving."

"Not long now," Alice replied, scooting across the floor and grabbing Ethan by the sides and tickling him. He howled and writhed dramatically, then ran off down the hall as Alice ran after him. Jimmy rose, walked over to the sink and washed his hands.

Dinner was fantastic. Alice had made a casserole with leftover turkey, bacon, peas and rice, all in a sauce that was two parts mushroom soup and one part something spicy that Jimmy couldn't quite put his finger on. There were hot, home-made rolls, muffins, stuffing, green beans and a mound of potatoes. Jimmy, who only ate this well when he was dining at Cabot's, packed it away.

Still, as much as he ate, he didn't come close to keeping up with Johnny. He'd been a little surprised and awed by the mountain of food that Alice prepared, as there were only five of them at the table, but as he saw it gradually dwindle away by way of Johnny's plate, he understood. He didn't know how many calories a day it took to keep Big Johnny big, but it was a whole heck of a lot.

He cleared the table with Johnny, and they washed the pots and pans together while Alice ran a bath for Ethan upstairs. Johnny wasn't much of a talker, but they somehow got on the subject of Eddie and that got him going. Like Coach, Johnny had nothing but good things to say about him, and Jimmy felt that he understood why. If the New Start guys were little more than boys, then that was all Johnny had been when Eddie had visited him in jail. He could imagine Johnny, big but less muscular and intimidating than he was now, trembling in his cell, crying silently in the darkness. Visits from Eddie would have been one of the few moments of respite in those hellish years before Johnny got big enough to take care of himself.

Take care of himself? Jimmy had watched Johnny on a few occasions before, but never for so long or in such a personal setting as today, and he wasn't at all convinced Johnny could take care of himself. He knew that when he wasn't staying at New Start overnight as a pseudo watchman, he had his own apartment, a small efficiency type place on the second floor above some old lady whom Alice knew, but he doubted Johnny spent much time there. He'd gathered from things said here and there that Johnny was usually with Alice and the kids when he wasn't at New Start.

And why not? Jimmy glanced at Alice as she entered the kitchen, the black sleeves of her turtleneck rolled up above her elbows and with wisps of red hair dangling in front of her beautiful face. With Alice and the kids for company, and with her cooking, why not be here? This was family, warmth, laughter and a full stomach. Why spend your evenings alone in an empty apartment? He thought of his own lonely existence. Major was good company, but a dog and a family were not the same thing.

"Are we ready for the movie?" Alice asked, smiling at them both.

"Yup," Johnny said, drying his hands on a dish towel.

The kids hung around for the first ten minutes or so of *The Wizard of Oz,* but shortly after the appearance of the Lollipop Guild, they drifted upstairs. Alice had suggested earlier that they probably would. They liked the movie, but Alice watched it with Johnny multiple times a year, and they didn't always stick it out. There was a small T.V. with a DVD player in the main bedroom, and they could be heard periodically down below, laughing at whatever it was they were watching.

There was no laughter downstairs, for even where the movie bordered on the comedic, there was a pall that had descended on the room that Jimmy didn't quite understand. He was in the big recliner, for Johnny had lain down on the sofa with his head in Alice's lap at the very beginning of the movie and hadn't stirred since. She sat in the dark, stroking his hair gently.

Even when the movie was over, they neither one moved as the credits rolled. Jimmy watched Alice and Johnny discreetly, and he could tell that though Johnny's eyes were closed, he wasn't asleep. He'd been crying. Jimmy had pretended to be entranced in the movie, so he didn't think they knew he'd noticed.

"It's getting late," Jimmy said eventually. "I should probably go."

"Wait a sec," Alice said, "and I'll walk you out."

"No, no," Jimmy shook his head. "It's so cold …"

"I'll get my jacket."

Johnny lifted up his head, and Alice jumped up to go get her jacket. Jimmy stood and retrieved his own coat from the chair in the hall where he'd set it on the way in.

"I'll go get the kids moving toward bed," Johnny called from the foot of the stairs.

"All right," Alice said as she came to the hall, still tying up her long, ankle length coat.

"You're crazy," Jimmy said. "Just walk me to the door. Don't go outside."

"I'll only be a minute," Alice said. "Besides, I've lived here all my life. I can handle a little cold weather now and again."

"All right," Jimmy said. They paused at the door. "Ready?"

"Ready," Alice replied with a smile.

Jimmy opened the door and stepped quickly out onto the porch, and Alice followed, pulling the inside door to. "I hope you don't get locked out."

"I won't," Alice said. "I checked the latch."

They walked briskly down the walk to the Bronco, and Alice followed Jimmy around to the driver's side door. He reached out for the handle and she grabbed his hand, stopping him. Her fingers lingered on his.

"I wish you'd been here last night."

"Why?" Jimmy asked, looking at her beautiful eyes, shining up at him.

"Because it's been a long time since I had someone to kiss when the ball dropped."

With that she stood up on her tip-toes and kissed him, her lips a warm infusion of life in the cold night air.

"Happy New Year, Jimmy."

"Happy New Year, Alice," Jimmy replied. He slipped into the Bronco and watched her walk back inside. She waved, and then the front door closed, and still he sat gazing at the front of the house. He started th e Bronco and let the engine warm up, then he backed out of the driveway and drove all the way home in a kiss-induced haze of surprise, happiness and confusion.

21

If it had occurred to Jimmy as even a remote possibility that the New Year's Day kiss from Alice might be the start of a torrid, steamy, love affair, he was mistaken. While the dynamic between them changed, and periodic dinners together and various more mundane events like joint grocery shopping became common, relational things progressed slowly.

Jimmy came, over tIme, to believe that one of the things holding them back from moving faster, perhaps even the main thing, was his reticence to speak of his own past. Alice had never pried, not really, though occasionally she dropped hints that she'd be interested in knowing more about Jimmy's life before Avalon Falls. She didn't ever say much about her own history, but she had said something, and that was more than he had done and more than he felt ready to do. So they settled into a casual routine that was more familiar and intimate than what they'd previously enjoyed, but not dramatically so.

One Monday in the middle of March, Jimmy left Cabot's with one of Alice's special dinners in a brown paper bag, which if it was as good as it was heavy, was going to be fantastic. There must have been half a pig or cow in whatever she'd cooked for him. He looked forward to showing it off, whatever it was, for he was routinely the envy of the lunchroom at the mill.

He dropped his dinner off in the fridge and headed to his locker to change into his work clothes and boots. A few others were there, but he was early and most would not be there until the last possible moment. He looked at his rough and callused hands as he laced up his boots. His skin had not been this thick and tough since high school when he'd worked for the county on road construction sites and perhaps not even then. Studying at UCLA and working at the bureau had left them smooth and soft, but they'd relearned and remembered their old strength and handiness when he'd called them back into service at the mill. Now, with more than a year's wear and tear from his hard manual labor, he wondered if they would ever be smooth and soft again.

He knew this musing was but the tip of a larger iceberg, since what was really on his mind was whether or not he could ever go back. Certainly not back to Chicago—he was done with that for good—and perhaps not even back to the bureau or law enforcement. But back, nonetheless, back toward the work he'd been trained to do. Back toward the kind of life in general if not the same life in particular that he'd left behind to come here.

As long as he'd lived outside of town in virtual isolation, numb to the larger world of people, ideas and existence beyond his own four walls, he'd been able to bury himself in a mindless routine of eating, working and sleeping. Now, though, as spending time with Alice was waking inside him stirrings of a larger world, he'd found that one of the unintended consequences of this change was that he was questioning for the first time since his coming to Avalon Falls how long he could continue at the mill.

Perhaps it had been inevitable. He'd come to Avalon Falls, decided to stay, and taken the first job he'd been offered. He'd never really tried to envision doing mill work for life, so it might well have been the case that sooner or later, whatever he'd done, he would have found himself at just this crossroads. He was certainly here now, and what he was going to do about it, he had no idea.

He'd taken the job so he'd be able to stay. With Alice and the beginnings of a new life here, he wanted to remain, but he was beginning to realize that the job he was currently doing was not something he could endure endlessly into the future. He could feel his brain, his past training, his intellectual core, though long dormant, returning. Flickering back to life. He wasn't at all confident that a job that would satisfy those stirrings existed in Avalon Falls. There was, as yet, no immediate crisis, but he suspected that one might just be looming.

He clocked in and went to watch the crew from first shift as they finished up and prepared to go home. He didn't notice his foreman at first, talking some distance away to a man in dirty blue jeans and a black t-shirt. When he did notice them, he stood rooted to the spot, staring at the grizzled face of the visitor.

By now, most of the workers from his shift had gathered or were gathering, so he had no trouble drifting slowly toward the back of the crowd as the foreman moved closer with his guest, but he couldn't leave the room entirely and was starting to have a sinking feeling in his stomach about why they were there and where this was headed.

"Listen up, everybody," the foreman called to them as they gathered round. "You guys know we've been a couple fellas short this last month or so, but we've got a new guy starting tonight, so welcome him and help him find his way around, all right?. This here is Dyson Beck, and George will be showing him around."

George Williams, one of the real veterans on the shift, stepped forward and shook Beck's hand. Some of the others drifted forward to welcome their new co-worker, but Jimmy held back. His worst fear had been realized. Beck wasn't visiting, he wasn't even there to apply—he'd already been hired and assigned to his shift.

He suddenly felt embarrassed. He'd never said anything untrue when he'd joined Gibbons in the interrogation room for Beck's questioning, but he'd certainly implied that he was an important player in the investigation and that Beck would be wise to keep that in mind. Even that wasn't so much false as incomplete. There'd been no reason to explain his past or his current occupation, and if Beck had made any assumptions about Jimmy's importance in the department and town as a whole, Jimmy had not felt obliged to disabuse him of these notions.

Once Beck had been released and was no longer a part of the investigation, there'd been no reason for further contact, and Jimmy hadn't seen him since except the one time at the grocery, so Jimmy assumed Beck had never been any the wiser. There would be further contact and fuller understanding now, of course, and while he couldn't be sure about how Beck would react to finding him there at the mill, working the same shift, he couldn't imagine, in any conceivable scenario, that he wouldn't lose face to at least some degree.

Just then, as Jimmy was wondering if he should just go forward and get the initial awkward encounter over with, Beck looked up and saw him. Recognition was immediate, even if understanding was not. Beck grimaced as he looked at him, and then he looked around as though to see if Sheriff Anderson or Detective Gibbons or any other surprises were lurking elsewhere. When he seemed satisfied that Jimmy was there alone, that his presence at the mill had nothing to do with him, and that in fact Jimmy was dressed like and almost certainly was a worker much like himself, that haughty, smirking grin slowly spread across Beck's face.

Beck started forward through the remaining shift workers, saying hello and shaking hands here and there, but moving steadily in Jimmy's direction. Having lost his chance to seize the initiative and control, somewhat, the nature of their first encounter, Jimmy held his ground and braced for whatever was coming.

"My, my," Beck said as he stopped in front of Jimmy, "I knew I'd landed in a real doozy of a nowhere town, but if this doesn't beat all. Tell me, what would possess a Sheriff to borrow a lumber mill worker to help out with a murder investigation? I was right, wasn't I? You really are some kinda junior detective, aren't ya?"

Jimmy stared coldly at Beck, but he didn't say anything. There were a lot of things he wanted to say, but he knew that there was probably nothing he could say that wouldn't be turned against him. The best thing to do was say nothing. He could tell Beck about his past in the Bureau, to set him straight, but it would be better if he let Beck find out as he inevitably would by asking someone else. That way, Beck would know that Jimmy hadn't felt him important enough to correct.

In the meantime, Beck stood gloating, and Jimmy decided he didn't need to take any more of it. He started to move away, and Beck reached out and grabbed his wrist. "Hey, Junior, we're gonna have to work together here. I'd hate to hear that you were spreading any lies about me."

Jimmy jerked his arm away and stepped closer to Beck, pointing right at his gloating face. "Don't ever touch me again."

"I won't, so long as you keep your mouth shut, Junior."

Jimmy could feel his anger boiling. He'd had suspects like Dyson Beck before—rapists, murderers, sex offenders and creeps of all varieties—say all kinds of things to him over the years, but between the power of his badge and the power of his gun, he'd never felt this helpless. Right now he missed both, though he probably missed his gun more. It was a good thing he'd gone back to locking it up at his house after he'd stopped working the Morrison case.

He steered as clear of Beck as he could, but there was no way to avoid him entirely. Every so often they'd end up near each other, and Beck persisted in calling him "Junior" in a familiar tone as though they were old friends. It was hard to stand within striking distance while holding a two-by-four and let the condescension pass, but he managed to hold his tongue and avoid violent retaliation before eventually taking refuge in the large Tupperware container full of Alice's pot roast at dinner time. It was amazing, as expected, but he ate at a table off on his own, the joy of his superior dinner lost at the sight of Beck sitting with a handful of the guys, talking merrily on the other side of the room as though they were all close, personal friends.

He had a good run after dinner, and he was almost able to put Dyson Beck out of his mind entirely until shortly before the end of the shift, when they ran into each other without anyone else near enough to hear them speak. Beck slowed down and stopped as Jimmy approached. "Hey, ex-FBI, huh? That's real impressive. You must have been one hell of an agent to end up exiled out here. What'd you do, Junior, shoot the wrong guy or something?"

Jimmy ignored Beck and kept walking, but Beck didn't let it go. He moved in front of Jimmy and blocked his way. His eyes were hard and taunting, a real glint of hatred evident. "Hey, you know why I took this job, Junior?"

Jimmy, stopped and waited, figuring silence was still the best policy. News of his past employment with the Bureau hadn't exactly had the desired effect, but there was still time to let it sink in. Beck's bravado might waver if Jimmy continued to ignore him.

"I'll tell you why I took this job, Junior," Beck said, leaning in closer so all he had to do was whisper. "Now that I don't start work until three, I have plenty of time to catch recess at the elementary school. It's even better than the grocery store. You have any kids there, Junior? There's a lovely park bench just across the street from the playground—"

Jimmy didn't hear how that sentence ended, because he reached out and grabbed Dyson Beck's shirt with both hands and drove the man sideways toward the mill's exterior wall. He slammed Beck against it and stood holding him, pinned up against it. Jimmy could feel himself shaking with rage.

"You have no idea why I'm in Avalon Falls or how many people I still know at the Bureau," Jimmy said, so close to Beck's face he could smell the onions and mustard on his breath, mixed with the inevitable reek of cigarettes. "I could seriously screw with your life, with or without proof of anything. So you shut the hell up, and if you go anywhere near that school, I will bury you. Do you understand? Bury you."

Beck's face was contorted with anger, but he did not fight back. After a moment of holding him against the wall, Jimmy suddenly released him, turned and stalked away. A few of the other workers from the shift had gathered at a bit of a distance, and they stared at him as he passed. He did not look at them.

He finished the shift in silence, avoiding everyone else, and they avoided him. When time was up, he clocked out, changed quickly, and headed home.

22

"It's so frustrating," Jimmy said, his body language betraying to Eddie his deep agitation. They were sitting together in the sanctuary of Calvary Baptist again. Eddie had been in his office at New Start when Jimmy pulled into the parking lot, so they'd gone across to the church to talk in some privacy.

"What is?" They'd been talking about Dyson Beck and the situation at the mill, as Jimmy had related the events of the previous evening. Their conversation had ranged widely, though, so Jimmy understood why Eddie wasn't exactly sure to which frustration he was referring.

"These guys, like Beck, it's never-ending." Jimmy said, fidgeting in his seat as he spoke. He could feel that he was worked up, could still feel the anger that had coursed through him the previous evening pulsating within, but he was with Eddie, so he knew he didn't have to act like it didn't bother him.

"I've worked my share of cases involving compulsive sexual predators, and it doesn't matter how many you catch and put away, there are always more waiting in the wings. Always.

"It's futile. You catch one and tell yourself you've made a difference, but that same day, somewhere in the same city or town or wherever, there are five more out there working up the courage to act on their compulsions. It's an epidemic, a flood, and there are too many holes in the dyke to plug.

"It's a war," Jimmy added, "a war that won't ever be won."

"Maybe not," Eddie said, "but that's a pretty ambitious goal. The world has always been full of people bent on pursuing their own desires, even if getting them can only come at the expense of their neighbor's happiness or property or life. We resist them, not because we think that stopping them will ensure there are no more like them, but because they ought to be resisted. We try to win the battles, if not the war, because we really can make the world better."

"It's like putting a band-aid on a deep, arterial cut," Jimmy said, making a cutting gesture across his arm as though to illustrate the absurdity of the notion, "or like using aspirin to cure cancer. It doesn't get us anywhere in the end."

"Well," Eddie said, a grin slowly spreading on his face, "I suspect you aren't really looking for a discussion of Original Sin and man's depravity, though I'd be happy to oblige you if you are, but I agree with your basic assertion that there's something fundamentally wrong with humanity that carefully honed civil codes and the best judicial system in the world can't fix. So I won't argue with you on that point.

"What I was meaning, though, was that the world isn't a place that is either all good or all bad. Some cultures and some countries, at various times and during various seasons, have been more peaceful and more just than others. Isn't that something worth fighting for?"

Jimmy shrugged and said nothing.

"Think about it, if you stop putting away the predators you can catch—and by you I mean people with the training and gifts and passion that you have—then the world would be just that much worse, right? The five new predators you mentioned, who are out there taking their first steps in their predatory ways, they're going to take those steps whatever you do, right?

"So the least we can do is plug as many holes in the dyke as we can. The least we can do is make the world as good a place as we're able. That's not a waste of time or effort, it's a really essential job, and I'm glad there are people out there like you, who have the stomach and determination to stare into the face of this kind of evil and not flinch. We need people like you, Jimmy."

Jimmy sat, staring at the carpet. "I'm only a mill worker now, Eddie. The world doesn't need me a whole heck of a lot."

Eddie shrugged, his smile returning. "I don't know about that. Even with modern technology, the world still needs lumber."

Jimmy didn't laugh, but a smile broke through and he felt himself relaxing. "Besides," Eddie added. "You didn't sound like a mill worker just now. Who knows, maybe one day you'll lay down your saw and take up your badge again?"

Jimmy looked up from the carpet and glanced at his friend, who sat watching him carefully. He'd not mentioned anything to Eddie about his second thoughts on his new career, but he was beginning to realize that Eddie always heard more than you said.

"Yeah, well, a mill worker is what I am for now," Jimmy said, and he knew that Eddie would take the hint that he wasn't ready yet to discuss his misgivings about his present employment or his questions about the future.

"Have you been up to the falls yet?" Eddie asked.

Though Jimmy had expected Eddie not to pursue his misgivings about the mill, this particular redirection came from out of nowhere and caught Jimmy by surprise. "No, I mean to, but I haven't yet."

"Come with me," Eddie said. "I think you'd enjoy it."

"Now?"

"No," Eddie laughed, "Not now. To do it right takes a whole day, a long day, so we'd have to leave well before dawn to get back the same night. I was thinking about the weekend, not this weekend, next weekend. I always go the first Saturday in April. It's a tradition I've kept pretty faithfully since high school. Why not come with me? It's beautiful up there. Maybe getting away would give you some perspective."

Suddenly, Jimmy really wanted to go. He'd not been more than ten miles from Avalon Falls in the last year, and the thought of getting away for a day and seeing something different, something beautiful, was very appealing. "All right, I'll come."

"Good," Eddie said. "We'll meet here next Saturday morning."

"What time should I be here?"

"Let me get back to you on that," Eddie said, smiling again.

"You're just not telling me so I don't back out."

"Maybe," Eddie said, laughing. "It'll be early, really early, but you can probably sleep a bit on the drive up there."

"Nice smooth ride, is it?"

Eddie laughed, and his non-answer told Jimmy what he needed to know.

Really early turned out to be four o'clock in the morning, and since Jimmy didn't get to sleep until almost two, he'd only slept for about ninety minutes when his alarm woke him. He dressed in darkness, grabbed his things and stumbled out to the Bronco to drive to Eddie's.

The kitchen light was on at the house, and Eddie had a pot of coffee waiting for them. They drank in silence before loading up the truck that usually sat next to the New Start building. It had been donated to New Start some years ago by a member of the congregation, and though it was still road-worthy, it didn't often leave the church grounds. Instead, the truck, like most other things New Start owned, had increasingly become part of the program in multiple ways.

Eddie believed that basic mechanical skills, as well as basic educational and social skills, were an important part of his job to equip the boys for re-entry into ordinary civilian life. In fact, a month or so before, when Jonathan, one of the older residents in the program had graduated from New Start and been released, he'd spoken at his graduation ceremony of his gratitude for just this insistence by Eddie that they all be equipped for a variety of tasks. He said that he'd come to see that he could do a lot of things he'd never believed he could do, and he thanked Eddie for that.

This morning, though, the truck was being appropriated for their trip to the falls, and even though Jimmy offered the Bronco, Eddie insisted that the truck wouldn't be missed for one day. So they loaded it up and Eddie backed it out of the long gravel drive. Before long, they were making their way along curvy back roads toward the falls for which this little town, nestled just at that place where the edge of the plains met the foot of the mountains, was named.

A few hours later, the early light of morning illuminated a sign indicating parking for those wishing to climb up to the falls, but Eddie ignored the sign and kept driving. "Wasn't that it?" Jimmy said, looking back over his shoulder at the turn-off.

"That's where most visitors park, and from there, it's a pretty straightforward hike up to the Falls. The problem, though, is that all you can do from there is get to the falls and come back. There's another, less well-known spot where you can climb up on the other side, and from there you can not only get a great look at the falls, but you can keep going up above them. That's ultimately where we're going, because the place I really want to take you is far above the falls themselves."

Eventually, Eddie turned into a dirt side road, and he drove slowly back over the bumpy stretch that severely strained the concept of a road, until he came across a grassy patch on the left where he turned in, stopped the truck and shut off the engine. "Here we are."

"Here we are," Jimmy answered, and they piled out of the truck and grabbed their gear. "There's a trail up to the falls here?"

"There sure is," Eddie said. "If you know where to look."

Once they were ready, Eddie led them along the edge of the grassy patch for about twenty yards or so, then suddenly he ducked under some overhanging branches and between two trees. They were immediately in the midst of thick undergrowth, and if it hadn't been for a bright strip of orange ribbon he saw tied to a branch overhead, Jimmy would quickly have despaired that they were anywhere near a path at all. As it was, his trust in Eddie and the slight hope given him by the apparent trail marker gave him enough patience to keep his mouth closed and keep going. After a while, he found that they were indeed hiking along something unmistakably path-like.

Though it was April, the air was crisp and quite cold. He was glad he'd let Eddie twist his arm and talk him into going shopping for some hiking gear a few nights before. His new jacket was warm and his ears were toasty under the hat Eddie had picked out. In fact, if anything, he could feel himself getting a little hot and sweaty as they pressed on, especially as the path grew steeper and their ascent more taxing. He knew, though, that had he worn what he'd first planned on wearing, he'd have been freezing.

As they climbed, Jimmy drank deeply of the cold air, scented with the fragrance of the ponderosa pines that rose everywhere around them. The canopy above was beautiful and dense, though Jimmy gradually became aware that through the trees on their left a void of empty space was growing. He had figured from Eddie's description of climbing "on the other side" of the falls that eventually it would be visible on that side of the trail. So when they reached a place about an hour into their hike where Eddie had stepped off of the trail to that side and motioned to Jimmy to come, he followed, wondering if they'd reached the falls already.

Eddie reached out and pulled a low-hanging branch back, indicating that Jimmy should look out through the now cleared opening. Jimmy poked his head out, but he saw nothing at first, beyond a small canyon or gorge, lying down below, between them and a mirroring wood on the far side. Then, it was as if his ears were suddenly opened, and he heard the distant sound of water echoing as it poured over rocks. He looked up, not down. In the distance, he thought he could make out the white spray of the base of the falls.

"They still seem a long way up."

"Better keep going then," Eddie said with a grin, and he was off, back to the trail.

He explained as they resumed their hike that while their current trail was superior in that it rose above the falls, unlike the trail more often used on the other side, it did, unfortunately, start from further down below the falls, so that it took a little longer to get up to the falls themselves. Jimmy noted out loud that Eddie had failed to mention this fact when reflecting on the advantages of this lesser-known trail earlier in the morning, and Eddie again just smiled and kept going.

The trail was now consistently steep and taxing, though not exactly treacherous. If Jimmy had feared that it might ascend with one side a sheer and precipitous drop into some distant abyss below, this was not the case. The gorge beneath the falls lay consistently a short walk through the trees on the left, so their was no immediate danger that if they lost their footing, they would tumble anywhere but backwards down the trail. However, the ground was in some places very steep, and Jimmy found himself needing to steady himself by using his hands like an animal on all fours in some places. It was a good thing he hadn't tried this too soon after coming to Avalon Falls, before his lungs had adapted to living in the thinner air in general. He would have found it a rough go.

The roaring of the falls grew louder. Jimmy knew they had to be close now, and he was not disappointed. A little further on they came to a place where the trees on the left opened up to form a marvelous vista of the falls, cascading down the mountainside. Eddie was already leaning against a tree, looking from the splendid vantage point, and Jimmy walked over and joined him. They were about a third of the way up the side of the falls, and they had an excellent view of the water in all of its grandeur as it poured over the edge of the ridge above and tumbled down majestically.

"Come on," Eddie said after a few moments. "There's another great view up near the top. In fact, the next one's my favorite."

They headed back up the trail, and this time it seemed like only a few minutes until Eddie was stepping off to the side again. This time they were roughly parallel to the top of the falls, and Jimmy got closer to the edge of the ridge along which they were climbing to look down. The view was indeed spectacular. When he didn't watch carefully, the water from the falls simply fell in an undifferentiated mass, but when he really focused, he felt he could pick out drops spiraling downward in the midst of the rest. For some reason, watching individual drops, or at least imagining that he could, provoked in him the strange thought that it would be peaceful to be washed over the falls.

This was, of course, ludicrous. Falling to your death on the rocks below would be tumultuous, noisy and painful, not peaceful, but he still found himself struck by the notion. For a drop of water, though, it might be a peaceful passage downward. For its whole existence, the drop was never alone, flowing in currents and swirling in eddies here and there at the side of the river or stream that carried it endlessly to the sea. It was always surrounded and always swallowed in a larger whole—whether it wished to be or not. But in that single, glorious moment, when it surged out over the edge of the falls and plummeted downward, perhaps time slowed for it, perhaps it felt free and independent and gloriously alone.

They did not talk much while they stood there, but Eddie did point out a few things in the view that he most appreciated. Then, they were off again. Still upward they climbed, stopping once more from some distance above the falls to look upon it one last time. Eddie said they would lose sight of it shortly, for the trail they were on would soon turn away from the falls and start working away from it. Jimmy didn't linger long; he preferred the up close view they'd had below and would have again on their way down.

The trail did indeed veer right, even as it continued going further up the mountain. Jimmy checked his watch and saw it was almost noon. They'd been climbing for six hours, and had it not been for the soreness in his legs, he would have been surprised. The time had passed swiftly. Suddenly, the trees began to thin on either side of the trail, and almost without warning they stepped out of the thick woods, emerging into a beautiful, mountain meadow. The midday sun hung warm and welcoming above, though the air up here was still cold and crisp, and Jimmy followed Eddie as though in a daze out from the meadow's edge into the middle of the open space all around them.

Waste high grass grew like wheat all round them, and mixed in with it were two or three varieties of wildflower, some white, some yellow and some a deep, beautiful purple. Jimmy heard the buzz of a bee hovering by one of the flowers nearby and looked around him at the splendor that stretched a good distance ahead, for he was just able to make out more trees on the far side of the clearing.

"He brought me out into a wide open place," Eddie said from nearby, "he delivered me, because he delighted in me."

Jimmy turned to Eddie. "A poem?"

"A Hebrew poem," Eddie said. "A slight paraphrase from Psalm 18."

"Oh," Jimmy said, turning back to the stunning meadow around them.

"Come," Eddie said, beginning to move through the high grass parallel to the woods from which they'd just emerged and motioning for Jimmy to follow. "There's a big rock over here where I like to sit and think. We'll have lunch. Set your burdens down a while and rest."

Unbidden and unwanted, tears formed in Jimmy's eyes.

23

Jimmy stood in the sun-drenched mountain meadow, a sea of billowing wild grass and flowers all around, hastily wiping tears from his eyes. Eddie hadn't noticed that Jimmy wasn't following. He continued in a line away from where they'd been standing for fifteen yards or so before he looked back over his shoulder and noticed Jimmy hadn't moved. He hesitated as he looked back, then looked away without moving on.

Jimmy wiped with both hands. The tears disappeared as quickly as they'd come, and he felt reasonably sure they wouldn't return. He stepped in Eddie's direction and called ahead, "I'm coming."

Eddie continued along, maintaining a course roughly parallel to the woods on their right. After a few moments, he veered inward a bit, and soon he was slipping his backpack off of his shoulders, lowering it to the ground beside the large slab of rock he'd referred to a moment before. "Ready for lunch?"

"Sure," Jimmy said, coming up to the rock. Eddie had carefully avoided looking at him directly, and even though Jimmy, much to his own surprise, was just then realizing that he didn't mind that Eddie had seen his tears, he appreciated his discretion all the same.

"Here we go," Eddie said, extending a saran-wrapped sub sandwich to Jimmy. "An Eddie special, the best cold-cut sub around."

"Thanks," Jimmy said, taking the sandwich gratefully. He hadn't eaten anything since the previous evening, and he was hungry. "It's all right, you know. We don't need to pretend like what just happened didn't happen."

"What did just happen?" Eddie asked, taking his own sandwich and sitting down on the rock.

"Well," Jimmy said, sitting down on the other side. "I'm not even sure I know."

"But you have an idea."

"I have an idea," Jimmy said, taking a bite and chewing while he thought. "Have you ever read *The Things They Carried* by Tim O'Brien?"

"Sounds vaguely familiar, but I don't think so."

"I'm not sure if you'd call it a novel or a collection of short stories or what, but it's basically a bunch of Vietnam stories."

"Still only vaguely familiar. I've read some Vietnam literature, here and there, but not much."

"My best friend from UCLA gave it to me a couple years after I started at the Bureau. He said that reading it had made him think of me, but he didn't say why. Anyway, when I read the title story, 'The Things They Carried,' I figured out why.

"The title story is about a young lieutenant, and one of his men gets shot. It's a simple story, really, but it has a pretty ingenious angle. Right from the beginning, O'Brien starts giving the reader lists of the objects that soldiers in Vietnam carried, lists and weights. He tells you how much their guns weighed, their ammo, their helmets and flak jackets, their cigarettes and food rations, their medical packs and boots. He goes on, list after list, in so much detail that its staggering. He lists the special items that only one guy in the platoon would have, like the radio or mines or bigger, heavier guns, and so on.

"Anyway, by the time you get a few pages into this thing, you feel the burden of all the weight they carried. You can't help but think of that hot, sweaty hell and those guys, 'humping it,' carrying all their gear from place to place, just waiting to be shot.

"Then, he pulls a switch. He starts listing, not the physical objects that they carried, but the intangible, abstract things. The fear, the hope, the memories of home, the dreams. By this point, the weight is unbearable, and it's easy for the reader to realize that the physical weight was the easy part. The rest of it—that was what broke you, that was what made every step so hard.

"For the young lieutenant, the weight he carried was love, unrequited love, or at least what he thought was love, for a young co-ed back home. It's her that he's thinking about when his man gets shot, and even though he couldn't have done anything about it, he feels guilty. He resolves to leave that weight behind so he won't be distracted, which is why the story ends with him burning her letters.

"When I first read the story, it was late at night in my apartment. I was alone in bed with my lamp on, and I suddenly realized that there were tears, streaming down my face. You know, like the Coldplay song."

Eddie shook his head slightly. "Sorry, I don't think I know it."

"Never mind. Anyway, at first, I thought those tears were for the soldiers, for those kids in their late teens and early twenties that we'd sent to that whacked out war. Kids we'd asked to carry all that crushing weight. But then, as I lay there feeling sorry for them, I realized that really, underneath it all,

I was feeling sorry for myself. I felt sorry for me, because I saw me in that young lieutenant. It was me, carrying around all those hopes and dreams, all the desires and fears that make us human, all the while trying to do a job that didn't make any sense—not any—a job that brought me face to face on a regular basis with the very worst of human nature. Then I understood why Sam had sent me the book."

Jimmy, who'd been increasingly animated as he talked, suddenly grew quiet, and after a moment, Eddie asked, "So what are you carrying now?"

Jimmy smiled and shook his head. "You don't beat around the bush, do you?"

"Should I?"

"No. At this point it would annoy me."

"Is it still the job?"

"No," Jimmy shook his head faintly, thinking of some of the more gruesome scenes permanently lodged in his memory. "There are times when it still haunts me, but that's not it."

Eddie finished his sandwich and dropped his balled up saran wrap in his backpack. He pulled out a bottle of water and handed it to Jimmy, then got out another for himself.

"Thanks," Jimmy said, unscrewing the lid and taking a long drink. "It was about six years ago now, I guess, when my team caught a case that took me to Chicago. A young woman had been murdered in her apartment. Gruesome, but I won't burden you with the details. Turns out she was a recent graduate of Northwestern Law, employed by a prestigious downtown firm, and she'd been out the night before with a couple friends from work, celebrating the fact that she and another friend had just passed the Bar.

"It was a really messed up case," Jimmy said, shaking his head as he thought about it. "Anyway—I'm botching this story—her friend from the law firm who had also just passed the bar was a woman named Nina. There was pretty strong mutual attraction between us, right from the beginning. It couldn't go anywhere, of course, since I don't get involved with people in cases I'm working. And yet, when we eventually solved the case and I told Nina, the first thing she said to me was, 'So does that mean you can ask me out now?'

"I've never forgotten that. There must have been thirty seconds of complete silence as I held my phone, thinking, what do I do now. Finally I just said, 'Yeah, I can ask you out now.' So I did, and we started seeing each other. I'd fly to Chicago or she'd come east. We were both making decent money, so the expense wasn't an issue. After a while, though, it got to be a drag, living so far apart, and about 8 months after we'd first met, we decided to get married.

"She was in a great job at the start of a promising legal career, and I'd been profiling for a decade already. There's a high burnout rate in my job, as you can imagine, so it wasn't hard to convince myself that I wanted a break. I transferred to the Chicago office, knowing my work was going to change in fundamental ways but thinking I was all right with that. Turned out I wasn't all right with it. I missed it. A lot. So my boss in the Chicago office helped me make some contacts at the Chicago Police Department, and before long, I was consulting with them on some of their more difficult cases.

"Nina didn't mind. At least she said she didn't, and at first I really think she didn't, since she was working super long hours herself. That was the problem, really. I was working full time for the Bureau plus additional hours with the CPD, while she was logging as much time or more, just at the firm, and the bottom line was that it felt at times like we'd seen more of each other when we lived in different cities.

"We went on like that for a few years, living life in the same space but running on parallel tracks, until we found out Nina was pregnant. All of a sudden, we had to work through all these things that hadn't been an issue before. It was amazing how even the thought of a child turned our lives upside down. Who was going to do what and how we'd look after the baby and where we would live—we couldn't agree on any of it. It was very stressful.

"For me, at least, it was a serious reality check. We'd gotten married, but we hadn't done any work forging a life together—you know, a shared life—but with the baby coming, we couldn't put that off anymore. So we starting working through some things, and though it was hard, it started to give me hope that we might be all right. It was only then that I realized I'd not had that hope for a while.

"Well, to make an already long story short, I decided to get her a special gift for our anniversary at the end of October, to tell her how grateful I was for her and for the baby and even for the hard stuff we'd been going through. There was a beautiful crystal vase that we'd asked for in our wedding registry, but we hadn't gotten it. We'd agreed to wait and get it for our fifth wedding anniversary, as a marker of sorts. Well, we'd only been married four years, but I was optimistic that she'd forgive me for going out and getting it, especially when I explained why.

"So the day of our fourth anniversary, I got permission to leave the office early so I could pick up the vase, take it home and stash it in our big storage closet until that night. Nina had a big case that she was working on, so we had plans to meet for a late dinner. I had plenty of time. When I got back to our apartment, though, I heard them back in the bedroom as soon as I entered. It didn't take an FBI agent to know what was going on in there, so I didn't even hesitate. I slammed the door behind me and started back through the apartment.

"Here's the thing. I'd left early, but I was still on call, so I had my gun. It's all like a really bad dream. I don't know what to tell you, but as I walked through that apartment, my hand glided to my holster and I drew my weapon. I carried it, barrel down, all the way back along our hallway.

"Well, the guy was one of the partners at Nina's firm—a super hair-gelled, smarmy, lawyer-type from somewhere in Alabama. You know, insincere southern charm oozing out of every pore, a guy who'd been married twice already with two ex-wives living pretty large on his considerable salary. Anyway, when he stepped out of our room, pants hastily pulled up and oxford shirt in hand, he saw my gun and fell over into the kitchen. I would have laughed at how pathetic he was if I wasn't so angry.

"Then, Nina appeared in the doorway, and she saw me walking toward them with the gun out and started screaming. Not scared, screaming. Mad screaming. There she was, caught red-handed, and she's furious with me for everything from coming home early to having my gun out in the apartment. Well, I don't know how I managed not to shoot them both. It was my deepest desire to do so, believe me.

"I held onto that gun like it was life itself, though, and a few seconds later, the guy bolted out of our back door carrying what clothes he'd not had time to put on as he went down the back stairs into the alleyway. Nina didn't budge. She just stood there going toe to toe with me, and I matched her verbally blow for blow.

"It got really, really ugly. Who even knows what all we said—though that's silly, I'm sure she does know. She never did forget things like that. She remembers everything. It's just how her mind works. Anyway, at the end of the night, the last thing she said to me was this. 'I'd been planning to break things off with him, but now I think I'll break things off with you instead.'

"And with that, she left the apartment and didn't come back. She didn't come back that night. She didn't come back the next day. She didn't come back that weekend. I waited at the apartment from Wednesday night until Monday morning. I called in sick. I called her cell. I called our friends. I called everywhere. On the following Monday, when I finally went back at work, she emptied all her personal belongings from the apartment. She left me a note that she already had legal counsel and recommended that I do the same.

"So that's how it ended. She made twice as much as I did, so she agreed to forego all present and future alimony claims to expedite the divorce. The affair had been going on for a year, so she didn't know who the father of the baby was. We agreed that she'd let me know the results of the paternity test after the baby was born.

"Most of this was at least roughly in place before I left Chicago that December, though some of it was arranged after I came here. I resigned from the FBI, and the only address I left my boss, my friends and my lawyer, was my sister's address here in Montana. She forwards all mail that comes for me, though by now that's nothing to speak of. I'd only been separated from Nina for about a month and a half when I got here, though now we're officially divorced, of course."

"Wow," Eddie said, when Jimmy stopped telling his story. "That is a lot to carry. And the baby? What did you find out?"

"You remember that day, last fall, when you and Big Johnny rescued me from The Rusty Nail?"

"Yes," Eddie said, looking curiously at Jimmy. "You're not saying that... you mean? Oh. Some things are falling into place."

"Yeah," Jimmy said, nodding. "That morning when I went to my mailbox, I had a letter from my sister. Inside that letter was an envelope from Nina. She'd sent it to my sister in August, but she'd been on vacation, so it had been delayed getting to me. Anyway, inside the envelope from Nina was a blank piece of paper wrapped around a picture. All it said was, 'She's yours, 5/24.'"

"Wow," Eddie said.

"Yes, wow." Jimmy nodded again.

Eddie raised his hand to his cheek, and for the first time, Jimmy noticed that tears were quietly running down his face. Eddie smiled as he wiped more aggressively. "Sorry about going all soft on you, like that."

"Don't be," Jimmy said. "It's just an empathy cry, right?"

"That's right," Eddie said, laughing. "It's all a sham."

They sat quietly on the rock, and Jimmy surveyed the beautiful scene around him. Large clouds moved over the sun, and a great shadow crept across the splendid meadow.

"You told me once that you have terrible dreams," Eddie said. "Is this what you meant?"

"Yes," Jimmy said. "They're never exactly the same, but they basically are. I dream I'm back in our apartment, and Nina and the baby are there in some form of darkness and decay. A wind blows the windows open or the roof off or something like that. It's always cold, always silent, always dreadful. They're dead or dying. Guilt for abandoning the baby or something. Perhaps guilt for abandoning both of them."

They sat, listening to the crickets hidden in the deep grass, and then Jimmy added. "I'm not sure what I'm supposed to do, Eddie. I have a daughter out there, who's almost a year old. I've never seen her or held her in my arms. I don't even know her name."

They talked a little more but didn't linger long at the rock. When there was no more left to say on the subject of Jimmy's divorce and shattered personal life, Eddie led them into the middle of the meadow. He pointed out interesting features of the landscape and indicated what was to be found if one wanted to explore further in various directions. Apparently, he'd first come across this place in April of his junior year in high school. That summer, he'd explored it pretty thoroughly, and almost every April since he'd been back, so that he managed to get up here at least once a year, sometimes more. It was, he said, his favorite retreat, a haven from the craziness of life.

On their way back down, they paused a few times again to view the falls. Jimmy enjoyed it, especially when they paused to watch it in the failing half-light of evening, but having seen the sunlit meadow up above, he understood why Eddie climbed this side, even if it was harder and took more time. The roar and turbulence of the falls only made the peaceful serenity of the meadow that much more striking.

It was dark by the time they reached the truck. They had their last water bottle and sat in the cab, resting and eating what remained of the food Eddie had packed. There was nothing left to stay for, but both felt somehow reluctant to start the truck and head back to town. Eventually Eddie did start it, and they drove slowly back toward Avalon Falls. Jimmy treated Eddie to a slice of pie at Cabot's, where they told Alice about their day—in very general terms. Then, as the hour was growing late, Eddie took Jimmy out to the church where he picked up his Bronco and headed out.

When Jimmy crawled into bed that night, he felt the weariness in his legs and body seep out. He could barely move. It felt good to lie down and even better to have finally unburdened his soul to someone, and he knew Eddie could be trusted. For the first time in a long time, despite his soreness and fatigue, he felt like the weight of the things he carried had decreased, even if only slightly. He slipped into a deep and peaceful sleep.

A persistent pounding woke him. He slowly became aware of it and of Major barking in the next room. Rain was heavy outside. He rubbed his eyes as he listened to the rain patter, to Major bark and to the pounding. It was coming from his door. He shuffled out to his living room, where light from headlights out front lit the room up faintly. He switched on the porch light and peeked through the small pane of glass at the top of his door. It was Sheriff Anderson and a deputy, but the Sheriff's head was down as he knocked stiffly on the door.

Jimmy swung his door open. Sheriff Anderson looked up. Rain poured off the brim of his wide hat, but all Jimmy saw was the ashen look on his face.

"It's happened again."

24

Jimmy stepped aside to let Sheriff Anderson and his deputy into his house. "I do have a phone," he said.

"Apparently, you don't believe in answering it."

"You called?"

"Yes, a few times."

"Sorry," Jimmy said. "I sometimes turn the ringer off when I go to bed after my shift at the mill. I must have forgotten to put it back on."

"Jimmy, did you hear what I said?"

Jimmy put his hand out and made an apologetic gesture. "Sorry, I was in a deep sleep when you woke me. I hiked the falls today, yesterday—whatever. I'm exhausted. You said something happened, or happened again or something?"

"Think Jimmy," Sheriff Anderson said. "Why would I be here in the middle of the night?"

Jimmy looked up, suddenly very awake. "When? Where? Who?"

"The body was found a little over an hour ago, about 1:30 AM. That's when we started calling you."

"Right. Sorry. A man, I presume? At the park? It's raining pretty hard, though, isn't it? Who'd be there on a night like tonight?"

"Not the park. An alley in town, about a block from Connelly's."

"An alley? Huh," Jimmy said. "That's a pretty big shift. I suppose you're here to escort me to the crime scene?"

"I was going to ask if you'd be willing first, but yes," Sheriff Anderson said. "We'll take you down if you'd like."

"That's all right. I'll drive myself—less complication that way when I'm ready to leave. I'll get dressed." Jimmy turned and was about to leave the room when the Sheriff added.

"It's Dyson Beck, Jimmy."

"Beck did it?" Jimmy said as he swung around. "You caught him?"

"No—the body, it's Beck."

Again, realization dawned, and he turned slowly away without saying a word. He walked to his bedroom. A moment later he re-emerged, dressed and holding his gun and holster. The Sheriff and the deputy, Greg, were standing where he'd left them, dripping on his floor and being watched by Major, who was lying a safe distance away so as to be well clear of the puddling.

"Sheriff," Jimmy said, putting his shoulder holster on and nodding toward his gun. "I assume that our previous arrangement still applies."

Sheriff Anderson glanced at his deputy before nodding his assent to Jimmy and turning for the door. "I'll ride down with you, if that's all right. Fill you in on the way."

"Sure thing," Jimmy said, turning off the light and shutting his door behind them. They stepped off his dark porch into the pouring rain, and soon both vehicles were slipping down his driveway and headed into town.

They arrived at the crime scene a little after 3:00 AM, and thankfully, the rain had slowed considerably. Gibbons and the deputies with him had had the good sense to erect a canopy over the body to protect it as much as possible from the rain, a technique Jimmy had only seen once or twice before, though Jimmy knew that in a rain like this, even minimal exposure would affect the amount of useful forensic evidence they could gather. Fortunately, there were things worth seeing that the rain couldn't wash away, so not all would be lost.

Jimmy approached the body slowly. When Sheriff Anderson had said the dead man was Dyson Beck, his snickering, mocking face had appeared instantly in Jimmy's mind. For a week and a half, Jimmy had put up with him at the mill, every night, all shift long. It wasn't a stretch to say Jimmy had harbored fairly intense ill will toward him.

And yet, he felt no guilt as he stood just inside the reach of the canopy, water still running down his raincoat, looking down at Beck's badly beaten body. The skull was crushed at the front, as before with Morrison, and his groin region was also severely battered, though this time the pants were not down as before. Jimmy noted the difference mentally as he walked around the body, studying it further.

Still no guilt. Maybe that would come later. He'd despised Beck and now Beck was dead, but if he was supposed to feel bad for wishing this man ill, he didn't. In fact, he continued to feel traces of something very different to guilt. When Sheriff Anderson had first mentioned Beck's name and Jimmy had turned back to his room, he'd found a distinct feeling of happiness inside.

He realized Beck was a human being and that being happy he was dead was probably not the ideal response, but he could think of little other than the man's insinuations about the school playground, his history of abuse and the likelihood, perhaps inevitability, that more victims would have come eventually. There were now, almost certainly, at least a few families in Avalon Falls that would not spend the rest of their lives dealing with the aftermath of abuse and the shockwaves that emanated from it. For that, at least, he was unashamedly happy.

He moved around the body, taking his own pictures and asking the medical examiner questions. After almost an hour, he stepped out from under the canopy to find the rain had almost completely stopped. He walked to the place where Gibbons stood in the drizzle, talking to Sheriff Anderson by one of their patrol cars.

"Certainly seems to be the work of the same guy. Too many similarities," Jimmy said. "Though I can't help but be struck by the differences."

"Care to elaborate?" Sheriff Anderson asked.

"On which part?"

"On all of it, if you like."

"All right," Jimmy said, leaning back against the car beside them and looking over at the body. "First of all, the obvious similarities. Beck's had his face and groin bashed in. More telling, though, is that the severity of the beating as a whole is roughly the same."

"Roughly the same?" Sheriff Anderson said. "Exactly, I'd say. They're both dead!"

"Yes, both men have been beaten to death, but that's not what I mean. They were both beaten well beyond death, and more to the point, beaten to about the same degree beyond death. No pictures of Morrison's body were ever printed in the paper, and no images appeared on T.V. So all told, there were maybe a dozen people who saw it or the crime scene photos.

"Even taking into account the possibility that some of the more gruesome details were shared with a friend or three over a couple beers down at the pub by various county employees—no offense intended or particular accusations leveled—I doubt these accounts circulated accurately even if they perhaps circulated widely. The print media accounts, always the most detailed in any crime report, didn't get specific enough for a copycat to figure out how to beat Dyson Beck so as to approximate the feel of Morrison's murder."

"No offense, Jimmy," Gibbons said, exchanging a glance with Sheriff Anderson. "This is kind of obvious. We weren't really thinking about a copycat."

"But if it's the same guy, why the differences?" Jimmy stood up straight and turned to face Gibbons and Sheriff Anderson directly. He motioned with his hands as his excitement grew. His mind was whirring, his blood flowing. This was the part he missed. The thrill of the chase, thinking out loud and processing information while he brought those who lingered a step or two behind up to speed.

"Let's start with the big thing, location. Look around, gentlemen. It's dark and somewhat secluded, yes, but just ten yards that way lies a street. More importantly, there's a streetlight on the other side of the entrance to this alley."

Jimmy pivoted and pointed in the other direction. "Fifteen yards in that direction lies another street. Now there's no streetlight, but still, you're exposed here on two sides. This is a much more risky place to kill a man. I don't know how long it takes this guy to beat a man to death and then keep beating until he's done, but it has to take a little while, doesn't it? It's no trigger pull followed by a clean get away.

Jimmy gestured toward the canopy. "This guy is methodical, thorough. He finishes the job he starts the way he wants to finish it. At two or three seconds per swing, he could get what, twenty swings into a minute? Even if he only gives ten to the head and ten to the groin, and he might well use more, he'd be standing over Beck for at least a minute. The jogging track was a far safer place than this. Now, maybe necessity, or perceived necessity drove him? Maybe it was just opportunity. Or maybe, and this is the truly frightening possibility, maybe he's just growing bolder. Maybe he ran his experiment at the park, and when he didn't get caught, maybe he was emboldened, this time running a greater risk. Maybe we're on a new timeline, too. Maybe he won't wait so long again."

"You sure about that?" Gibbons asked.

"I'm not sure of anything—just thinking out loud," Jimmy said. "I do that at a crime scene. I process while I talk. Old habit, sorry. Back to the dissimilarities, another big one would be Beck's pants. They're up, not down. A big part of the mystery around Morrison was how the killer got Morrison's pants down without a struggle. Right? There was no evidence that Morrison fought back, and yet his pants were down. It was hard to figure, and now we have Beck's body, beaten in much the same way, but with his pants up not down. Why?"

Jimmy stood, the question rolling around in his head as he gazed at the canopy and the work going on under it. "If there's significance in the fact that the blows are to the head and groin, which there has to be, then why didn't it matter to the killer that Beck be exposed like Morrison to receive them? Why didn't he do whatever he did to Morrison to get him into the proper position?"

"As you've already noted," the Sheriff said, "this is a more vulnerable place. Maybe the killer didn't have time to do things in exactly the same way."

"Maybe, but it's puzzling. If this guy is compulsive, and it certainly seems that he is, and if getting Morrison's pants down was part of the compulsion, then the risk wouldn't stop him. He'd have to do it."

"So location and pants," Sheriff Anderson said. "Is there more?"

"Yes," Jimmy said. "The murder weapon. No overhanging branch to use here, obviously, and it shows on Beck's skull. The blows that landed more to the side of Beck's head, the ones that remain discernible among the mess that's left, they look smooth and symmetric. I'd expect a heavy pipe of some kind, though who knows if we'll ever find it."

"We already have," Gibbons said, again exchanging looks with the Sheriff while Jimmy talked. "That's what we were discussing when you came over from the canopy."

"What?" Jimmy said. "I'm right, aren't I?"

"Yes," Gibbons replied. "A sweep of the alley found a bloody pipe in the dumpster over there."

Gibbons indicated a dumpster in the direction of the street where there wasn't a streetlight illuminating the intersection with the alley. Jimmy looked from the body to the dumpster. "He didn't spare much effort getting rid of it, unlike the end of the branch that broke off at the park. Another difference. He didn't care if we found it. Perhaps he wore gloves this time and wasn't worried about forensics. Or, perhaps he assumed the rain would take care of his fingerprints. Can I see it?"

After Jimmy examined the pipe, he returned to Anderson and Gibbons, so animated that he paced in the alley. "It's a solid pipe, decent length. There's a good chance he may not have found it here, I'd say, suggesting this might be different from Morrison in another respect. The broken branch felt spontaneous, improvised, but the pipe suggests premeditation."

Jimmy stopped and rubbed his chin aggressively with his hand. "That brings me to another thing. Beck. What's different about Morrison and Beck?"

"One was visiting and the other lived here," Sheriff Anderson offered.

"True, though Beck is still pretty new," Jimmy said. "Even more obvious."

"Beck's a sex offender and Morrison wasn't."

"Not that we could find, anyway, and we looked, didn't we?"

"We did," Gibbons agreed.

"Why?" Jimmy said, getting excited. "Why did we look?"

"Because of the sexual overtones of the case."

"Bingo," Jimmy said, pointing at Gibbons. "This crime fits. Morrison's murder didn't. Beck's a pervert. An abuser. If this had been the first body we found, not the second, we'd have understood right away. Sex offender beaten in the groin and face until he's unrecognizable. Grisly? Yes. Mysterious? I don't think so. But nothing about Morrison fit the profile."

"So our killer got the wrong guy the first time?" Sheriff Anderson asked.

Jimmy shrugged and ran his fingers through his wet hair. "Could be. Beck was living in Avalon Falls at the time, as we later found out. I guess the killer could have confused them somehow, but they don't really look alike. I don't know, I can't quite put the pieces together yet, but there's something here. I know it."

Sheriff Anderson looked at his watch. "Look, it's almost 4:30. Do you need more time here, Jimmy?"

"No, I have what I need."

"Then why don't we take this back to the station, dry off and get some coffee."

"Sounds good to me," Jimmy said.

"All right, we'll see you there."

They started away and Jimmy watched them go. He looked at Beck's motionless form. He felt alive. Maybe he'd feel guilty for that later, too. For now, he reveled in the excitement.

25

Jimmy sat on the back of the sturdy chair, his feet planted solidly on the seat to maintain his balance. He liked sitting up high—above the table and photographs—so he could get a bird's eye view without having to stand up.

He was back in his old room at the station with the same table and chair, this time with two different sets of crime scene photos spread around. He was also dry, finally, and it felt good not to be dripping wet. He'd spent a long time sifting and sorting the Morrison and Beck photos, then arranging them just the way he wanted. He identified key images from both sets, putting Morrison's on the left, Beck's on the right. He'd added, removed, revised and rearranged until he was finally happy with the layout. Ever since, he'd been sitting, staring, and thinking.

He yawned and glanced down at his watch. It was almost ten. There had been moments during the hours since the Sheriff woke him, like this one, when he'd felt powerfully tired. Of all nights to be summoned from his bed after so little sleep, why this one? He'd been up since before the crack of the dawn, after a less than satisfactory sleep, and he'd hiked all day. Both mind and body were paying the toll.

He yawned again.

He glanced over at his empty, styrofoam cup. He could have used some more coffee, but he'd had half a pot already, and he almost couldn't bear the thought of more station coffee. Maybe Gibbons and the Sheriff would let him go out for some. He looked back at the pictures, though, and he knew that he wasn't going anywhere. Not yet. His mind had been racing since leaving the crime scene, and a careful examination of the pictures had only confirmed his suspicions.

He'd been trying, for the last half hour or so, to make the case to himself that the second murder had been committed by someone else, but despite the important differences, he remained unconvinced. He kept coming back to the same fundamental conviction that Beck and Morrison had been killed by the same man. So why the changes? What had happened? Or, perhaps a better question was, what was happening? Was this evolution? Was the killer becoming bolder, more confident and more reckless? Where would this new trajectory take him?

The door opened and Gibbons entered. He'd been in and out a lot earlier, but he'd left Jimmy alone to his musings while he tracked down information on Beck's whereabouts the previous evening. Gibbons stopped just inside the door, and after a moment, Jimmy looked up. "Hey, Eric, did you find anything that would challenge the bartender's testimony about the timeline?"

"No," Gibbons said. "In fact, two other patrons from Connelly's also confirm that Beck left pretty close to 12:30."

"And the M.E. hasn't said anything that would suggest he might revise his original estimate that the time of death was about 12:30?"

"Nope."

Jimmy nodded. "So when he left Connelly's, Beck only had a few minutes left to live."

"Looks that way," Gibbons said. "Hey, I don't want to interrupt you here, but the Sheriff was hoping you'd come to his office."

Jimmy, whose attention had been drawn back to his layout of photographs, pulled his eyes away and looked back at Gibbons. There was something in Gibbons' face that suggested something might be amiss, but as quickly as it appeared it was gone, and Jimmy didn't think about it further. "All right. I could use a stretch."

Jimmy followed Gibbons to the Sheriff's office, where Anderson sat behind his desk, massaging his temples gingerly. He looked haggard, and Jimmy was reminded that what was for him an opportunity to shake the rust off of his investigative skills and try his hand again at the work that had once animated and invigorated him, was for the Sheriff something very different.

To the Sheriff, this drizzly April morning must have felt like the peace and harmony of his happy little town had been shattered beyond repair, lost beyond recall. He'd seen it before, that look in the eyes of those who'd spent a lifetime serving as the guardians of their communities, the deep and abiding fear that normalcy was gone for good, irretrievably lost in the surreal nightmare of some senseless act of violence or another. That was the look he'd seen in Sheriff Anderson's face when he'd looked up as Jimmy opened his door in the pouring rain.

"Headache, Sheriff?" Jimmy said as he stopped in front of Anderson's desk.

"In every conceivable way," Anderson replied. "Please, sit down Jimmy."

Jimmy sat. The Sheriff still hadn't looked up, and when he glanced at Gibbons, Gibbons looked away. Jimmy frowned. "What's going on?"

At last, Sheriff Anderson looked up. Weariness was in his eyes, but also a certain wary consideration, as though he was re-evaluating Jimmy. "You neglected to mention, Jimmy, that Dyson Beck began working your shift at the mill a couple weeks ago."

"A week and a half ago, to be precise," Jimmy corrected him. He sat up straight, body tensing. There was only one reason the Sheriff would bring this up now, like this, but he couldn't believe it was happening.

"What does this have to do with anything?" Jimmy said, cold and calm.

"You also failed to mention that on Beck's first night on your shift, the two of you got into a fight."

"A fight? What are you talking about? I didn't get into a fight with Beck."

Sheriff Anderson looked at Gibbons, and Jimmy shifted in his chair to see what the Sheriff was looking at Gibbons for. "Eric? You have some questions you want to ask me?"

"Take it easy, Jimmy," Gibbons said, looking from the Sheriff to Jimmy.

"Don't tell me to take it easy, damn it," Jimmy snapped. "I see where you're headed. Well? Go on, let's do this. Let me hear what ingenious conjecture is passing for police work here."

"There's no need to be belligerent, Jimmy," Sheriff Anderson said, an edge in his voice.

Jimmy gave the Sheriff a hard, icy stare. "I'll decide for myself if belligerence is called for. Now stop stalling and ask me your questions."

"Perhaps 'fight' is a bit strong," Gibbons said. "The people we talked to from your shift talked about a heated exchange that ended up with you shoving Beck against the wall. Perhaps 'altercation' would be more to your liking?"

"Yeah, we had an argument," Jimmy said, deliberately refusing to use any of the labels offered him. "Do you want to know why?"

"Why?"

"It's not what you think. If you've talked to people on my shift, you probably know that Beck liked to have a little fun at my expense at the mill. The details aren't important."

"We'll decide what's important, Jimmy," Sheriff Anderson said.

"No, you won't," Jimmy said. "You're trying to discover what's important, but you won't decide what's important. There's a difference. I already know what's important, so I'm going to save you some time and tell you. I slammed Beck against that wall because of what he said, and it had nothing to do with me specifically."

"What'd he say?"

"He told me that the best thing about his new job at the mill was that it left him free to hang out by the Avalon Falls elementary school during the day."

Jimmy finished his sentence, then shut up, so the picture it painted could hang in the air for a moment. Neither Sheriff Anderson nor Gibbons said anything to that, and after a moment, Jimmy continued. "That's what he said. And like you guys, I've read his jacket. I know what he's done, and like you, I could see him targeting more victims as I heard what he was saying. He as good and taunted me with the fact that he was on the prowl again. So I grabbed his shirt and got up in his smug little face and slammed him against that wall. And you know what? I don't regret it. I'd do it again. I don't know who killed him tonight, but I'm not especially broken up that he's dead. Are you?"

Neither Gibbons nor the Sheriff answered, so Jimmy said, "Can I get back to work now?"

"Not quite yet, Jimmy," Sheriff Anderson said, and he nodded to Gibbons to continue.

"Where were you last night at 12:30?"

"I was in bed, like I told you."

"You never told us you were in bed at 12:30."

"I did say," Jimmy replied, turning to Sheriff Anderson, "when you came banging on my door, that I'd been up to the falls—with Eddie Carlson, by the way—and that I'd come home and gone to bed because I was exhausted."

"Nothing in that precludes the possibility you were out at 12:30."

"O.K., let me spell it out for you. Eddie took me back to my car about 10:00 or so. Maybe a little later. I drove straight home, barely took the time to undress and get into bed. I was zonked in no time, and I didn't do anything else until you roused me from my deep and wonderful sleep at 2:30—apparently to come help you solve a murder I'd just committed a few hours before. Ask Eddie, when he dropped me by my car, he'll tell you the same thing."

"We've already asked him."

"You've already asked him?" Jimmy said, turning around to Gibbons. "What do you mean you've already asked him? You didn't know I was with him?"

"We've made some calls," Gibbons said.

"Some calls," Jimmy whispered. He clenched his fists, growing more irate by the minute. "Let me get this straight. I've been in the back room, working this case, while you've been out here investigating me? Calling my friends. Finding out what I've been up to. How long have you been doing that?"

Silence.

"And what did you tell him, anyway? Did you say you were investigating me? Of course, even if you didn't, what's he going to think if you called to ask about my whereabouts last night?"

"We didn't tell him anything," Gibbons said. "We just asked him if you two had been together yesterday, and he confirmed that you two hiked the falls and that he dropped you at your car around ten, like you said."

"Like I said."

"Which in itself, proves nothing," Sheriff Anderson chimed in, "since there would have been plenty of time for you to do a lot of things between ten o'clock and 2:30. That might even explain why you didn't pick up your phone when we called earlier."

Jimmy clenched his teeth as he stared angrily at the Sheriff. "This is insane. So I didn't like Beck because he was a pedophile. Does anyone like a pedophile? Do you? Would you like working with one? Would you just stand there and laugh as he taunted you with his habit of hanging out by the playground?"

"Of course we wouldn't, but that's not the point."

"What is the point?"

"What's the point?" Sheriff Anderson said. "The point's this, Jimmy. We know you're ex-FBI, but what else do we really know about you? How do we know that you didn't leave your job because you couldn't take guys like Beck anymore? Do you want to know what my gut instinct—my first, strong, abiding instinct—was, the first time I met you?"

"What?"

"That you were running away from something. That you were in Avalon Falls because it was a town where you'd never be found. I didn't follow that up because your background check didn't raise any red flags and because you were available and willing to help on the Morrison case. But I still think there's more to who you are and where you've come from then you've told me, so don't you sit there and act like this is crazy, like we're supposed to really know you and should be ashamed of ourselves for daring to ask you a few questions, because the truth is, other than your former employer, we don't know jack about who you were before you got here."

Jimmy sat, looking from the Sheriff to Gibbons and back. He felt a lot of the vehemence and the heat that had been building up inside him drain away.

"All right, fair enough," he said at last. "You don't really know me, not well anyway. Still, I'd say you know enough to know some things about me, like the fact that whatever I might or might not be running from, I'm not a killer."

"We wouldn't have thought so," Gibbons said. "Convince us you're not."

"All right," Jimmy said. "You just mentioned Morrison, Sheriff. If I'm your guy, why did I kill him? Even if Beck ticked me off, why would I kill Morrison? I had no beef with him."

"We thought about that," Gibbons said. "That's why we didn't come to you sooner."

"Well, you did come to me, so you must think you have an answer."

"Maybe you didn't kill Morrison," Gibbons said, "but maybe you used the fact that we didn't catch Morrison's killer to give yourself cover. You knew the Morrison case as well as any of us. Better, even. You could have made them look related to cast suspicion away from yourself."

"Yeah, I could have, but I would have done a better job," Jimmy said, scoffing as he spoke. "I wouldn't have changed the M.O. so much. I wouldn't have killed Beck in an alley, in town, where anyone could have seen me. That's generally not a good move if your goal is to be sneaky and get away with something. I would have found a pretense to lure him out of town into the park or a place like it. I wouldn't have used a pipe and then dropped it in the dumpster. In general, I would have tried to make it look as much like the original crime as possible."

"But, like you said earlier, maybe that was too hard. Maybe getting Beck's pants down presented too much of a challenge. Maybe a branch was too unwieldy, or maybe a heavy pipe was a better bet. Maybe you knew Beck would never let himself be caught alone with you in some out of the way wood or secluded spot. Maybe it wasn't even premeditated. Maybe you had a couple drinks at Connelly's after you left Eddie's place—after all, we know you've had a few too many on occasion—and maybe you ran into Beck who popped off to you and you took care of him."

Jimmy sat and shook his head. "I can't believe this. This is absolutely insane. You have nothing whatsoever that resembles proof or motive. You can't put me at the crime scene and no forensics of any kind links me to Beck tonight. None. Did any of the patrons at Connelly's mention seeing me? Did you even check? All you can say for sure is that I didn't like him. Wow, I didn't like the town pedophile who liked to mock me—I must have killed him. You got me."

No one said anything for a moment, and all three men sat silently, with hard, determined looks on their faces. Just then, a small commotion outside the office caught their attention. Sandy was standing at the front desk, talking to a bedraggled, middle-aged woman who looked angry and worked up about something, and to a girl who appeared to be in her late teens, crying into a Kleenex.

As they looked up, Sandy turned away from them and knocked on the door. The Sheriff called for her to come in. She stepped into the room and said, "Sheriff, I think you'd better hear what this woman has to say."

26

For a moment the Sheriff sat, immobile. He blinked as he looked at Sandy, who waited expectantly with her head inserted through the slightly open office door. Behind her, by the front counter, the woman and the girl stood, appearing for all the world to Jimmy as though they weren't entirely at ease with being left alone together.

"Thanks, Sandy," Sheriff Anderson said at last. "Please make sure they're comfortable and see if they'd like a drink. I'll be out in a few minutes."

"Will do," Sandy said as she withdrew from the room and closed the door behind her. All three men watched her shuffle back to the front counter and show the woman and the girl to the waiting area. Gradually, Jimmy's attention drifted back to the issue they'd been discussing, and he snorted as he thought about where it now left them.

"Well," he said, "It looks like you have a decision to make, Sheriff."

"Yeah? Which decision would that be?"

Jimmy restrained himself from rolling his eyes. "You know which decision, Sheriff. The one where you decide if you're going to arrest me based on the weight of all your 'evidence,' handcuff me and lead me away to one of your fine holding cells, or if you release me because you're not ready to file charges at this time and tell me not to leave town.

"Or—and this would be a real stunner—perhaps you've come to your senses. Maybe you'll apologize and ask me if I'd continue helping you with this case by listening to this woman's story with you."

"Ah, that decision," Sheriff Anderson said, leaning back in his chair. He didn't look to Gibbons this time, but he kept his eyes fixed steadily on Jimmy. Jimmy met his gaze without looking away, matching him, look for look, unflinching. "You know what, Mr. Wyatt?"

"What?"

"I don't think you killed Dyson Beck."

"You don't?" Jimmy said, feigning surprise. "But what about the damning facts that I didn't like him and don't have an alibi since I was mysteriously sleeping at 12:30?"

"Your sarcasm is growing tiresome."

"I'm so sorry about that, Sheriff," Jimmy said. "Next time I'm asked to help with a murder investigation and then I'm interrogated like a suspect by the man who asked me to help, I'll try to remember that my sarcasm could become tiresome."

Sheriff Anderson blinked, then continued as though Jimmy had never said anything. "I don't think you killed Dyson Beck, for a few reasons. First, I do think that if you'd set out to be a copycat, that you'd have made the second murder look more like the first. All though, I suppose, as an experienced profiler, you may have planned for this, to use it as a defense.

"Still, even if you had, I don't think you would have pointed out at the crime scene just how small the pool of candidates is that knows the details of the first murder, not if you had just committed a copycat crime. Not that we wouldn't have figured out how small the pool was, mind you, it's just that I don't think you'd have gone out of your way to make that point unsolicited.

"The other reason why I don't think you did it, and perhaps for me the main one, is that the same gut instinct that told me you were running from something when I first met you, tells me that whatever it might have been, you're not our guy. I think you really were asleep when we came to your house, and I think you really were surprised when we told you it was Beck that was dead. I think you would have tried harder to look at least a little saddened by the news of his brutal murder, if you were the murderer, whereas you didn't appear sad at all. You were down to business, matter-of-fact, 'let's go see the scene,' right from the start. You would have been more self-conscious about your lack of remorse than that, if you were our guy."

"Why, thank you, I guess, for crediting me with that much intelligence. Though, Sheriff, you do seem to be saying that your chief evidence on my behalf is that I would have given it away with bad acting if I was really the killer."

Jimmy sat, watching the Sheriff watch him. After a moment, the Sheriff sat forward and leaned over his desk. "Now, Jimmy, I don't mean this as a slight, though I realize you may take it as such, but I am not going to apologize to you for the questions we asked today."

"Why not?"

"For the same reason you didn't apologize to me for asking for deputies to watch the park when you thought you'd seen someone there. For the same reason you didn't apologize for going out to New Start and interviewing all of Eddie's boys, even though we told you that was a dead end. You didn't apologize for those things, because, however slim the chance might have been that they'd lead somewhere worthwhile, you believed they needed to be done, that due diligence required it.

"Well, I wasn't convinced you were our guy, but I had what I considered sufficient grounds to ask you the questions and see how you'd react. So while I will be sorry if you can't get past this and keep working with us, from where I sit, it was a chance I needed to take to answer a few of my own questions. And ultimately, Jimmy, I'm the one answerable for the safety of the people of Avalon Falls. That, at least, is something I think you can understand, unless I've totally misjudged you."

"No, Sheriff," Jimmy said. "You haven't totally misjudged me. You will excuse me, though, if I don't apologize for my belligerence and sarcasm and whatever else I did or said that you didn't like. You had your questions, but I have my good name and self-respect. But unless I've misjudged you, those are things I think you can understand."

"I can," the Sheriff nodded. "So will you stay and hear whatever this woman has to tell us?"

Jimmy took a breath. "I will."

"All right, Gibbons," the Sheriff said, finally taking his eyes off of Jimmy and looking at his subordinate. "Go tell Sandy to show them in."

A moment later, Sandy was showing the woman and the girl into the office. The woman looked to be in her early forties and had medium length blonde hair pulled back in a ponytail. She also looked like she'd passed a long and unpleasant night but was running on a high dose of caffeine. The girl wore black jeans and a sweatshirt, and she looked like she'd rather have been just about anywhere other than the Avalon Falls Sheriff's office. All three men stood as they entered, and Sandy introduced them. "Sheriff, this is Doris Benson and her daughter, Katherine."

Sheriff Anderson came around from behind his desk and shook their hands. "Thanks for coming in today. Please, take a seat. Make yourselves comfortable."

The girl, Katherine, took the chair closest to the door. Jimmy scooted the chair he'd been sitting in over and set it beside hers, so Doris could sit beside her daughter. The chair where Gibbons had been seated earlier was the only one left, at that point, and Gibbons motioned to it and nodded to Jimmy, but Jimmy waved his hand as though to say, 'Take it. Don't worry about me. I'll stand.'

The Sheriff, having returned to his own seat while these details were being looked to, sat down and leaned forward with his elbows on his desk. "Benson," he said as though thinking out loud. "Do you by any chance work at the Philips 66, over on Highway K?"

"I own it," Mrs. Benson said proudly. "My late husband and I bought it in 2000 and ran it together, but for the last three years, I've run it on my own."

"Right," Sheriff Anderson said. "I thought I'd seen you there. So what can we do for you today, Mrs. Benson?"

Mrs. Benson looked sideways at Gibbons in his chair and Jimmy standing against the wall beside him. "I'm sorry," the Sheriff added. "I should have introduced the others in the room. That's Detective Eric Gibbons, my senior officer here at the department, and standing beside him is Jimmy Wyatt. He's helping out with a case we're working. You may not have heard yet, but unfortunately, we had a murder in Avalon Falls last night."

"I did hear," Mrs. Benson said, turning toward the Sheriff as she perked up in her chair. "That's why I'm here."

"Oh?" the Sheriff said. "You have some information for me?"

"Well," Mrs. Benson said, sounding more measured and less eager as she spoke this time. "I don't know for certain that it's information about the murder, but that's why I'm here, isn't it? I don't know if there's a connection yet or not."

"Why don't you tell us what brought you in today, Ma'am."

"Last night, I had to go in to the station. I've been working the late shift all week because my usual clerk is out of town. So like I said, I went to work, only I wasn't feeling very well. I do get awful headaches on these rainy nights, you know. Something about the barometric pressure, I think."

"So," the Sheriff said, trying to gently redirect her back to the matter at hand. "You went to work but weren't feeling well. Did you see something suspicious?"

"No, not at work," Mrs. Benson said, looking a bit ruffled that she'd been interrupted in the first place. "But as I said, I wasn't feeling well myself, so a little after midnight I closed up, turned off our sign and headed home. Well, I got back about a quarter after twelve and what did I find? I'll tell you what I found. One of those New Start hooligans was in my living room, getting cozy with my seventeen year old daughter!"

"I'm eighteen in a month. He's only nineteen, and we were only kissing," Katherine piped up, speaking vehemently and shooting her mother an angry look. "It's not like it's a big deal."

"It's a big deal to me," Mrs. Benson replied curtly. "Besides, I know, just like everybody else in Avalon Falls knows, that those boys have a curfew. They're not supposed to be out late like that. That boy shouldn't have been in my house, Sheriff."

"No, Mrs. Benson, he shouldn't," the Sheriff acknowledged, looking for the first time during the brief interview at Gibbons and Jimmy.

"What happened then?" Jimmy asked. Several things were running through his mind. The timeline might well fit, and depending on which of the boys she indicated, things could get interesting.

"I told him to get out, that's what happened. They hadn't been expecting me home, that much was obvious. Just makes one wonder what might have happened if I'd not come home then, doesn't it?" She looked angrily at Katherine, who, for her part, was now doing her best to pretend like her mother wasn't even in the room.

"So you told him to go and he left?" the Sheriff asked.

"More or less."

"Do you remember about when that was?"

"Well, the whole thing couldn't have taken more than a few minutes. He grabbed his jacket and left by the front door while I was taking charge of the situation."

"Taking charge of the situation?" Katherine said, returning to life next to her mother. "You were screaming like a madwoman, even when he opened the front door. Everyone on the street could hear you. It was so embarrassing."

"He had no right to be in my house with you when I was at work!" Mrs. Benson said, rounding on her daughter angrily.

"Please, Mrs. Benson," the Sheriff said, speaking firmly to assert control over the situation. "I'm sure you will have some things to discuss with Katherine later, but if you wouldn't mind answering just a few more questions? You're sure about the timeframe you've given? You arrived around quarter after twelve and the lad was gone a few minutes later?"

"Absolutely."

"And where do you live?"

"Only about five minutes walk from Connelly's."

Jimmy didn't listen very carefully as the Sheriff pursued getting a specific address from her. He was growing anxious about the question that would be coming next. There was only one boy at New Start he'd ever had any real suspicion about. If she indicated him, he'd have to take this seriously, which would mean another trip out there. This time, a far more serious trip.

"And do you know the boy's name?"

The Sheriff had asked the question. Jimmy did not betray his interest in the answer externally, but internally, he was on edge, straining to hear what Mrs. Benson would say.

"I didn't know his name when I saw him, though I'd seen him around with that lot of course. Katherine called him Nathan."

It was Nathan, Jimmy thought. The wrestler. His had been the only background that had suggested a penchant for violence, and it had been primarily to sit down with Nathan that he'd gone out to New Start the last time. He'd felt pretty confident afterward that Nathan hadn't had anything to do with Morrison's murder, but he'd been wrong about such things before. Now, to find out that Nathan had been out after hours and near Connelly's just five or ten minutes before Beck was killed. He had a sinking feeling. Eddie wouldn't like this, but it couldn't be ignored.

Sheriff Anderson was thanking Mrs. Benson for coming in, and Mrs. Benson was saying something about how she'd planned to give that Carlson a piece of her mind first thing this morning for not keeping closer tabs on the boys in his program and allowing them to run all over town at all hours, when she'd heard about the killing on the radio over breakfast and known, simply known, that it was probably that good for nothing boy who'd been in her house with her daughter the night before.

They'd probably come within a hair's breadth of being killed in their sleep themselves, she was adding when the Sheriff cut the rant off at the pass. He thanked her again, stood and indicated that there was a deputy who would take down all the details of the event in an official report if she wouldn't mind spending just a few more minutes of her time at the station. Mrs. Benson indicated her willingness and left through the door that Gibbons had opened. Katherine rose to follow but stopped at the doorway.

"I know my opinion probably doesn't count for much," she said tearfully to the three men standing behind her in the Sheriff's office. "But I know Nathan didn't kill anyone. He's had some problems in the past, but he's not a killer."

"Your opinion does count for something," Sheriff Anderson said gently. "We won't rush to any conclusions. We'll look into it, like we do any report that we receive, and Nathan will be treated with all the respect and rights he possesses under the law, just like anyone else would be. We know all about his past, and it won't be held against him."

"Thanks," Katherine said. Jimmy could see the wind taken out of her sails by the Sheriff's reasonableness, and the girl was probably realizing that her issue at that moment was with her mother, not him. She turned and walked toward the nearby desk where Mrs. Benson was already seated and waiting for Sandy to fetch a deputy.

Gibbons closed the door. "Isn't Nathan the one you were interested in before, Jimmy?"

Jimmy nodded.

"Well," Sheriff Anderson said, sighing. "Looks like we'll all be headed out to New Start this time."

"Eddie won't like it," Jimmy said.

"No, but when he hears about Nathan's curfew breaking, if he hasn't already, he'll understand. We can't just let this go. He'll see that."

"I hope so," Jimmy said

"Well, if he's mad," the Sheriff said, "he'll have to be mad at me this time, because I'm authorizing the investigation and coming along myself."

"I'm not really worried about him being mad, Sheriff. Eddie and I worked things out before and will again if need be." Jimmy said. "Actually, I'm more frustrated with myself right now. I was sure it wasn't Nathan. I just can't see how I went so wrong."

"You may not have," Sheriff Anderson said. "We know he was out after hours last night. We don't know that he killed anyone."

"True," Jimmy said. "Let's go find out."

27

Jimmy got into the back seat of the squad car and rubbed the sleep out of his eyes. It was only a little after 11 a.m., but he was exhausted. His mind was racing from the questions surrounding the case, the brief but intense exchange in Sheriff Anderson's office, and now the complications regarding the boy from New Start. He thought back to that first day he'd met Eddie and the others, when Nathan had shoved the guy that gave him the hard foul and then sat out the rest of the game. It seemed so long ago.

Sheriff Anderson got in the passenger's seat and Greg, the deputy who usually drove the Sheriff around, backed the car out. Jimmy leaned forward. "Sheriff, do you mind if we stop at the 7-11 that's more or less on the way out to Eddie's place?"

Sheriff Anderson turned halfway around, eyebrows raised. "We're on our way to interview a possible murder suspect."

"I know," Jimmy said. "But give me a break. I got dragged out of bed at 2:30 this morning, I've not had any decent food since—sorry, but squad room coffee and danishes don't count—and I'm dying. I need a decent cup of coffee and something resembling real food. The mere fact that I'm asking for the 7-11 should tell you how desperate I am. I'll run in, grab something to go, and be as quick about it as I can. Promise."

"All right," the Sheriff said, sounding exasperated about the whole thing.

A few minutes later they pulled into the 7-11, and Jimmy popped out and darted inside. There was a meager selection of pre-made deli sandwiches in one of the refrigerated sections, and Jimmy grabbed a six inch turkey sub that actually looked like it could have been reasonably fresh, though he was of course, skeptical. He got the biggest coffee he could grab and a handful of sugar packets, just in case it was really awful, and in no time he was crawling back into the squad car.

"See, Sheriff, it didn't take long at all." The Sheriff sort of grunted by way of reply, and they were back on their way.

Eating the passable but less than remarkable turkey sub—nothing like a Carlson special—reminded Jimmy of the striking beauty of the mountain meadow high above the falls. He couldn't believe he'd been there just the day before. He thought about sitting on the big rock with Eddie in that peaceful place, gazing at dozens of small, delicate white and yellow butterflies floating all around them in the afternoon sun. It felt like a journey taken, not to a real place outside of town, but to an alternate dimension outside of all the ludicrous acts of human cruelty that had been the fabric of Jimmy's days and nights for the better portion of his adult life.

How did one reconcile these two realities? Places of unspoiled beauty, essentially untouched by human hands, that seemed to lift the spirit into transcendent wonder, and dark, rain-soaked alleyways that concealed the bestial brutality of man that was far too common to be considered abnormal or unusual.

Jimmy sipped his coffee and wadded the remaining crumbs from the sub he'd wolfed down in the saran wrap. The coffee was no treat, but it was better than the muck at the Sheriff's Department. He swallowed, closed his eyes and leaned his head against the window. How could he face Eddie today, with these suspicions about Nathan? As much for Eddie's sake as for Nathan's, he hoped desperately that there would be some kind of easy answer that would clear everything up, something that would spare everyone involved the difficulty of a full investigation.

The car hit a bump and Jimmy whacked his head against the window. Gritting his teeth, he reached up and held the side of his forehead where it was now stinging from the blow. The sound of it must have caught the attention of the men up front, because both acknowledged it in different ways. The Sheriff turned his head slightly at the sound and Greg said, "Sorry about that, hit a pot hole."

"I'm all right," Jimmy grumbled, but he didn't rest his head on the window again. He took another drink from his mammoth coffee cup and remained upright the rest of the way out.

Gibbons and the other deputy were already on the scene when they pulled in, but they'd waited for the Sheriff's car to arrive before going up to the New Start building. Gibbons stared in mild surprise at Jimmy's coffee as they piled out of the squad car, and the Sheriff intervened before Gibbons could do or say anything by waving him off, rolling his eyes and saying, "Don't ask."

Gibbons looked at Jimmy who just shrugged his shoulders and took another long swig, and then all five men started moving along the gravel walkway that led from the Calvary Baptist parking lot to the New Start building. It appeared, though, that their presence had not gone unnoticed, for they hadn't gotten very far when Coach came out of the building and started walking over to meet them.

"Good morning, Sheriff," Coach said with a friendly smile. "You're here with quite a few of the boys. Looks serious."

"It is, Sam," Sheriff Anderson said, and it took a minute for Jimmy to remember that Coach actually had a name and it was Sam McAllister. "You've heard about the man killed in town last night?"

"We have," Coach said, growing sober but not looking all together surprised. "A terrible thing, to be sure, but why does it bring you out this way?"

"Well, a woman's come by the station this morning and filed a report that one of your boys was out that way about the time it happened, which was after his curfew. She knows because she found him with her daughter."

"Ah," Coach said, "Nathan and Katherine Benson."

Jimmy saw mild surprise register on the Sheriff's face before he regained full control and put his calm and unflappable mask back on. "You mean you know about them?"

"Well," Coach said, "you should probably talk to Eddie. There'd been signs before this, but we only found out this morning for sure."

"So he was caught?" Jimmy asked.

"No, I don't believe so."

"He volunteered the information?" Jimmy said, his turn to be surprised.

"That's right," Coach said. "I think the deception was bothering him, so he might have admitted to it before long anyway, but when we heard about what happened in town, he asked Eddie if they could talk."

"Really?" Jimmy said

"I think, Jimmy," Coach added, "That he was thinking about you asking those questions the last time, and he didn't want Eddie to get any surprises. They talked for about an hour, and Eddie was planning on heading into the station to report the matter personally. I guess he won't need to now."

"No," the Sheriff said, "he won't, but we'll need to talk to Nathan and Eddie both."

"Of course," Coach said. "Come on up to the building. Nathan's there, and I'll get Eddie. He went back to the house about twenty minutes ago."

"That's all right, Coach," Jimmy said, nodding toward the house up on the hill. "Looks like he's already on his way."

They all turned to see Eddie walking down his steps and starting across the lawn. They waited for him to reach them.

"Eddie," Sheriff Anderson said, stepping forward to be the first to shake his hand. "I'm sorry about this, but we need to talk to Nathan."

"I thought you might," Eddie said, looking from the Sheriff to the others. "But there are so many of you. Why?"

"Detective Gibbons, Jimmy and myself are here for the interview, and if it would be all right with you, I'd like to have my deputies search the property."

"Search the property?" Eddie said. "Did you come with a warrant?"

"No, but I can get one if necessary."

"No, that's not what I meant," Eddie said. "Of course they can look around, provided they're respectful of our property. We have nothing to hide. It's just that I can't believe Nathan's curfew breaking alone is sufficient to merit this kind of attention. There must be something else going on."

"We have a witness that puts Nathan a few minutes' walk away from where the body was found, just before the murder was committed."

Eddie nodded. "I was aware of that, which is why I was about to drive Nathan into the station so we could report the matter, but I still don't see how that's enough to get this kind of attention. There must have been a lot of people within a few minutes walk of where the murder happened at the time."

"There may have been," the Sheriff said, agreeing, "but they weren't all breaking curfew from New Start."

"More to the point," Jimmy said, speaking up for the first time since Eddie had arrived. "Nathan's history makes him of special interest. You know he's the main reason why I made my trip out the last time. It may be a coincidence that the one boy in your program we were interested in was the one violating his curfew, but we'll need to look into it a bit more to find out."

Eddie looked at Jimmy, and much to Jimmy's relief, there was no anger in his eyes, only sadness and resignation. Eddie nodded, as though he understood everything Jimmy was saying, and even the things that Jimmy had not yet said. "Look, I understand that from your point of view, this must look bad. I know what it looks like when you look over Nathan's record without really knowing the details. He hurt his father, and that's shocking—"

"He put him in a coma, Eddie," Jimmy said.

"I know, I know," Eddie said, "but if you'd been talking to Nathan for the better part of the last year, like I have, and if you'd heard the stories about his dad that I've heard, and what he did to Nathan, you'd understand why. I'm not excusing him, I'm just saying it wasn't a senseless and random act like these killings."

"How do you know the killings were senseless and random?" Gibbons asked.

"Look, I don't know that much about them, just what I've heard on the news and read in the paper. What I mean is that Nathan didn't know either of these men, so for him to hurt them, it would be senseless and random. See what I mean? He only hurt his father under great provocation. He didn't have cause to hurt these men."

"Look, Eddie," the Sheriff said. "I think we're all getting ahead of ourselves. There's no presumption of guilt here. We're just asking you for two things. We'd like to talk to Nathan, which you're welcome to sit in on if you'd like, and we'd also like to look around. All right?"

"All right," Eddie said. "Let's go ahead in."

Sheriff Anderson gave the deputies instructions for their search and then followed the others up to the New Start building. They entered the front room, and Jimmy noticed that although all the guys appeared to be gathered in the T.V. room, the T.V. wasn't on. Nathan sat in an arm chair in the corner, looking frightened, and Jimmy felt his heart go out to the kid. He'd probably known as soon as he'd heard about the murder that a moment like this would come, just not so soon.

Jimmy turned to Eddie. "Should we go back to the office?"

"It's too small to be comfortable for us all," Eddie said. "We'll go to the dining area."

Eddie stood in the middle of the room. "You guys know why the Sheriff is here, so here's the deal. We know Nathan didn't do anything, but they don't. They need to ask their questions, and we need to be courteous and cooperative. I want you all to stay right here with Coach. I'm going with Nathan and these gentlemen into the dining room. We are not to be disturbed. Two of the Sheriff's deputies are looking around, so if they ask you anything, be polite, be respectful, and tell them what they need to know. Understood?"

There were general murmurs of agreement and consent, less begrudging than Jimmy might have expected, and Nathan rose and followed Eddie through to the dining room. Jimmy, the Sheriff and Gibbons also followed them through, and when they were all in, Jimmy pulled the door closed. Soon they were all settled in around the table.

Jimmy looked at Gibbons, but Gibbons nodded back at Jimmy, as though to indicate that he should go ahead. Jimmy had assumed Gibbons would take the lead, but it made a certain amount of sense that Gibbons would defer since Jimmy had already spoken with Nathan about the first murder. So Jimmy leaned in across the table and began.

"Nathan, we're going to be a little more formal this time than we were last time, you understand? I'm not here on my own to ask general questions of all the guys, questions about sneaking out after hours—we're here to talk to you because we know you were out last night, we know you were near the murder scene not long before it happened, and we know there's violence in your background. Do you understand?"

"I never killed anybody, Jimmy."

Jimmy raised his hands. "I'm not saying you have, and I shouldn't have started without making sure you were aware that you don't have to talk to us right now. You do have the right to remain silent, just like all the police shows say you do, and if you'd rather have a lawyer here, we can arrange for that. There are lawyers that the county will provide if you don't have money to hire one yourself."

"I don't want a lawyer," Nathan said. "My court-appointed lawyer last time didn't do jack to help me."

"All right, you don't have to have one, but let me also say that since you're nineteen, you're a legal adult and don't need a parent or guardian here. We've asked Mr. Carlson to join us, but if you'd rather he left, that's up to you."

"I want Eddie here."

"All right, then we'll get right to it. You were with Katherine Benson last night, correct?"

"I was."

"Was this the first time you'd broken curfew to go meet her?"

"Yes, I swear. I only met her a few months ago at church."

"At church?"

"She came with a friend, and we met there. Not that first time, but eventually, you know?"

"If I may," Eddie said. "Katherine came for the first time to the Christmas Eve service. I was serving as a greeter and remember speaking with her and a couple of the other visitors at the service."

"And she's come back since?" Jimmy asked.

"Yes, she's been pretty regular about it," Eddie said. "I don't know if she's been back because of her interest in the church or her interest in Nathan, but I'd say the latter was almost immediate."

Nathan blushed. "Yeah, it didn't take long."

"All right, I think I'm getting the picture," Jimmy said. "You met at church and saw each other there each week. Was last night the first time you'd met in private?"

Nathan hung his head, "No sir, like I told Eddie earlier, a few weeks back, I said I was sick one Sunday morning and didn't go to church, and Katherine came late and met me up here behind the building. That was the first time we made out, and that was when we started talking about me maybe sneaking out one night and meeting up."

"So last night was the first time?"

"Yes."

"When did you get to Katherine's house?"

"I had to wait until everyone was asleep to sneak out, and Katherine was waiting for me just down the road in her car. We'd only been back at her house for like five minutes when her Mom came home."

"Mrs. Benson's report indicated that you were perhaps a bit angry when you left. Would that be a fair description?"

"Sure," Nathan said, sitting up. "She was threatening to tell Eddie on me, and I was upset about that and about having to go so soon after I got there, and about not having any way back. I had to jog all the way, and it was kinda cold."

"I can imagine."

"Did you head straight back to New Start?"

"Yes sir, straight back, and I didn't go anywhere near that bar or that man and didn't hear nothing about the murder until this morning."

"When did you get back, would you say?"

"Maybe a quarter to two."

Jimmy nodded. "And the clothes you were wearing last night, where are they?"

"They're in my hamper, but I can get them."

"Actually, if you'd point them out, we'll collect them for you and take them back to the station," Gibbons said. "It would be helpful if you'd come to the station as well. We'll get an official statement and run a few tests. Have you showered since last night?"

"Yes sir, this morning. I got pretty sweaty running home last night."

"Well, no matter, we'll do the tests anyway, unless you object?"

Nathan looked at Eddie and Eddie nodded. "O.K. Can Eddie come, too?"

"Of course."

At that point, the door opened and the two deputies walked in, faces flushed with excitement. The first walked over and extended a gloved hand that was holding a pipe which looked a lot like the bloody pipe that had been recovered from the dumpster in the alley. "We found this lying in a back corner in the basement, along with about five or six other pieces just like it. I think it's the same type and length."

Jimmy thought about the floor hockey games they'd played downstairs and the corner where various leftover odds and ends from the construction of the building were stored. It hadn't occurred to him to check that stash for a match to the murder weapon, but it looked like one had been found, nonetheless.

"And," the other deputy said, stepping forward. "I was looking through the dumpster behind the church, and I found this stuffed inside a cereal box."

He held up a yellow, rubber, dishwashing glove, with dark stains that looked like blood spatter all over it. The silence in the room was complete. Everyone at the table stared at the glove.

Nathan pushed his chair back from the table and leapt up. "I've never seen that before! I didn't do nothing!"

The room sprang to life. The deputy holding the pipe dropped it and drew his weapon, pointing it at Nathan. The one holding the glove moved his free hand to his holster to be ready, in case his help should be necessary. Meanwhile, all the men at the table leapt up, either to calm down Nathan or the deputies or both. It was chaotic for a moment, until Eddie convinced Nathan to stand still and hold his hands out in front of his body.

"It's all right, Nathan," Eddie said as Nathan was handcuffed. "I don't know what's going on here, but we'll get to the bottom of this."

"Take him out that way," the Sheriff said, pointing to the door that led outside from the kitchen.

"I want to come with him to the station," Eddie said.

"Fine, but this just got a whole lot more serious, you understand."

"I can see that, and though I can't explain what's going on here, I know Nathan had nothing to do with this murder."

"Are you sure you know that, Eddie?" the Sheriff said while the deputies escorted Nathan toward the back door.

"Absolutely. He didn't do this."

The Sheriff looked at Jimmy, and Jimmy shrugged. "Don't look at me. I don't know what the hell just happened. My gut's with Eddie, but there's a pipe in the basement and a bloody glove in the dumpster. Something's going on."

The Sheriff started walking toward the back door and Gibbons followed while Jimmy lingered, waiting for Eddie. Eddie, who was standing there, looking lost, turned to him after a moment and said. "Go ahead. I'll meet you all out front. I need to tell Coach what's happening."

Jimmy knew Eddie was confident about Nathan's innocence, but his own confidence about the boy's lack of involvement had taken a serious blow.

28

Jimmy leaned against the back of the squad car, reeling from the developments of the past few minutes. Sheriff Anderson was talking to his deputies about twenty feet away. Gibbons was waiting by the driver's side door. Eddie was talking to Coach outside the New Start front door while the rest of the New Start guys peered down at the scene from the large front window, and Nathan sat handcuffed in the backseat of the other cruiser.

Jimmy glanced in through the window at the nervous boy. He was trying to hold it together, but Jimmy could tell he was teetering on the brink. He was scared, and he had every right to be. If forensics showed the stain on the glove to be Beck's blood, it almost didn't matter if there was a direct link to Nathan or not. He might be convicted based on the circumstantial evidence alone. Jimmy had seen a good prosecutor get a conviction with less.

Eddie started toward the car and Coach went back inside. The Sheriff started over toward the car as well. As Eddie approached, though, the sound of a large vehicle coming up the road toward the church broke through the surreal silence of that sunny, April midday that would have been, all other things being equal, quite beautiful. Jimmy stood up straight and craned his neck to see what was making the sound, and both Gibbons and the Sheriff turned to look too.

Jimmy caught a glimpse of the vehicle through the trees at the bottom of the drive. A hulking garbage truck swung wide in the two-lane road to make the turn into the drive that led up to the church parking lot. It took a moment for what was going on to register, and then it seemed to dawn on all of them at the same time. The Sheriff, Gibbons and Jimmy all started suddenly out into the parking lot, waving their arms to get the driver's attention.

No doubt these steps were unnecessary, for the presence of not one but two cars from the Sheriff's Department would have gotten his attention had none of them bothered, but nothing was left to chance. The driver stopped in the middle of the parking lot, leaving the loud, rumbling engine to idle while the Sheriff walked up to the driver's side of the cab, followed closely by Gibbons and Jimmy.

"Something wrong here, Officer?" the driver said to the Sheriff, showing either his nervousness or ignorance of the local police hierarchy.

"Nothing for you to worry about," the Sheriff said. "There won't be any need for a pick up today."

The man blinked and looked past the Sheriff at Gibbons and Jimmy, and beyond them at the cars and deputies. "You don't want me to empty the dumpster?"

"I do not," the Sheriff answered.

"Well," the man started, not quite sure how to proceed. "I think I need to call my supervisor. I get in trouble if I miss any stops, and I don't want him to send me all the way back out here later."

"He won't," the Sheriff said. "I'll put in a call as soon as you leave."

The driver looked like he might push the matter further, but another quick sweep of the landscape and he thought better of it. He shifted the truck into reverse and started turning around. Jimmy, along with the Sheriff and Gibbons, moved back and out of the way. They waited until the roar of the truck heading off up the road had faded to a reasonable level before talking.

"That could have been a disaster," Gibbons said.

"Yes," the Sheriff replied, turning to Gibbons. "If they'd been searching inside and that truck had arrived three minutes later, can you imagine? It might have gotten that dumpster emptied before they even noticed it was here."

"It might have," Gibbons said.

"We're leaving Greg and Andy to secure the scene," the Sheriff added. "Whatever might still be here to find, I want it found."

The Sheriff talked to the deputies and returned to the car. He sat up front with Gibbons driving, and Eddie and Jimmy crowded in the back on either side of Nathan. Jimmy wasn't used to riding in the back of squad cars with murder suspects. It did feel a bit odd, but the fact that he knew Nathan reasonably well and Eddie even better mitigated the awkwardness. If anything, he realized as they drove back into town just how nervous Nathan was. He felt echoes of the boy's trembling, reverberating through the seat, all the way to the station.

They were halfway back into town before Jimmy realized he'd left his unfinished coffee on the table in the New Start dining area. He'd had most of it, but he still felt a slight pang of regret. The way this was looking, it could be a long afternoon and evening, and he doubted he'd get a chance to slip out for anything. It looked like there was nothing for it but to face another long, bleak stretch of the Department's coffee.

Gibbons led Nathan into the station while the Sheriff took charge of the evidence they'd gathered. Jimmy and Eddie followed Gibbons and Nathan to the back room, and they waited in the hall while Gibbons cleared the crime scene photos that Jimmy had left spread out on the table. Jimmy saw Eddie look through the window at the pictures as Gibbons gathered them up. He seemed to be drawn in by them for a moment, then he closed his eyes and looked away.

Gibbons opened the door, took Nathan in and seated him, then left to retrieve an extra chair for Eddie as there were only three in the room. Jimmy went ahead and took the seat directly opposite Nathan. It occurred to him that perhaps he should wait and see if Gibbons wanted it, but he sat down anyway. Gibbons had already passed on taking the lead in this, and Jimmy wasn't about to relinquish it now. Something didn't fit. A sense of unease had been growing in his mind all the way back from New Start, and it only grew as he sat across the table from the trembling nineteen year old who was supposed to be the vicious killer of not one, but two men.

Gibbons returned, and if he was irked about being displaced from the chair he'd occupied while interrogating Beck, it didn't show. He took his seat quietly and Jimmy began.

"All right, Nathan," Jimmy said. "You said you got back from Katherine's around 1:45, is that right?"

"Yeah, about then, maybe a little later."

"And you say you went straight back to New Start—no detours? Are you sure about that?"

"Yes, sir, I went straight back. I jogged the whole way, even up the big hill. I was aggravated and just wanted to get home to bed."

"Now," Jimmy said, leaning in. "It's important that you tell me the truth, Nathan, because if you tell me one thing, and a witness puts you someplace you're not supposed to be, and I realize you've lied to me, it'll make me wonder. It'll make me wonder, 'if he lied to me about this, what else is he lying about?'"

"I'm not lying, Jimmy."

"All right, I just want to make sure you know, that if for any reason you're altering your story to cover something up, maybe something you don't want me to know or Eddie to know, the stakes are way too high for playing games with the truth. Got it?"

"Yes, sir."

Jimmy smiled and turned to Gibbons. "Would you mind getting both files for me, Beck and Morrison?"

"Sure," Gibbons said and rose, slipping from the room.

"He'll just be minute." Jimmy leaned in and put his elbows on the table as he folded his hands in front of his face. "Nathan, while he's out, let me say something I probably wouldn't say with Detective Gibbons in the room. My gut says you didn't do this, but right now, it doesn't look good. You have to promise to tell the truth, no matter how bad it makes you or Katherine or anyone else look. Do you understand?"

"Yes," Nathan said, sitting up higher in his chair as he answered. "You really believe me?"

"I do," Jimmy said, looking from Nathan to Eddie. "But it doesn't really matter what I believe. It only matters what the Sheriff thinks and what a prosecutor thinks he can prove. I have no jurisdiction here."

The door opened, and Jimmy turned to smile at Gibbons as the detective handed him the two folders he'd brought with him. "Thanks, Eric."

Jimmy took both folders and made sure that the names written on the tabs weren't visible to Nathan. He opened the Morrison folder, pulled out the Missoula salesman's photo that had been sent to them by his ex-wife and slid it across the table in front of Nathan as he watched the boy carefully. "Have you seen this man before?"

Nathan looked intently at the photo for a moment, then sat back and looked at Jimmy, shaking his head. "No sir, I don't think so. Is he the dead guy?"

"Yeah," Jimmy said, "He's the dead guy."

He flipped open Beck's folder and removed Beck's updated file photo that they'd taken when he'd come in to register in the fall. "What about this guy, have you seen him before?"

Again, Nathan peered at the photo. This time, he lingered a little longer. "I'm not sure about this one. He looks a little familiar. I may have seen him around somewhere, but I can't remember where."

Jimmy pulled both photos back from the other side of the table, placing them back in their respective folders. He glanced at Gibbons as he did, and he could tell from the look on Gibbon's face that the detective had noticed Jimmy's switch.

"Was that the other guy?" Nathan asked.

"What other guy?"

"The guy from before. The one you came out to New Start to question us all about?"

"Speaking of my coming out to New Start," Jimmy said, ignoring the question. "At the time, you said you hadn't been out the night in question. In the light of these events and your promise to tell the truth, are you sure you don't want to revise your statement?"

"Yes, sir, I'm sure. Like I said then, I wasn't out that night. The other guys said so too, remember. No one was out that night."

"Did any of the other guys know you were out last night?"

"Not when I left, I don't think, but I think I woke Steven when I came back in."

"You did," Eddie said. "After you talked to me this morning, he told me that he'd known you'd been out."

"Do you think he could confirm Nathan's testimony about when he returned to New Start?" Jimmy said, trying not to betray any sense of eagerness. If they could corroborate Nathan's arrival time, then show that from Katherine's it would take over an hour for a fit person to jog to New Start, then they might have at least the beginnings of a defense.

"I doubt it," Eddie said, putting an end to that hope. "I asked him when Nathan came in, and he said he didn't know. He just heard the door open, stirred and saw Nathan slipping into his bed."

"You see, it's impossible to get out and back without somebody knowing," Nathan said eagerly, as though seeing an opening to get himself off the hook. "If I'd been out after curfew last time, somebody would know."

"It may be difficult to get out and back in without waking someone," Jimmy said, "but impossible is stretching it. Besides, you're leaving out the obvious, namely, that even if one of the others heard you leave or return, they might be covering for you."

"They weren't covering for me," Nathan said, starting to slump again in his seat.

"Maybe not," Jimmy said, leaning in again. "Nathan, I want you to think. Is there anything you can think of from last night, anything at all from the time you left the Benson's to the time you returned to New Start, that you could tell me, that might in some way, validate or confirm your version of events?"

Nathan shook his head. "I wish there was, Jimmy. I've been trying to think of something, anything, but it was so late and I only saw the headlights of a couple cars on the way, and I ducked off the side of the road when I saw them so no one would catch me, you know, since I was breaking curfew and all."

"I'm sorry, Nathan," Gibbons said when Jimmy was silent. "But you're going to have to stay a while. We need to wait and see if anything turns up on your clothes or the glove that might shed some more light on all this. We can't let you go. Out after curfew, not far from the crime scene, what looks like a bloody glove in the dumpster New Start shares with Calvary Baptist— it doesn't look good."

"Sit tight," Jimmy added as he stood and started toward the door. He turned to Gibbons when he knew neither Eddie nor Nathan could see his face and used his eyes to indicate his desire for Gibbons to follow him out, then he turned back to the others. "Stay with Nathan, Eddie?"

"Sure," Eddie replied, sitting back in his chair with his arms crossed.

Once Jimmy and Gibbons were both out, Jimmy motioned to Gibbons to follow him down the hall. "What's it, Jimmy?"

"Have somebody watch the door and come with me to the Sheriff's office, if you don't mind."

Gibbons took care of it and joined Jimmy outside there. They entered together, and the Sheriff looked up and waited for one of them to speak.

"I don't think this kid is our guy," Jimmy said.

"What makes you say that?" the Sheriff asked.

"A lot of things, but particularly the fact that I switched Beck's and Morrison's photographs when I showed them to Nathan. He thought he was seeing Beck when he was really seeing Morrison, and he thought he was seeing Morrison when he was really seeing Beck. When I did this, he said he'd never seen Morrison but might have seen Beck, which of course would have been counterintuitive for him to say unless it was true."

Sheriff Anderson blinked. "I didn't understand a word of that. What are you talking about?"

"Sorry, I realized about halfway through that it might sound a little confusing."

"A little?"

"What I did was this. I had Gibbons get the folders for Beck and for Gibbons. While he did, I continued to urge Nathan to tell me the truth, saying that lying about little things would only make us suspicious about the big things. When Gibbons came back, I got out Morrison's photo first, when we hadn't even talked about the first murder, when anyone sitting in the room would have expected me to get out Beck's photo.

"Anyway, he looked at it, studied it, and said no, he'd never seen him before. Of course, by itself, that's not surprising, since denial would be expected, but as soon as he denied it he asked me if Morrison was the dead guy, meaning Beck. Of course, if he'd killed them both, he'd have known exactly who it was. Eric can speak for himself on this point, but if the boy was trying to pull one over on us, he was really smooth. Way too smooth for a petrified, nineteen year old kid."

"The denial looked sincere," Gibbons said.

"It sure did," Jimmy agreed. "And more to the point, when I showed him Beck's photo, knowing he'd assume it was our first victim if he was innocent and had never seen him, he said he may have seen him around. That makes no sense unless it's true. In any other scenario he'd just lie—'nope, don't know him.' There's no reason to admit possibly having seen him."

"Why not?"

"Well, if he knew the second photo was Beck, not Morrison, the man he'd killed last night, why would he admit it? Surely he knows by now, like the whole town does, that Morrison was just passing through Avalon Falls. If Nathan was just playing the part of an innocent accused, pretending not to know which man was which and going along with my ruse, he wouldn't indicate that he might have seen or had contact with a man that he knew I was passing off as Morrison, a man who'd only been in town for mere hours before being killed. It makes no sense."

Sheriff Anderson frowned slightly, "I think I see what you're getting at, but it seems thin to me, given all the other evidence."

"What evidence? It's circumstantial, all of it. Yeah, he was at the Benson's, but nobody puts him in the alley."

"Not yet, anyway."

"Understood, and if someone puts him in the alley that's different, but at the present, no one has put him there. We've only said he *could* have gotten there in time to kill Beck, but that's a whole lot different then saying he *did* go there. As for the glove, it was found in the dumpster at New Start, but until forensics proves both that it has Beck's blood on it and that Nathan has touched it, we can't put it in, much less on, his hand. It's possible that the glove got into that dumpster some other way."

"All right, there's nothing definitive, but you know as well as I do that often there isn't."

"I know that, but that's my point. In the absence of definitive proof, what do I have, Sheriff? What am I left with? Two
things. I have my gut. Like you trusted yours about me earlier,
I trust mine with Nathan. My gut tells me this kid didn't do
this."

"Maybe you just can't admit it to yourself," Gibbons said,
"because in your mind, you'd already cleared him. I understand how that happens. It's always hard for me to admit I'm
wrong when I'm wrong."

"It's hard for me too, but I don't think this is just me being stubborn. My gut tells me he didn't do this. It doesn't fit.
There's no real connection to Beck, even less to Morrison. And
Eddie's right. What violence there is in his past doesn't fit terribly well with murders like these."

"And the second thing?"

"The second thing," Jimmy said, reaching back to pick up
the thread of reasoning he'd begun a moment before. "Is my
knowledge of human nature. I showed Nathan the wrong picture. I slid it across the table and put Morrison in front of him
when he must have been expecting Beck. And I watched him.

"There were any number of ways he might have proceeded if
he was our guy, but he would have been surprised and the surprise would have shown. He would have had to try and guess
at what I was up to, showing him the wrong photo, and he'd
have had to develop a strategy to respond. Both are discernible,
I think, if you know where to look. A guilty man knows he has
to play innocent. An innocent man can be himself.

"What I'm saying is this. If he was our guy, I think he
would have tipped me off. It's just the way people are. He's
nineteen, seems like a nice enough kid, but he's no rocket sci-
entist. There's no way he could bluff and lie his way through
without giving me a sign. I laid a simple trap, because simple

traps work. They may not tell me anything that I can hand to a prosecutor to use in a court of law, but they work. I've tripped up more clever suspects than him with less well-laid traps than this. I'm telling you, he did not know who these men were or which one was which. That means he didn't kill them."

"Well," the Sheriff said, "I see you feel pretty strongly about it."

"I do."

"But I can't just let him go because you say so. We're going to have to wait to see what the tests show, and that could take a while."

"I understand."

"And even if they prove inconclusive, Jimmy," the Sheriff quickly added. "I don't think I can let him go. There's just too much here to do that. I'm afraid that lacking a more likely suspect, he's our guy."

"And if the real killer is still out there? Does this kid have to take the fall?"

"Again, we're getting ahead of ourselves. Let's just wait and see what the tests show."

"All right," Jimmy said. "I just hate to see the wrong people in handcuffs."

"We all do," Sheriff Anderson said. "But when things are this unclear, we need to err on the side of caution."

"Again, I understand," Jimmy said, making a deferential motion as he looked from the Sheriff to Gibbons. "I don't really feel that I need to ask him any more questions at this point, so I'm going to look over the case files again, if that's all right you two."

"Sure, Jimmy," the Sheriff said. "We'll let you know when we hear something."

A few hours later Jimmy was standing outside the department on the front steps, getting a bit of fresh air. It was early evening and the sun was hanging low in the sky. The afternoon had brought no decisive news, but it had brought more circumstantially bad news for Nathan. A second glove had been found in the dumpster, hidden in a plastic grocery bag. It was also covered with what looked to be blood, and Jimmy found himself working hard to avoid thinking about the perplexing question of just what those gloves were doing in the dumpster if Nathan hadn't put them there. As he tried to avoid thinking about this, the Sheriff came outside and stood beside him.

"Any news?" Jimmy asked, suppressing a yawn that had come over him suddenly.

"No, Jimmy, which is why I'm here."

"What do you mean?"

"Look, you had a long day yesterday, very little sleep last night, and it isn't fair to ask you to hang around. There's nothing you can do right now. Why not go home and get a little sleep?"

Jimmy nodded. He couldn't argue with anything the Sheriff had said. "You'll call me if you hear anything I need to hear?"

"You'll turn the ringer on you phone on?"

"Yeah," Jimmy said. "I'll turn the ringer on."

"Then I'll call."

"All right, I am pretty tired," Jimmy said, stepping down the stairs. "Thanks, Sheriff."

Jimmy pulled out of the station and started home through town. Sleepiness had started to come over him almost as soon as he'd gotten behind the wheel. He just needed to fend it off until he could get home, so he pressed on.

He was stopped at the light at the end of Main Street, gazing vacantly out his window, when a car sped up beside him and stopped suddenly. The beeping of the car's horn interrupted his sleepy reverie, and he looked over. It was Alice. He leaned across his front seat and rolled down the passenger's side window. "Alice?"

"Jimmy," she said, and he could hear the panic in her voice. "I need your help."

"What's going on?"

"It's Johnny. I haven't seen him since early last night, and I'm starting to get worried."

29

The light turned green. Jimmy pointed to the angled parking spots off to the right, just past the intersection. "Pull over. We'll talk."

Alice pulled through the intersection and parked, and Jimmy merged right and parked next to her. Alice was already getting out of her car, so Jimmy leaned over and unlocked his passenger side door so she could get in. The door swung open and Alice stepped into the Bronco, looking worried.

"What's going on?"

"I'm sorry Jimmy, I must have startled you. It's just that after what happened last night, I'm so worried something's happened to Johnny."

"You don't need to apologize. Why don't you start at the beginning?"

"O.K.," Alice said, taking a deep breath and trying visibly to calm herself. She reached over and took his hand in hers, adding softly. "It's so good to see you."

Jimmy smiled gently and held onto her hand. "I'm sorry you've been worried. Just tell me what's happened, and we'll go from there."

"Yesterday afternoon, Johnny brought Ethan home from playing at the school playground, and he was beside himself. Johnny just doesn't get angry. I mean, he does, but it's rare and he usually keeps it inside. The only reason I know he's mad when he gets mad is because I'm his sister and I know these things. But yesterday, he was furious. I think even Ethan was a little freaked out."

Jimmy listened as Alice spoke, the deeply unsettling unease that had begun at the stoplight growing. The world whirled around him as the case as he'd known it crumbled into pieces and rapidly reconstituted itself in a different shape in his brain. Trying to restrain his anxiety, he asked. "What happened Alice?"

"After lunch, Johnny took Ethan to the playground, and some of Ethan's friends were playing there too, so they got wrapped up in some game or other and Johnny sat in the grass. He's so big, you know, he often doesn't feel comfortable on public benches if they're narrow or don't feel sturdy or whatever. Anyway, after a while he lay back, closed his eyes and nodded off. He doesn't no how long he was asleep, but when he woke up he couldn't see the boys.

"Well, he panicked. He jumped up and looked around, and it only took a few seconds, but he found them. They were standing by a tree on the other side of the street. Johnny said they looked to him like they were looking at something hidden behind the tree next to them, only it wasn't a something, it was a man."

Jimmy closed his eyes, picturing the scene. He knew exactly where this was going. "Beck."

"What's that?"

Jimmy, opening his eyes and seeing the quizzical look on Alice's face, realized the name wasn't familiar to her. "I'm sorry, continue."

"Beck? Who's that? Why'd you say, 'Beck,' Jimmy?"

"I'm sorry, Alice. I shouldn't have interrupted. I'll explain later."

Alice didn't continue. She looked at him, fear growing in her face in addition to the worry already there. "Beck is the name of the man they found near Connelly's last night, isn't it? You think the man behind the tree is the man that got murdered."

Her eyes grew wide. "Jimmy, you don't think that…"

"I don't know what happened last night, Alice, I don't," Jimmy said, forestalling the question so he didn't have to lie. "I blurted out a name and shouldn't have. Just tell me what happened to Ethan and the boys that made Johnny so angry."

"Well," Alice started again. "He saw the boys, and he said his panic left. He started walking over to see what they were looking at, but as soon as he could see it was a man, he said his intuition immediately told him something was wrong, really wrong. He started running across the street, and he said that as soon as the man talking to the boys saw Johnny coming, he turned and fled as fast as he could. Johnny wanted to go after him, but he wanted to see if the boys were all right first.

"Apparently, they acted kind of nervous, claiming there was nothing going on, and the two boys Ethan had been playing with took off pretty quickly to go home. Since they were headed the opposite direction as the man, Johnny let them go. He pressed Ethan, though, to tell him what happened."

"What did happen?"

A flicker of anger showed in Alice's eyes before slipping away, replaced just as quickly by the fear and anxiety. "I'll tell you what Johnny said Ethan told him. I haven't pushed Ethan to talk about it yet. Ethan said the man approached them on the playground and told them that he'd found a dead cat among the trees across the street and thought the boys might want to check it out. Well, they're fourth grade boys, aren't they? Of course they wanted to check it out. They followed him to the trees.

"Then, the story gets a little fuzzy. Ethan's not as clear on what happened next, but the gist of it all is that the man started talking about something Ethan didn't understand—something sexual no doubt—because he started touching himself, you know, with his hand down his pants. It was right about then that the man looked up, saw Johnny and took off."

"I bet he did," Jimmy said, thinking about Dyson Beck looking up and seeing the mountain that was Johnny running toward him. His heart must have just about stopped to see him coming. Unfortunately, any pleasure he would otherwise have derived from the thought of Beck's fear and flight was lost amid the sinking realization that his worst fears were being realized. There was no longer any question in his mind why Johnny was missing or how the gloves had come to be at New Start.

"So Johnny brought Ethan straight home?"

"Yes."

"Then what?"

"I tried to calm him down. He was stalking around the house, pacing up and down, saying things that didn't make any sense. He wasn't even coherent. It took at least half an hour before he was able to stand still enough and compose his thoughts to tell me what had happened. A little later he said he had to go make sure Ethan and the other boys were safe, and that he'd be home for dinner."

Alice clutched Jimmy's arm "I thought he meant he was going to the Sheriff's Department to report it. I didn't think he meant he'd hurt the man, Jimmy. Do you really think he did this?"

Jimmy looked at Alice. He couldn't lie to her, and he realized as he wrestled with what to say that it would be useless to try. She could see he believed, and he could see that she did too.

She started to cry. "You don't think he killed that other man too, do you?"

Jimmy held her trembling hand. "I don't know Alice, but I would have said a little earlier today, before I knew what I know now about Johnny, that I'm pretty sure we're looking for one killer, not two."

Alice sobbed. "Oh, Jimmy, he's my little brother. Where is he? What's he doing? What's going to happen to him?"

The flood of tears and questions streamed out, and Jimmy wasn't sure where to begin. He thought about trying to offer comfort, but he knew he couldn't tell her anything she wanted to hear that would also be true. He was unwilling to offer false hope, so he said none of the things he might have wanted to say but that wouldn't have meant anything. He held onto her and said, "Alice, right now, we need to find him. You haven't seen him since he went out?"

"No, I haven't. Mrs. Byerly, his landlady, says he was definitely there in the late afternoon. After he left my house, I mean, but she hasn't seen him since and doesn't think he was home last night. She assumed he'd stayed with us like he often does."

"O.K.," Jimmy said. Alice's tears slowed and she seemed to be regaining control. "Are Ethan and Ellen at home?"

"They're next door, with Mrs. Gregory."

"That's probably a good thing. See if she can keep them."

"All right," Alice said.

"Do you think you'll be all right to drive home?"

"Sure, but aren't we going to go look for Johnny."

"I'm going to go look for Johnny. I want you to go home."

"I want to come with you."

"I don't think that's a good idea."

"But I want to help."

"You can help," Jimmy said gently. "Go home. There's no reason to think Johnny knows that we know. We didn't catch him last time, if it was him. He may not suspect we've figured things out this time, even if he's laying low because he's scared. So he may come back to you since your house is his haven. If he does, I want you to call me. If you can't get me, I want you to call the Sheriff. Will you do that?"

Alice wiped her eyes and nodded her head. "I can do that."

"Good," Jimmy said.

"What will you do?"

"I'm going to Johnny's place. If I don't find him there, I'm going to call the Sheriff and tell him what we suspect so his men can start looking, too. We've got to bring him in. Sheriff Anderson has men at New Start right now, so if he is out there or returns there, they need to know about this."

"You'll call me if you find him?"

"Of course."

"All right," Alice said, moving to open the door. Jimmy didn't let go of her hand though, and he pulled her gently toward him. She stopped moving and turned back toward him. He pulled her close and kissed her softly on the forehead.

"I'll do everything I can for him."

That brought fresh tears, but Alice fought valiantly to wipe them away. "Try to keep him alive, Jimmy."

"I will, Alice."

She thanked him and got back into her car. He watched her back out and drive away before backing out himself. He pulled a u-turn across Main Street and headed through the early evening to Johnny's apartment.

He'd only been there once before, and only to drop Johnny off. He found Mrs. Byerly's house, parked on the other side of the street, got out and crossed over.

There were lights on downstairs, but upstairs it appeared dark. There were external stairs that went up to a door on the second floor, an odd architectural feature in Avalon Falls. He didn't think many people in such a harsh climate wanted an external stairwell, but Johnny had lived there since returning to the town and apparently didn't mind.

Jimmy looked around as he stood at the base of the stairs. The evening light was fading, and he knew darkness would cover the town soon. He didn't see anyone watching him, but of course he couldn't be sure. He drew his gun and slipped quietly up the stairs.

At the top, he knocked lightly on the door. "Johnny?"

There was no answer.

"Johnny? It's Jimmy. I just saw Alice and she's worried about you. Says you were supposed to have dinner last night and you didn't show up."

Again, no answer. He reached down and tried the handle. It was locked. He looked around again. Still, he'd attracted no attention that he could see. He stepped back on the little wooden landing and then threw himself at the door. The lock busted and the door flew open.

Jimmy stepped in quickly, gun raised. The room was dark, but the blinds were partially open and a dusky light filtered through. He scanned it quickly and found neither any trace of Johnny nor any obvious hiding place. He walked silently through to the hall that led from the main front room back to the little kitchen, bathroom and bedroom. When Jimmy was satisfied that the apartment was empty, he walked back to the front room, pushed the door to and turned on a lamp in the corner.

He looked around the room. There was an oversized chair in front of a T.V., and on the other side of the room was a desk with a computer and printer. He walked over to the computer and reaching down, jiggled the mouse. There was a slight delay, then a hum from the tower beside the desk and the screen glowed to life.

He found Johnny's browser icon on his desktop and clicked on it. It was a dial-up connection, so it took a moment, but soon he found himself staring at Johnny's personalized Yahoo! homepage. He clicked on the most recently viewed website and before it could open he knew what he would see. Sure enough, it was a website designed to make available information made public from Megan's Law, a site that informed communities about sex offenders in their midst. That was how Johnny had found Beck.

Jimmy disconnected and picked up the phone on the desk. He dialed the Sheriff's Department, and when Sandy picked up, he asked for the Sheriff. "Sheriff?" he said once Anderson was on the line. "We need to pick up Johnny Cabot."

When Jimmy had finished talking to the Sheriff and after he'd called Alice to let her know he'd come up empty, he left Johnny's apartment. The broken door would be a sure giveaway to Johnny that someone had been there, so he'd had to ask the Sheriff to dispatch a deputy in an unmarked car to wait there.

He wasn't sure at first where he was headed when he left Johnny's, but as he got in the Bronco, he knew he was headed home. With deputies at New Start, Alice at home and a man on his way to Johnny's, almost any other place would be a shot in the dark. Besides, if Johnny was out there in the gathering dark, Jimmy wasn't sure he wanted to try to make that arrest on his own. If Johnny chose to be violent, Jimmy knew he'd have no hope except in using his weapon, and he didn't want to shoot Johnny any more than he wanted to explain to Alice about why he'd shot her brother. It was perhaps a little self-serving, but if somebody had to bring Johnny in and Johnny wasn't going to come quietly, Jimmy was perfectly willing to let somebody else try.

So he pulled out and drove home. The weariness that he'd been holding off while he checked out Johnny's place came washing back over him. The sun was sinking below the mountains now, and streaks of red and orange painted the horizon while a dark glow fell above them in the night sky. He turned in at his place at last, parked the Bronco and headed up to the door, yawning as he walked.

He reached up to put the key in, but when he took hold of the doorknob, it turned slightly. He jiggled it and found that it wasn't locked. He yawned again as he opened the door and went in. He'd been tired and a little out of it when he left with the Sheriff that morning, he thought as he entered, but not locking the door was unlike him.

A swift movement out of the corner of his eye was all he saw. Something heavy struck him in the back of his head.

He fell into darkness.

30

Jimmy opened his eyes. He was on his couch, and his head throbbed painfully. He looked around the room and saw Johnny, sitting on the hearth of his fireplace, holding Jimmy's gun.

Jimmy kept his eyes on Johnny as he let them adjust to the light. He sat up, slowly. Though his head hurt, he felt better about being upright. For his part, Johnny sat quietly too, watching Jimmy closely.

"You hit me," Jimmy said, feeling the back of his head where a large bump that was somewhere between a golf ball and tennis ball in size was already rising.

"Sorry, Jimmy," Johnny said, almost bashfully.

"What did you hit me with?"

"Your iron," Johnny said. "You left it out."

"My mistake," Jimmy said, suddenly immensely grateful that he'd gotten the cheap, flimsy, lightweight one instead of the heavy-duty expensive one he'd first considered. Suddenly, Jimmy looked around. He didn't know how long he'd been home, since he didn't know how long he'd been out, but it had been long enough that Major should be here. "Where's Major?"

"Tied to a tree out back."

"Out back?" Jimmy asked, incredulous. He never used a leash, so he couldn't imagine how Johnny had managed to tie the dog up. "How'd you manage that?"

"I managed."

Jimmy thought about the big man and the big dog, and he thought that as big as Major was, he'd not like to bet against Big Johnny. Besides, Major had been around Big Johnny before, and if he'd been gentle enough, maybe force hadn't been needed.

"What's going on here, Johnny? You're in my house. You whacked me with an iron. You have my gun. Where's this going?"

"I killed Dyson Beck." Johnny said matter-of-factly.

Jimmy didn't betray shock at this straightforward admission, saying simply. "I know, Johnny."

Puzzlement passed over Johnny's face. "You know?"

"Yes."

"But you've arrested Nathan? I saw you take him in."

It was Jimmy's turn to be puzzled. "You saw?"

"Yeah, I'd been out most of the night, and I was coming back when I saw the two cars from the Sheriff's Department pull in, so I stayed out of sight and watched. I didn't know how you guys had figured it out already, but I thought you were there for me. Then, after a while, you came out of the building with Nathan in handcuffs, and I couldn't believe it. After you guys were gone, I got out of there, but I called Coach from a payphone. I acted like I didn't know anything, and he told me the whole story.

"I knew right then, Jimmy, that I had to tell you. I had to tell you Nathan didn't do it. That boy can't go to jail for what I done. You understand, don't you Jimmy? Of all people, I can't have someone going away for what I did."

There were tears in Johnny's eyes as he spoke, and they began to fall, rolling steadily down his cheeks. "Nobody should ever go to jail for something they haven't done."

"No, Johnny, they shouldn't. You were right to come forward."

They sat quietly, Johnny holding on tightly to the gun and crying, and Jimmy watching, wondering where this was headed. "Give me back the gun, Johnny."

"I'm afraid I can't do that, Jimmy. I came to set you straight on Nathan, but I can't let you take me into custody. I'm never going back to jail, Jimmy. Never."

"Johnny," Jimmy said, hearing the determination in Johnny's voice, and searching desperately for an angle to take. "I know what prison is like, Johnny, and I can imagine, or at least begin to, what you went through. I also know what Beck was like, so I can understand why you were so mad yesterday. A jury might be sympathetic, Johnny. You never know. Given the time you've already served, for a crime you didn't commit, given the mitigating factors …"

"Come on, Jimmy," Johnny said, impatient. "I'm not the smartest guy around, but don't treat me like an idiot. I hate being treated like the dumb guy just because I'm big. Don't tell me I might not go to jail if I turn myself in. That's exactly where I'm going, and this time I'll never get out. There are no mitigating factors, or whatever you call 'em, that could get me off the hook for killing two people. And I told you, I'm never going back. When I walked out of the gate of the Montana State Prison, I vowed that I'd never go back. The only way they could get me back inside those walls would be to kill me and drag my dead body in. There ain't no other way."

Johnny stopped, and again they sat in silence. He'd admitted, more or less, to killing Morrison, too. Jimmy had known it without the admission, but now it was confirmed. He also knew there was no way he was going to talk Johnny into giving back his gun. Johnny wasn't going to take his chances in the legal system, because he didn't think he had a chance—and he was right. If Johnny turned himself in, he would go to jail for the rest of his life. The only open question was whether the state of Montana would elect to artificially shorten what was left of it.

Unless …

"You're right, Johnny," Jimmy said. "You're not walking away from this. But I think there's a good chance you could avoid prison. The state might opt to commit you …"

"I ain't crazy," Johnny said.

"I never said—"

"I ain't!" Johnny shouted.

With that gun in his hand, Jimmy didn't want Johnny worked up. He let it go.

When Johnny looked like he had calmed down a bit, Jimmy said. "So if you're not turning yourself in, what are we here for? You've told me about Beck, presumably so I can tell the Sheriff and get Nathan out of trouble. What now?"

"We wait."

"Wait? For what?"

"For Alice. I called her while you were unconscious. I want to see her one more time before I go."

"Alice is coming here?"

"She is. I told her to come alone, and she said she would. She should be here in the next five to ten minutes."

Jimmy nodded. He didn't like the thought of Alice being drawn into this, but he couldn't imagine Johnny hurting her, not on purpose anyway. Whenever a gun was involved, though, there was always a risk. Accidents happened.

"Johnny," Jimmy said. "I can understand why you killed Beck, given your history and what he was doing …"

"It isn't just what he was doing," Johnny said. "He was a predator. He was going to keep on going unless someone stopped him."

"You're probably right about that," Jimmy said, "but my question isn't actually about Beck. It's about Morrison. Why'd you kill him?"

Johnny didn't answer at first, and when he did, it was clear that he was more reluctant to talk about Morrison then Beck. "That was an accident."

"An accident?" Jimmy said, leaning forward, incredulous. "Johnny, I saw the crime scene. He was beaten beyond recognition. How can you call that an accident?"

"I don't mean an accident like that. It was an accident because I got it wrong. He wasn't like Beck."

"No, he wasn't, but why would you have thought he was? You'd never met him before, had you?"

"No," Johnny said sheepishly. He took the gun in his other hand and wiped his right hand on his jeans, then put the gun back in it. He was nervous, and that made Jimmy nervous.

"I'd been sitting on the rock by the lake that night," Johnny started again. "It's a favorite spot of mine. Anyway, I was walking back up to the path when I heard somebody laughing. It startled me because it was late and I thought I was alone. I crept up to the path and saw a guy not far away. It was dark, and at first I couldn't tell what he was doing. I stepped on a twig underfoot and the guy swung around. His pants were down and he was holding himself.

"I lost it, Jimmy. I just lost it. All these memories of the guys from prison came flooding back. I wasn't going to let that happen again. I reached up and grabbed the branch overhead and snapped it off, and before the guy even knew what was going on I hit him. I hit him and hit him and hit him. I tell you what, Jimmy, every swing felt better than the one before. It was like I was hitting all of them. I saw their faces. I heard their voices, and I beat them all until they were still and quiet and dead.

"It was like a dream, but then I came to my senses. I looked around, and I knew I'd just killed a man and was holding the murder weapon. I broke off the end I'd been holding, just in case my prints or were on it, and I took it with me. A few days later, I burned it in the fireplace at Alice's house. It wasn't easy to burn, but I got it done."

As Jimmy listened, the whole episode unfolded before his mind's eye. He saw it all. The gentle giant, enjoying the beautiful night. He'd left his painful past in prison behind, but he'd never really been able to leave it behind. Suddenly, life confronted him with this unlikely chain of events, a trigger that unlocked and unleashed a rage that was equal parts self-protection and righteous anger against those who had tormented him.

The bottle was uncorked, and the genie that came out could not be controlled.

Alex Morrison, the hapless, unlucky and unremarkable carpet salesman had just been in the way. He'd been drinking a beer and taking a leak late at night in a remote corner of the Avalon Falls park, and he must have barely had time to wonder what was happening before the pent up rage in Johnny was fatally vented upon him.

"Was it you?" Jimmy asked.

"Was it me what?"

"When I was at the crime scene with Major that night? Down at the lakeside, by your hangout. He scented something and chased it up the hill—was it you?"

"Yes," Johnny said.

"Why were you there? Why go back?"

"I killed a guy who hadn't done me any harm, Jimmy. As good as it felt, hitting him when it happened, that's how bad I felt later. I was miserable. I was in hell. I was a murderer. I'd actually done the thing I'd been falsely accused of before. It felt like a bad dream. I went back to see if it had really been real."

Jimmy nodded. He'd thought a dynamic like this might have been at work. He'd just not known all the things he'd needed to know to understand who had been drawn back and why. As he sat, massaging the sore spot on the back of his head, another question occurred to him.

"Johnny, why'd you put those rubber gloves, covered in blood, in the New Start dumpster? Why so careless this time?"

"I didn't think I was being careless," Johnny said. "I knew the dumpster would be emptied around midday. Once that stuff was in the dump, I figured it probably wouldn't ever be found, and if it was, it wouldn't be traced back to New Start. How was I to know policemen would come out and look in that dumpster so soon? When Morrison died, no one looked anywhere at New Start. You came out and talked to the boys, almost a week later, but no one looked anywhere."

"But you said you came back at midday, when the police were already there. Why'd you still put them in the dumpster?"

"I didn't put them in then," Johnny said. "The gloves were already there, Jimmy. I put them there in the middle of the night. I went back and grabbed the change of clothes I keep there before I went to a spot I know where I could incinerate my bloody clothes, the same place where I incinerated my clothes before."

"You incinerated your clothes at this place, but not the piece of branch? Why?"

"I didn't find this place until almost a month after I killed Morrison. By then, I'd already burned the branch."

"A month? Where'd you keep the clothes, Johnny?"

"Hidden in my apartment."

Jimmy groaned internally. Bloody clothes had been lying there to be found at Johnny's apartment for a whole month, but no one had ever looked.

The sound of a car coming up the gravel driveway and the flash of headlights through the front window announced Alice's arrival. Johnny had Jimmy peak out through the window just to be sure, and he confirmed it was indeed Alice. Johnny then made Jimmy sit down again, and he called to Alice to come in when she knocked.

She entered and took a few steps into the room before stopping. "Why are you holding a gun, Johnny?"

"I had to make sure Jimmy didn't call the Sheriff or try anything until I had a chance to see you Alice."

"I'm here now, Johnny," Alice said gently. "You can put the gun away now, can't you?"

"I'll hold onto it until I go."

"Where are you going?"

"That's not important."

"Johnny ..."

"Alice, I've been over all this with Jimmy. I don't want to go over it again. I'm running out of time."

"What do you want?"

Johnny patted the stone hearth beside him. "I want you to sit down with me."

Alice walked over and sat beside her brother. They sat silently side by side. Tears were running silently down her face. Though her hands were clenched tightly in her lap, she leaned her head against his broad shoulders.

"Sing *Rainbow* for me, Alice."

Her tears were no longer silent. They burst from her as she shook her head.

"I can't sing now, Johnny."

"Please? One more time?"

More silence. All three sat motionless in the lamplit room. Then, Alice broke the silence. She began to sing. Softly, and shaky, but she sang.

> *Somewhere over the rainbow*
> *Way up high*
> *There's a land that I heard of*
> *Once in a lullaby*
>
> *Somewhere over the rainbow*
> *Skies are blue*
> *And the dreams that you dare to dream*
> *Really do come true*
>
> *Some day I'll wish upon a star*
> *And wake up where the clouds are far behind me*
> *Where troubles melt like lemondrops*
> *Away above the chimney tops*
> *That's where you'll find me*

Somewhere over the rainbow
Bluebirds fly
Birds fly over the rainbow
Why then, oh why can't I?

Some day I'll wish upon a star
And wake up where the clouds are far behind me
Where troubles melt like lemondrops
Away above the chimney tops
That's where you'll find me

Somewhere over the rainbow
Bluebirds fly
Birds fly over the rainbow
Why then, oh why can't I?

If happy little bluebirds fly
Beyond the rainbow
Why, oh why can't I?

Alice stopped singing. Jimmy felt the weight of the silence crowding the room. In the end, it was Alice who broke it. "Oh, Johnny, when will you stop paying for what you didn't do?"

"But I did, Alice. This time I did." Johnny said softly, wiping the tears from his face. A new look of confidence and resolve seemed to come over him. "Alice, get some water for Jimmy and me from the kitchen."

"Why Johnny?" Alice asked. She'd detected the shift in tone and looked warily at her brother.

"Because I'm thirsty, and I'd guess he is too. Don't worry, I'm not going to hurt him."

Alice looked at Jimmy, who nodded that it was all right, and she stood to walk toward the kitchen. Halfway there she stopped and turned back. "Where are you going, Johnny?"

"I can't tell you that, Alice."

"I want a kiss before you go."

Johnny stood but kept his tight grip on the gun. He walked to Alice, keeping one eye on Jimmy, then slipped his arm around her, bent over, and kissed her gently.

"Goodbye, Johnny," she whispered.

"Goodbye, Alice," he answered, and she walked into the kitchen.

Johnny walked over to Jimmy. "She's worth more than both of us put together. Take good care of her, Jimmy."

Before Jimmy could say anything, Johnny whacked him on the head again, this time with the gun.

Jimmy didn't pass out, but he fell to his knees on the floor, pain radiating out through his head. He heard Johnny run out the door, and he heard Alice call out to him as she rushed back into the main room. She ran to Jimmy and got down on her knees to see if he was all right. They heard the sound of Alice's car starting, and then the sound of wheels squealing as it flew down the driveway.

"Help me up," Jimmy said, grimacing from the pain.

Two sharp blows to the head on the same night from Big Johnny. He hurt like crazy but felt lucky to be alive. Johnny had definitely taken a little something off the second hit, and Jimmy was grateful.

"Jimmy, I'm so afraid he'll hurt himself."

"I know," Jimmy said. "We need to call the Sheriff and go after him."

Alice called, and when she finished, she helped Jimmy, still wincing from the blow, get up from the couch. "I don't think I should drive," he groaned as the room swirled around him. "Take my keys."

Alice didn't hesitate, and they were soon outside, getting into the Bronco.

They sped into town. If Johnny was leaving Avalon Falls, then their chance of guessing what direction he was going was minimal, but if he was intent on hurting himself, he was likely to do it someplace familiar, Jimmy said. So Alice drove like mad, her headlights on full beam the whole way, looking for any traces of Johnny in her car down every street they passed.

Before long, they were roaring up Main Street. They drove past Alice's house, past Cabot's and past Mrs. Byerly's. No sign of Johnny.

"The park," Jimmy said suddenly, as they sat at a traffic light, waiting to turn back onto Main Street. "Go to the park."

Alice didn't wait for the light to turn. She pulled through the red light and turned left, heading to the park.

Her car was already there. Johnny had pulled it in, shut off the engine and the lights, then left it behind, the driver's side door slightly ajar.

Alice pulled in next to it.

"He's gone to the rock by the lake, near where Morrison died," Jimmy said.

"Let's go, then."

"He has my gun, Alice," Jimmy said. "You have to stay here."

"No, he doesn't have your gun."

"What?"

"He left it on the table by your front door. Didn't you see it?"

"No," Jimmy said. "I could barely see anything back there."

"I'm sorry, Jimmy. I should have told you. I thought you'd seen it."

Jimmy thought about his gun lying on the table and the fact that he'd really rather have had it here, but in a way he was relieved. He knew that Johnny wouldn't hurt Alice if they caught up to him, and probably all Johnny would do to Jimmy was whack him again, which was bad, but without his gun along he'd have an excuse not to shoot him. What exactly he'd do if they found him alive he hadn't figured out yet.

"All right," Jimmy said, getting out with a grimace as his head throbbed. "Come on."

They ran through the darkness across the grassy park to the place where the path disappeared into the woods. Moonlight and starlight gave them limited visibility that only diminished once they were on the path. They ran until Jimmy thought they'd gone far enough, and they slowed to try to find the opening that led down to the rock and the lakeside. It felt like it took a long time, but eventually they found it and scrambled down to the rock.

The big rock sat lonely in the moonlight, beside the placid water. No Johnny. Jimmy walked over to the rock with Alice, and they saw them.

"Johnny's shoes," Alice said.

They turned and looked out at the water. There was no sign of him. Alice leaned against Jimmy and began to cry.

"We'll call the Sheriff and have a Search and Rescue team come and scour the lake."

She said nothing. He turned from the water. She reached her arms around him and held him tight.

31

Jimmy pulled up outside Eddie's house and turned off his engine. Eddie came out on the porch and sat on the top stair. Jimmy got out and walked over to sit beside him.

"How's Alice doing?"

Jimmy shrugged. "She holds it together for the most part, but it's pretty rough."

"It's a lot to deal with," Eddie said.

"Yeah," Jimmy said. "Not just that he's gone, you know, but what he did."

They sat, looking out at the bright blue sky. "She said to tell you how much she appreciated your words at the service, by the way."

"Thanks," Eddie said. He sighed. "I still can't help but feel that I failed him."

Jimmy looked at Eddie. "Even as good as you are at helping people, Eddie, you can't blame yourself for this."

Eddie looked down. Jimmy stared across the green lawn.

"What happened to Johnny," Jimmy said, "that doesn't just go away."

"I know," Eddie said. "I can't expect to fix every problem. I don't even expect that of God, not yet, anyway. It's just hard for me to understand the why sometimes."

"It's a messed up world," Jimmy said. "I've found it hard to understand my whole life."

Eddie looked over at the Bronco. "Car's packed. Going somewhere?"

"I am," Jimmy said, looking down. "That's why I wanted to come by."

"Thought so."

"Of course you did," Jimmy said. "I mean, you guess everything else, so why not this? How'd you know?"

"I don't know," Eddie said, shaking his head, "but when you called and said you wanted to stop by for a minute, I had a gut feeling it was to say goodbye."

"Not for good, of course," Jimmy said. "I've left Major with Alice and the kids as a pledge of my return, so don't get too sentimental on me."

Jimmy smiled, and Eddie laughed. "I won't."

They sat for a moment, and Eddie spoke again. "You told Alice then?"

"I did."

"How'd she take it?"

"About Nina or about me going back?"

"All of it."

"Pretty well, I think. With everything that's going on, she just seemed pretty relieved to know there weren't any secrets between us. She made me promise not to keep anything from her anymore."

"Sounds like a good idea," Eddie said. He looked at Jimmy. "What's the plan then?"

"I don't know. All I know is that I have a daughter and I want to meet her."

"That's good, Jimmy."

"Everything I was running from, I brought it with me," Jimmy said. "You can't run from yourself, Eddie. You taught me that."

"I taught you that?"

"Yeah, you did, though maybe it wasn't just you. Maybe Avalon Falls taught me that."

Eddie nodded again, quietly.

"Avalon Falls," Eddie said, mouthing the words carefully. "I remember being in fourth grade and reading about King Arthur and his knights. I was shocked to find out there was a city in the story named Avalon. I hadn't known that. Even though I grew up here. All I'd known about that name was that the first settlers here had thought this place beautiful and wanted to name it Avalon, I didn't know why. Then, as the town became known for the nearby waterfall, its name was officially changed to Avalon Falls.

"I was much, much older before I understood the irony. Avalon Falls. Paradise, at least on earth, never lasts."

Eddie rose. "I won't keep you, Jimmy. You've probably got a big day ahead."

"I do," Jimmy said, standing too. "I want to cover some serious ground before I stop tonight. Besides, I haven't had a really good cup of coffee in over a year."

"Ouch," Eddie said. "Don't let Alice hear you say that."

"I know," Jimmy said. "She's a great cook, but the coffee at Cabot's is only average at best."

They stood in the sunshine for a while. Jimmy closed his eyes and tilted his face up so he could feel the warmth on his skin without hurting his eyes. "You said once," he said, without moving, "that Johnny thought there might be some purpose or plan in what happened to him. Still think that?"

"I never said the world wasn't a mess, Jimmy, or that what happened to Johnny wasn't terrible."

"I know."

"Bad things don't stop being bad," Eddie continued, "just because God sometimes brings good things from them."

"So who's responsible?" Jimmy said, looking over at Eddie.

"We are."

"Isn't God responsible for us?"

Eddie smiled. "Should we talk about that when you get back?"

"Sure," Jimmy said.

"Well," Eddie said, extending his hand. Jimmy took it and they shook. "I wish you all the best. We'll be looking forward to your return."

"Thanks," Jimmy said. He walked to the Bronco, stopped and looked back. "I owe you a lot, Eddie."

"You don't owe me anything. As my favorite fictional character, from my favorite novel said, 'I am a weak and sinful man, but God put his hands on me, that is all.'"

"Well, you're the best argument for God that I've ever heard, I'll tell you that much."

"Maybe you've not heard very good arguments," Eddie said. "We'll have to remedy that when you return."

"We'll add that to the list," Jimmy laughed. "Take care, Eddie."

"I will. Drive safely."

"Will do," Jimmy said. He got into the Bronco, started it up, turned around and headed down the hill, beeping twice when he turned out onto the road.

Eddie stood on the porch, waving, until the car had finally driven out of sight. He stood there for a long time, then descended the stairs and headed across the grass to New Start.

The End

ACKNOWLEDGMENTS

For something that has a reputation for being, and quite often is, a somewhat solitary venture, I find at the end of most writing projects that I am indebted to a great many people. I am all too likely to have neglected some of those here, but a short list of acknowledgements is very much in order, starting with my family, who bear with me patiently.

I also need to thank my good friend Pat Biggers, who read a very early version of *Avalon Falls* and lent his law enforcement expertise to help ensure that those elements of the story weren't terribly unrealistic. As did another good friend, Shane Lankford, who lent his similar expertise in car sales, and he did so with patience and good humor, despite the less than enthusiastic portrayal of the car salesman in question, to whom Shane bears no resemblance, whatsoever.

I would also like to thank Tom Wenger, Jonathan Rogers, Luke Davis and Larry Hughes, all of whom read and gave feedback on *Avalon Falls* at various stages, contributing in their own way to the many revisions and much improved final shape of the story.

My largest editorial debt is owed to Matt Crossman, who read this in its entirety, both in its earliest, roughest form and also at the 11th hour, when final corrections had to be made. His keen editorial eye and writer's sensibilities make him invaluable to me, and as long as he keeps offering to read the things I'm working on, I'll keep sending them.

I would also like to thank Wayne Batson, for helping to start me down this road of exploring the world outside the mainstream of conventional publishing, Abe Goolsby for his work on the beautiful cover, and 52 Novels for their work on the interior design.

Last, but not least, I need to thank my mother, Anna Graham, whose financial generosity has made this possible. I'm not entirely sure I'm a wise investment, but that doesn't deter her in the slightest.

ABOUT L.B. GRAHAM

L.B. Graham writes contemporary adult fiction and fantasy/sci-fi. His novel Beyond the Summerland was a finalist for a Christy Award in 2005. Check out his website www.lbgraham.com for more information on his previously published works and his forthcoming titles. He lives in St. Louis with his wife and two children.

ALSO BY L.B. GRAHAM

The Binding of the Blade
A five volume, epic fantasy series, consisting of…

Beyond the Summerland, Book 1

Bringer of Storms, Book 2

Shadow in the Deep, Book 3

Father of Dragons, Book 4

All My Holy Mountain, Book 5

Coming Soon from this Author

The Raft, the River and the Robot – A futuristic novel inspired in part by *The Adventures of Huckleberry Finn*. (Fall of 2012)

The Darker Road – Book 1 of a new fantasy trilogy called *The Wandering*. (Spring of 2013. Books 2 & 3 of that series will follow in '14 and '15)

The Promise – The first book of an adult contemporary trilogy called *These Three Remain*. (Release Date to be Determined)

CPSIA information can be obtained
at www.ICGtesting.com
Printed in the USA
LVOW11s1617080517
533722LV00001B/103/P